Praise for the novels of Debbie Macomber

"Charming and funny, the latest installment of the Blossom Street series has many touching moments, too. Here's to the adventures of Lydia and her friends continuing for a long, long time."
—*RT Book Reviews* on *Summer on Blossom Street*

"Macomber's assured storytelling and affirming narrative is as welcoming as your favorite easy chair."
—*Publishers Weekly* on *Twenty Wishes*

"Macomber spins another pure-from-the-heart romance giddy with love and warm laughter."
—*BookPage* on *The Snow Bride*

"Debbie Macomber has written a book that is absolutely unputdownable...one of the most compelling books I've read in a very long time."
—*The Best Reviews* on *Changing Habits*

"Even the most hard-hearted readers will find themselves rooting for the women in this hopeful story while surreptitiously wiping away tears and making their own list of wishes."
—*Booklist* on *Twenty Wishes*

"Debbie Macomber writes characters who are as warm and funny as your best friends."
—#1 *New York Times* bestselling author Susan Wiggs

Debbie Macomber "can weave a story that will keep you enthralled for hours, not wanting to put it down."
—*RomanceJunkies.com* on *8 Sandpiper Way*

"Debbie Macomber is...a bona fide superstar."
—*Publishers Weekly*

Also by Debbie Macomber

DEBBIE MACOMBER

The Man You'll Marry

MIRA®

Recycling programs for this product may not exist in your area.

ISBN-13: 978-0-7783-2783-7

THE MAN YOU'LL MARRY

Copyright © 2010 by MIRA Books.

The publisher acknowledges the copyright holder of the individual works as follows:

THE FIRST MAN YOU MEET
Copyright © 1992 by Debbie Macomber.

THE MAN YOU'LL MARRY
Copyright © 1992 by Debbie Macomber.

www.MIRABooks.com

Printed in U.S.A.

Dearest Friends,

It's hard to believe I wrote these two stories for romance "bridal collections" back in the early 1990s. My daughter Jenny had recently become engaged and while I did research for her wedding I made copious notes regarding these stories. In the years since, Jenny and Kevin have given my husband, Wayne, and me three adorable, talented and highly entertaining grandchildren. As a bonus, their daughter Maddy just happens to have been born on my birthday. My daughter always did have a wonderful sense of timing.

I don't remember how I came up with this romantic comedy idea of a supernatural wedding dress. What I *do* remember is that writing *The First Man You Meet* and *The Man You'll Marry* brought back some hilarious memories of my own wedding to Wayne. It all started with the bachelor party. My father and brother took Wayne and his friends out for a night on the town and then in the wee hours of the morning they invaded the kitchen. My mother and several of my aunts had spent days preparing traditional German dishes for the wedding dinner. As you might have guessed, the members of the bachelor party arrived ravenous and my father ever so generously emptied the contents of two refrigerators. The men promptly devoured a good portion of what was intended for dinner that day. It took Mom years to forgive my dad for that one.

Then, the morning of the wedding, I discovered to my horror that my dress no longer fit. I'd given up eating lunch in order to save money and my lovely wedding dress hung on me like an oversized burlap bag. (I should be so lucky now!) Between them, my mother and aunts managed to adjust it with safety pins so that it was presentable. I remember Mom circling me as my aunts fidgeted, mumbling in German with her hands over her mouth in horror. Later at the dinner—and yes, there was still plenty of food after some frantic grocery shopping and last-minute menu revisions—Wayne and I headed for a mountain resort where we were to spend our wedding night…only there was a girl tucked away in the trunk of the car! It was a joke that quickly brought us back to the reception—where everyone was waiting for our return. Oh, the memories…

I hope you'll enjoy the story of Great-Aunt Milly's infamous wedding dress and what happens when Shelly Hansen receives it, knowing the family legend that she'll now marry the next man she meets. Then the dress goes off to Jill Morrison and the magic starts all over again. And if it so happens that reading these two stories stirs up a happy memory of your own wedding or someone else's, all the better. Sit back, reminisce and enjoy!

Warmest regards,

Debbie Macomber

P.S. I love to hear from readers. You can reach me at www.debbiemacomber.com or P.O. Box 1458, Port Orchard, WA 98366.

CONTENTS

THE FIRST MAN
YOU MEET

For James Jordan Buckley,
the other writer in the family.

One

It had been one of those days.

One of those nightmarish days in which nothing had gone right. Nothing. Shelly Hansen told herself she should have seen the writing on the wall that morning when she tripped over the laces of her high-top purple running shoes as she hurried from the parking lot to her dinky office. She'd torn a hole in the knee of her brand-new pants and limped ingloriously into her building. The day had gone steadily downhill from there, with a package lost by the courier and—worst of all—the discovery that her bank account was overdrawn because a client's check had bounced.

By the time she returned to her apartment that evening she was in a black mood. All she needed to make her day complete was to have her mother pop in unannounced with a man in tow, convinced she'd found the perfect mate for Shelly.

She could only hope that wouldn't happen, but it was exactly the kind of thing Shelly had come to expect from her dear, sweet *desperate* mother. Shelly was twenty-eight now and still single, and her mother tended to view her unmarried status as a situation to be remedied. Since her father had decided not to retire, and her two brothers were both living out of state, Shelly had become the focus of her mother's obsessions. Marriage, closely followed by grandchildren, were the first and second items on Faith Hansen's agenda for her only daughter.

Never mind that Shelly felt content with her life just the way it was. Never mind that she wasn't interested in marriage and children…at least not yet. That time would come, she was sure, not now, but someday soon—or rather, some *year* soon.

For the moment, Shelly was absorbed in her career. She was proud of her work as a video producer, although she continually suffered the cash-flow problems of the self-employed. Her relaxation DVDs—seascapes, mountain scenes, a flickering fire in a brick fireplace, all with a background of classical music—were selling well. Her cat-sitting DVD had recently caught the attention of a major distributor, and she couldn't help believing she was on the brink of real success.

That was the good news.

Her mother hounding her to get married was the bad.

Tossing her woven Mexican bag and striped blue

jacket onto the sofa, Shelly ventured into the kitchen and sorted through the packages in her freezer until she found something that halfway appealed to her for dinner. The frozen entrée was in the microwave when the doorbell chimed.

Her mother. The way her day was going, it *had* to be her mother. Groaning inwardly, she decided she'd be polite but insistent. Friendly but determined, and if her mother began talking about husbands, Shelly would simply change the subject.

But it wasn't Faith Hansen who stood outside her door. It was Elvira Livingston, the building manager, a warm, delightful but insatiably curious older woman.

"Good evening, dear," Mrs. Livingston greeted her. She wore heavy gold earrings and a billowing, bright yellow dress, quite typical attire. She clutched a large box protectively in both hands. "The postman dropped this off. He asked if I'd give it to you."

"For me, Mrs. L.?" Perhaps today wasn't a total loss, after all.

Elvira nodded, holding the package as though she wasn't entirely sure she should surrender it until she got every bit of relevant data. "The return address is California. Know anyone by the name of Millicent Bannister?"

"Aunt Milly?" Shelly hadn't heard from her mother's aunt in years.

"The package is insured," Mrs. Livingston noted, shifting the box just enough to examine the label again.

Shelly held out her hands to receive the package, but her landlady apparently didn't notice.

"I had to sign for it." This, too, seemed to be of great importance. "And there's a letter attached," Mrs. Livingston added.

Shelly had the impression that the only way she'd ever get her hands on the parcel was to let Mrs. Livingston open it first.

"I certainly appreciate all the trouble you've gone to," Shelly said, gripping the sides of the box and giving a firm tug. Mrs. Livingston released the package reluctantly. "Uh, thanks, Mrs. L. I'll talk to you soon."

The older woman's face fell with disappointment as Shelly began to close the door. Obviously, she was hoping for an invitation to stay. But Shelly wasn't in the mood for company, especially not the meddlesome, if well-meaning, Elvira Livingston.

Shelly sighed. This was what she got for renting an apartment with "character." She could be living in a modern town house with a sauna, pool and workout room in a suburban neighborhood. Instead she'd opted for a brick two-story apartment building in the heart of Seattle. The radiators hissed at all hours of the night in perfect harmony with the plumbing that groaned and creaked. But Shelly loved the polished hardwood floors, the high ceilings with their delicate crystal light fixtures and the bay windows that overlooked Puget Sound. She could do without the sauna and other amenities, even if it meant occasionally dealing with an eccentric busybody like Mrs. Livingston.

Eagerly she carried the package into the kitchen and set it on her table. Although she wondered what Aunt Milly had sent her, she carefully peeled the letter free, then just as carefully removed the plain brown wrapper.

The box was an old one, she noticed, the cardboard heavier than that currently used by stores. Shelly gently pried off the lid. She found layers of tissue paper wrapped around...a dress. Shelly pushed aside the paper and lifted the garment from its box. She gasped in surprise as the long white dress gracefully unfolded.

This wasn't just any dress. It was a wedding dress, an exquisitely sewn lace-and-satin wedding dress.

Surely it couldn't have been Aunt Milly's... No, that couldn't be... It wasn't possible.

Anxious now, her heart racing, Shelly refolded the dress and placed it back in the box. She reached for the envelope and saw that her hands were trembling as she tore it open.

My Dearest Shelly,

I trust this letter finds you happy and well. You've frequently been in my thoughts the past few days. I suppose you could blame Dr. Phil for that. Though now that I think about it, it may have been Oprah. As you'll have gathered, I often watch those talk shows these days. John would have disapproved, but he's been gone eight years now. Of course, if I wanted to, I'd watch them if he were still alive. John could disapprove all he wanted, but it wouldn't do him a bit of good. Never did. He knew it and loved me, anyway.

I imagine you're wondering why I'm mailing you my wedding dress and what Dr. Phil and Oprah have to do with it. (Yes, that is indeed my infamous wedding dress.) I suspect the sight of it has put the fear of God into you. I wish I could've been there to see your face when you realized what I was sending you. No doubt you're familiar with the story; everyone in the family's known about it for years. Since you're fated to marry the first man you meet once the dress is in your hands, your instinct is probably to burn the thing immediately!

Now that I reconsider, I'm certain it was Dr. Phil. He had a show recently featuring pets as companions to the elderly, lifting their spirits and the like. The man being interviewed brought along a cute little Scottish terrier and that was when the old seamstress drifted into my mind. Her name was Mrs. McDonald—or was it McDonnell? At any rate, I must have fallen asleep, because the next thing I knew the six-o'clock news was on.

While I slept I had a dream about you. This was no ordinary dream, either. I saw you plain as day, standing beside a tall young man, your blue eyes bright and shining. You were so happy, so truly in love. But what astonished me was the wedding dress you were wearing.

Mine.

The very dress the old Scottish woman sewed for me all those years ago. It seemed to me I was receiving a message of some sort and that I'd best not ignore it. Neither should you! You're about to embark on the grandest adventure of your life, my dear. Keep me informed!

Believe me, Shelly, I know what you're thinking. I well remember my own thoughts the day that seamstress handed me the wedding dress. I'd ordered something completely different from her—a simple evening gown—so I was shocked to say the least. Marriage was the *last* thing on my mind! I had a career, back in the days when it was rare for a woman to attend college, let alone graduate from law school.

You and I are a great deal alike, Shelly. We value our independence. It takes a special kind of man to be married to women like us. And you, my dear niece, are about to meet that one special man just the way I did.

All my love,
Aunt Milly

P.S. You're only the second person to wear the dress. Never before have I felt anything like this. Perhaps it's the beginning a new tradition!

With hands that trembled even more fiercely now, Shelly folded the letter and slid it back into the envelope.

Her heart was pounding, and she could feel the sweat beading her forehead.

The phone rang then, and more from instinct than any desire to talk, Shelly picked up the receiver.

"Hello." It hadn't dawned on her until that moment that the caller might be her mother, wanting to bring over a man for her to meet. Any man her mother introduced would only add to the growing nightmare, but—

"Shelly, it's Jill. Are you all right? You sound... strange."

"Jill." Shelly was so relieved that her knees went weak. "Thank heaven it's you."

"What's wrong?"

Shelly hardly knew where to begin. "My aunt Milly's wedding dress just arrived. I realize that won't mean anything to you unless you've heard the family legend about my aunt Milly and uncle John."

"I haven't."

"Of course you haven't, otherwise you'd understand what I'm going through," Shelly snapped, then felt guilty for being short-tempered with her best friend. Making an effort to compose herself, she explained, "I've just been mailed a wedding dress—one that's been in my family for over sixty years—with the clear understanding that I'll be wearing it soon myself."

"You didn't even tell me you were dating anyone." Jill hadn't managed to disguise the hurt in her voice.

"I'm *not!* And I'm not getting married, either. If anyone should know that, it's you."

"Then your aunt intends you to wear it when you do get married."

"There's more to it than that," Shelly cried. "Listen. Aunt Milly—who's really my mother's aunt, a few years older than my grandmother—became an attorney just after the Second World War. She worked hard to earn her law degree and had decided to dedicate her life to her career."

"In other words, she'd planned never to marry."

"Exactly."

"But apparently she did."

"Yes, and the story of how that happened has been in the family for years. It seems Aunt Milly had all her clothes professionally made. As the story goes, she took some lovely white material to an old Scottish woman who had a reputation as the best seamstress around. Milly needed an evening dress for some formal event that was coming up—business-related, of course. The woman took her measurements and told her the dress would be finished by the end of the week."

"And?" Jill prompted when Shelly hesitated.

"And…when Milly returned for the dress the old woman sat her down with a cup of tea."

"The dress wasn't ready?"

"Oh, it was ready, all right, only it wasn't the dress Aunt Milly had ordered. The Scottish woman said she was gifted with the 'sight.'"

"She was clairvoyant?"

"So she claimed," Shelly said, breathing in deeply.

"The old woman told my aunt that when she began the dress a vision came to her. A clear vision that involved Milly. This vision showed Milly getting married. The old woman was so convinced of it that she turned what was supposed to be a simple evening dress into an elaborate wedding gown, with layers of satin and lace and lots of pearls."

"It sounds beautiful," Jill said with a sigh.

"Of course it's beautiful—but don't you see?"

"See what?"

It was all Shelly could do not to groan with frustration. "The woman insisted my aunt Milly would marry within the year. It happened, too, just the way that seamstress said, right down to the last detail."

Jill sighed again. "That's the most romantic story I've heard in ages."

"It isn't romance," Shelly argued, "it's fate interrupting one's life! It's being a...pawn! It's destiny whether you like it or not. I know that seems crazy, but I've grown up hearing this story. It was as though my aunt Milly didn't have any choice in the matter."

"And your aunt Milly mailed you the dress?"

"Yes," Shelly wailed. "*Now* do you understand why I'm upset?"

"Frankly, no. Come on, Shelly, it's just an old dress. You're overreacting. You make it sound as if you're going to marry the next man you meet."

Shelly gasped audibly. "How'd you know?" she whispered.

"Know what?"

"That's *exactly* what happened to Aunt Milly. That's part of the legend. She tried to refuse the dress, but the seamstress wouldn't take it back, nor would she accept payment. When Aunt Milly left the dress shop, she had car problems and needed a mechanic. My uncle John was that mechanic. And Aunt Milly married him. She married *the first man she met*, just like the seamstress said."

Two

"Shelly, that doesn't mean *you're* going to marry the next man you meet," Jill stated calmly, far too calmly to suit Shelly.

Perhaps Jill didn't recognize a crisis when she came across one. They were talking about fate here. Predestination. Okay, maybe, just maybe, she was being a bit melodramatic, but after the ghastly day she'd had, who could blame her?

"Aunt Milly came right out and said I'm going to get married soon," Shelly said. "According to the family legend, the first man you meet when you get the dress is the man you'll marry."

"It's just coincidence," Jill reassured her. "Your aunt probably would've met her husband *without* the dress. It would've happened anyway. And don't forget, she's an old woman now," Jill continued soothingly. "I know this wonderful old lady who comes into the pharmacy every few weeks and she always insists *I'm* going to get married soon. I smile and nod and fill her prescription. She means well, and I'm sure your aunt Milly does, too. She just wants you to be happy, the way she was. But I think it's silly to take any of this prediction nonsense seriously."

Shelly exhaled sharply. Jill was right; Aunt Milly was a lovely woman who had Shelly's happiness at heart. She'd had a long, blissful marriage herself and wanted the same for her great-niece. But Shelly had plans and goals, none of which included meeting and marrying a stranger.

The story of Aunt Milly's wedding dress had been handed down through the family. Shelly had first heard it as a child and had loved it. She'd ranked the story of her aunt Milly and uncle John with her favorite fairy tales of Cinderella and Sleeping Beauty, barely able to distinguish truth from fantasy. However, she was an adult now. Her heart and her life weren't going to be ruled by something as whimsical as a "magic" wedding dress or a fanciful legend.

"You're absolutely right," Shelly announced emphatically. "The whole thing is ridiculous. Just because this wedding dress supposedly conjured up a husband for my aunt Milly sixty-plus years ago doesn't mean it's going to do the same thing for me, no matter what she claims."

"Well, thank goodness you're finally being sensible about this."

"No one bothered to ask me what I thought before shipping off a so-called magic wedding gown. I don't want to get married yet, so I certainly don't need the dress. It was a nice gesture, but unnecessary."

"Exactly," Jill agreed.

"I'm not interested in playing déjà voodoo." She paused to laugh at her own joke.

Jill chuckled, too. "I wouldn't be, either."

Shelly felt greatly relieved, and the tight muscles along the back of her neck began to relax. Jill was, as usual, full of practical advice. Aunt Milly was a wonderful old lady, and the legend was a delightful bit of family lore, but it would be laughable to take any of this seriously.

"How about meeting me for lunch tomorrow?" Jill suggested. "It's been ages since we got together."

"Sounds good to me," Shelly said. Although they'd been close friends since college, it took some effort on both their parts these days to make time in their hectic lives to see each other. "When and where?"

"How about the mall?" Jill asked. "That would be easiest for me since I'm scheduled to work tomorrow. I can get off a few minutes before twelve."

"Great. I'll see you at noon at Patrick's," Shelly promised. Meeting her friend for lunch was just the antidote she needed after her terrible day. But what did she expect on Friday, April thirteenth?

Shelly overslept, then got stuck in a traffic jam on her way to meet Jill the following morning. She detested being late, although she often was. Rather than fight for a convenient parking spot in the vast lot that surrounded the mall, she took the first available space and rushed over to the nearest entrance. Patrick's, a cozy, charming restaurant on the mall's upper level, was deservedly popular for business lunches. Shelly had eaten there often and especially enjoyed the spinach-and-shrimp salad.

A glance at her watch told her it was already after twelve, and not wanting to keep Jill waiting, she hurried toward the escalator, weaving her way through the crowd.

Her mind must have been on the salad she intended to order instead of the escalator because the moment she placed her foot on the first tread, she lost her balance.

"Oh…oh!" Swinging both arms out in a futile attempt to remain upright, she groped at thin air. She tried frantically to catch herself as she fell backward.

Landing in someone's arms shocked her as much as having lost her balance. Incredulous, she twisted around to thank her rescuer but this proved to be a mistake. Her action caught the man off guard, and before he could prevent it, they went crashing to the floor. Once again Shelly expected to experience pain. Instead, her waist was surrounded by arms that were surprisingly strong. His grip was firm but gentle, protective. As they fell, he maneuvered himself to take the brunt of the impact when they landed. Sprawled as she was above him, Shelly found herself staring down at the most attractive man she'd ever seen. Her heart thrummed. Her breath caught. Her body froze.

For a moment neither of them spoke. A crowd had

gathered around them before Shelly managed to speak. When she did, her voice was weak and breathless. "Are you all right? I'm so sorry…"

"I'm fine. What about you?"

"Fine. I think."

She lay cushioned by his solid chest, their faces mere inches apart. Shelly's long hair fell forward, framing his face. He smelled of mint and some clean-scented soap. Her gaze wandered curiously over his features; at such close range she could see the tiny lines that fanned out from the edges of his sapphire-blue eyes, as well as the grooves that bracketed his mouth. His nose was classically straight, his mouth full and sensuous. At least his lower lip was. It didn't take her long to recognize that this man was uncompromisingly male. His eyes held hers reluctantly, as if he, too, was caught in the same powerful trance.

Neither of them moved, and although Shelly was convinced the breathless sensation she felt was a result of the fall, she couldn't seem to breathe properly even now.

"Miss, are you hurt?"

Reluctantly, Shelly looked up to find a security guard standing over her.

"Um…I don't think so."

"Sir?"

"I'm fine."

The arms that were holding her securely began to loosen.

"If we could have you both sit over here for a moment," the guard instructed, pointing at a bench. "We have an ambulance on the way."

"An ambulance? But I told you I'm okay," she said.

The guard helped Shelly to her feet. Her legs were shaky and her breathing still uncertain, but otherwise she was unhurt.

"Officer, there's really no need," the man who'd fallen with her protested.

"Mall policy," the guard said. He hooked his thumbs into the wide leather belt and rocked back on his feet. "It's standard procedure to have all accident victims checked immediately."

"If you're worried about a lawsuit—"

"I don't make the rules," the guard interrupted her rescuer. "I just see that they're carried out. Now, if you'd sit over here, the medical team will arrive in a couple of minutes."

"I don't have time to wait," Shelly insisted. "I'm meeting someone." She glanced longingly at the upper level, wondering how she could get word of her delay to Jill. Needless to say, she'd forgotten her cell—could anything else go wrong? It didn't reassure her to notice the number of people clustered by the railing, staring down at her. Her little escapade had attracted quite a bit of attention.

"I've got an appointment, as well," the man said, looking pointedly at his watch.

The security guard ignored their protests. He removed a small notebook from his shirt pocket and flipped it open. "Your names, please."

"Shelly Hansen."

"Mark Brady."

He wrote down the information and a brief account of how they happened to fall.

"I won't have to go to the hospital, will I?" Shelly demanded.

"That depends," the guard answered.

This whole thing was ridiculous. She was perfectly fine. A little shaken, true, but uninjured. She suddenly realized that she hadn't thanked this man—Mark, was it?

"I'm terribly sorry about all this," she said. "I can't thank you enough for catching me."

"In the future, you might be more careful." Mark glanced at his watch a second time.

"I will be. But if it ever happens again, might I suggest you just let me fall?" This delay was inconvenient, but that wasn't any reason to be quick-tempered. She studied her rescuer and shook her head slightly, wondering why she'd been so impressed. He looked as if he'd stepped off Planet Nerd. Dark blue suit and tie, crisp white shirt, polished loafer-type shoes. This guy was as original as cooked oatmeal. About as personable, too.

If she was giving him the once-over, she discovered he was eyeing her, too. Apparently he was equally unimpressed. Her sweatshirt was a fluorescent orange and her jeans as tight as a second skin. Her ankle-high boots were black, her socks the same shade of orange as the sweatshirt. Her hair cascaded about her shoulders in a layer of dark frothy curls. Mark was scowling in obvious disapproval.

The wide glass doors at the mall entrance opened, and two paramedics hurried inside. Seconds later, when the ambulance arrived, two more medical people entered the building. Shelly was mortified that such a minor accident would result in all this scrutiny.

The first paramedic knelt in front of her while the second concentrated on Mark. Before she completely understood what was happening, her shoe was off and the man was examining her ankle. Mark, too, was being examined, a stethoscope pressed over his heart. He didn't seem to appreciate the procedures any more than she did.

It wasn't until he stood up that she realized how tall he was. Close to six-five, she guessed. A good match for her own five feet ten inches, she thought automatically.

It hit her then. Bull's-eye. Aunt Milly's letter had mentioned her standing beside a tall young man. Mark Brady was tall. Very tall. Taller than just about any man she'd ever met.

Aunt Milly's letter had also said something about Shelly's blue eyes. She'd ignored it at the time, but her eyes weren't blue. They were hazel. Mark had blue eyes, though. The kind of vivid blue eyes women generally found striking… Nor could she forget her initial reaction to him. She'd been attracted. Highly attracted. It'd been a long time since a man had interested her this much. Until he stood up, anyway. When she got a good look at him, she'd known immediately that they had nothing in common. She'd bet he didn't own a single article of clothing that wasn't blue, black or tan. Mark Brady was clearly a man without imagination or flair.

On a sudden thought, she glanced worriedly at his left hand. No wedding ring. Closing her eyes, she sagged against the back of the bench and groaned.

"Miss?" The paramedic was studying her closely.

"Excuse me," she said, straightening. She jerked impatiently on Mark's suit jacket. He was involved in a conversation with the ambulance attendant who was interviewing him and didn't turn around.

"Excuse me," she said again, louder this time.

"Yes?" Mark turned to face her, frowning impatiently.

Now that she had his attention, she wasn't sure she should continue. "This may seem like an odd question, but, uh…are you married?"

He frowned again. "No."

"Oh, no," Shelly moaned and slumped forward. "I was afraid of that."

"I beg your pardon?"

"Do you have a girlfriend? I mean, you're a good-looking guy. There's got to be someone important in your life. Anyone? Please, just think. Surely there's someone?" She knew she was beginning to sound desperate, but she couldn't help it. Aunt Milly's letter was echoing in her mind, and last night's logic had disappeared.

The four paramedics, as well as Mark, were staring at her. "Are you sure you don't want to come to the hospital and talk to a doctor?" one of them asked.

Shelly nodded. "I'm sure." Then before she could stop herself, she blurted out, "What do you do for a living?"

"I'm a CPA," he answered wearily.

"An accountant," she muttered. She should've guessed. He was obviously as staid and conventional as he looked. And as boring. The kind of man who'd probably never even heard of DVDs for entertaining bored house cats. He probably wouldn't be interested in purchasing one, either.

Her aunt Milly *couldn't* have seen Mark and Shelly together in her dream. Not Mark Brady. The two of them were completely ill-suited. A relationship wouldn't last five minutes! Abruptly she reminded herself that she wasn't supposed to be taking Milly's prediction seriously.

"May I go?" she asked the paramedic. "I'm not even bruised."

"Yes, but you'll need to sign here."

Shelly did so without bothering to read the statement. Mark, however, seemed to peruse every sentence. He would, of course.

"Uh, Mark…" Shelly hesitated, and Mark glanced in her direction.

"Thank you," she said simply.

"You're welcome."

Still she delayed leaving.

"Is there anything else?"

She didn't know quite how to say this, but she felt the need too strongly to ignore it. "Don't take offense— I'm sure you're a really great guy—but I just want you to know I'm not interested in marriage right now."

Three

Jill was seated at the table, doodling on the paper place mat, when Shelly arrived. "What kept you?" she asked. "I've been here for almost half an hour."

"I—I fell off the escalator."

Jill's eyes widened in alarm. "My goodness, are you all right?"

Shelly nodded sheepishly. "I'm fine."

"Shouldn't you see a doctor?"

"I already have," she said, avoiding eye contact with her friend. "Well, sort of. The security guard called in the paramedics."

"No wonder you're late."

"I would've been, anyway," Shelly admitted as she reached for a menu, although she knew what she was going to order—the same thing she always did.

"This has really got you flustered, hasn't it?"

"It's more than the fall," Shelly explained, lowering the menu. "It's the man who caught me."

Jill arched her eyebrows jokingly. "Aha! I should have guessed there was a man involved."

"You might try to understand how I felt," Shelly said reproachfully. "Especially since I haven't recovered from receiving Aunt Milly's wedding dress yet."

"Don't tell me you're still worried about that first-man-you-meet nonsense."

"Of course not. That would be ridiculous. It's just…it's just I can't help feeling there might be *something* to that silly wedding dress."

"Then mail it back."

"I can't," Shelly said, slapping the menu down on the table. "Aunt Milly warned me not to. She didn't use exactly those words, mind you. She said I shouldn't ignore the dress. I mean, how can I? It's like an albatross around my neck."

"I still think you're overreacting."

"That's the crazy part. I *know* I am, but I can't seem to stop myself. I grew up hearing the legend of that wedding dress, and now it's in my possession. I've got a piece of family history hanging in the back of my closet. What if my mother hears about this?" She shuddered at the thought.

"So you hung the dress in your closet."

"I tried keeping it under my bed, but I couldn't sleep, so I finally got up and stuck it in the closet." She closed the menu and set it aside. "That bothered me, too. I tossed and turned half the night, then I remembered Aunt Milly had done the same thing when the seamstress gave her the dress."

"She put it under her bed?"

Shelly nodded slowly. "I seem to remember hearing that. She'd tried to refuse it, but the old woman insisted Aunt Milly take the gown home with her. By the time she got to her apartment she'd already met my uncle John, although she still didn't know she was going to marry him."

Jill raised a skeptical eyebrow. "Then what? After she put it under her bed and couldn't sleep, I mean?"

"Well, she did the same thing I did," Shelly said. "She shoved it in her closet." Shelly felt as if she was confessing to a crime. "I didn't want the thing staring me in the face so I hung it in the back."

"Naturally." Jill was trying, unsuccessfully, to disguise a smile. Shelly could see how someone else might find her situation humorous, but she personally didn't think any of this was too amusing. Not when it was her life, her future, being tossed around like…like some cosmic football. At this rate, she'd be married by nightfall!

"That's not the worst of it," Shelly added. She exhaled slowly, wondering why her heart was still beating so fiercely.

"You mean there's more?"

She nodded. The waitress arrived just then and took their orders, returning quickly with glasses of iced tea. Shelly took a deep breath before she continued. "I literally fell into that man's—Mark Brady's—arms."

"How convenient."

"It's very nice of him to have broken my fall," she said sternly, "but I wish he hadn't."

"Shelly!"

"I mean it." She glanced around to make sure no one was listening, then whispered, "The man's an accountant."

Jill reacted in mock horror, covering her mouth with both hands. "No! An accountant?"

"Think about it. Could you honestly picture me married to an accountant?"

Jill mulled over the question for a moment. "Hmm, a CPA," she repeated slowly. "You still haven't memorized your multiplication tables, have you? You freeze up whenever you have to deal with numbers. No, I guess you're right, I can't see you with an accountant."

Shelly raised both hands, palms up, in a dramatic gesture. "I rest my case."

Jill reached for some bread, carefully selecting a whole-wheat roll. "Just because you fell into his arms doesn't mean you're going to marry him," she said in a matter-of-fact voice.

"I know that."

"Then what's the problem?"

"I can't make myself *believe* it," Shelly said. "I feel like one tiny pin fighting the force of a giant magnet."

"That's preposterous."

"I know," Shelly agreed readily. "I just wish I hadn't said anything to Mark."

Jill set the roll on her plate with exaggerated care. "You told him about your aunt Milly's wedding dress?"

"Of course not!" Shelly said. "I told him I couldn't marry him."

Jill's mouth dropped open. "You didn't! Did you?"

Shelly nodded. "I don't know what made me say anything so ludicrous. I can't imagine what he must think of me. Not that I plan on seeing him again, of course. Unless—"

"Unless what?"

Their lunches were served. Jill had ordered a hot spinach salad with slices of chicken. Shelly's spinach salad was piled high with shrimp, egg slices and black olives.

"Go on," Jill urged once the waitress had gone. "You don't plan on seeing Mark again unless—"

"Unless it's absolutely unavoidable."

"I take it this means your aunt Milly's first encounter with your uncle John wasn't her last." Jill giggled. "Silly me. Obviously it wasn't."

"No. Even though Aunt Milly didn't want to see him again. My uncle was a wonderful man, don't get me wrong, and he was perfect for Aunt Milly, as it turned out, but they were as different as night and day. Aunt Milly was a college graduate and Uncle John never completed high school."

Shelly sighed wistfully. At one time the story of their romance had been like her own personal fairy tale. But now she didn't find it nearly as enthralling. "He helped Milly fix her car the night it broke down. The very next day she was in court defending a client in a lawsuit—"

"Let me guess," Jill interrupted, "your uncle John was the man suing her client."

Shelly nodded. "Yes, and that was only the beginning. Every time they turned around they were bumping into each other."

"How soon after they met did they get married?"

This was the question Shelly had dreaded most. She closed her eyes and whispered, "Ten days."

"Ten days," Jill echoed with an incredulous look.

"I know. It seems that once they kissed, they both realized there wasn't any use fighting it."

"Did your aunt tell John about the seamstress and the wedding dress?"

Shelly shrugged. "I don't know, but my guess is she didn't...at least not at first." She hadn't touched her salad yet and paused to savor a forkful of her favorite seafood. Then she said abruptly, "They eloped without telling anyone."

"Children?" Jill wanted to know.

"Three boys. My mother's cousins."

"What about granddaughters? You'd think your aunt Milly would want to hand the dress down to one of them."

"All three of her sons had boys themselves. I guess you could say I'm the closest she's got to a granddaughter."

"Ten days," Jill repeated. "That's really something."

Forking up another succulent shrimp, Shelly continued her story. "That old Scottish woman knew about the wedding even before the family did. When Aunt Milly and Uncle John returned from their hon-

eymoon, there was a wedding card from the seamstress waiting for them."

Jill propped her elbows on the table and gazed at
Shelly. "Tell me what Mark Brady looks like."

Shelly frowned, trying to form her impressions of him
into some kind of reasonably articulate description. He
was compelling in ways she didn't quite understand. She
sensed that he was principled and headstrong, but what
made her so sure of that, Shelly couldn't explain. "He's
tall," she began slowly. "And he was wearing a suit."

"How tall?"

"Basketball-player tall. He must be about six-five."

"Brown hair?"

Shelly nodded. "With blue eyes. *Really* blue eyes. I
don't think I've ever met a man with eyes that precise
color. They seemed to…" She hesitated, unsettled by the
emotion that stirred within her when she thought about
Mark. Although their encounter had been brief, Shelly
was left feeling oddly certain that she could trust this
man, trust him implicitly. It wasn't a sensation she could
remember experiencing with any other man. She didn't
like the feeling; it made her uncomfortable. Until Jill
had started asking her about Mark, Shelly didn't realize
she'd experienced *any* emotion toward him—except for
embarrassment, of course.

"Why do you want to know?" she asked.

Jill gave her a knowing grin. "Because if he's as tall
as you say, with dark brown hair and deep blue eyes, and
he's wearing a suit, he just walked into this restaurant."

"What?" Shelly felt her stomach sink. "Mark's here? Mark Brady?"

"That's not so unusual, is it? This is, after all, the same shopping mall where you, uh, met—" Jill made a show of glancing at her watch "—thirty or so minutes ago."

"He's here." She reminded herself that Jill was right: Mark's choosing to have lunch at Patrick's was just a coincidence. Too bad she couldn't convince her racing heart to believe that.

"He's on the other side of the room," Jill whispered.

"Has he seen me yet?"

"I don't think so."

Without being obvious—or at least Shelly hoped she wasn't being obvious—she turned to look in his direction. At that same instant, Mark happened to look up. Their eyes met. Despite herself, she gasped. Her hands shook and she felt herself break out in a cold sweat.

Mark scowled and quickly looked away.

She couldn't blame him. He seemed surprised to see her there. Unpleasantly surprised.

"Well, is it him?" Jill demanded.

Shelly couldn't find her voice, so she answered with a nod.

"I thought it might be. What are you thinking?"

"That I've lost my appetite." Shelly doubted she'd be able to finish her lunch.

"You want my advice?" Jill asked, grinning broadly. "I don't have a lot of experience with magic wedding dresses, but I recently read a fascinating book on home remedies."

"Sure." At this point Shelly was feeling reckless enough to try just about anything.

"Garlic," Jill said solemnly. "Wear a garlic rope around your neck. Not only does it deter vampires and prevent colds, but it might ward off potential husbands conjured up by a magic wedding dress."

Four

Hard though she tried, Shelly had a difficult time ignoring Mark Brady. He sat there, stiff and unapproachable, at the other side of the small restaurant. Just as stiff and unapproachable as she was. Jill wanted to linger over her coffee before returning to her job at the PayRite Pharmacy in the mall, but Shelly was eager to be on her way. The sooner she left, the sooner she could put this bothersome encounter behind her.

"Don't forget Morgan's baby shower on Tuesday night," Jill said as Shelly reached for her purse.

Shelly had completely forgotten about their friend's party, which was understandable given her present state of mind. Most of their college friends were married and several were now having babies. Rather than admit how absentminded she'd suddenly become, Shelly asked, "Do you want to drive over together?"

"Sure," Jill said. "I have to go directly from work so I'll stop off at your place and we can leave from there."

"I'll be ready." She tried to imagine their excitable classmate as a wife and mother. It was Morgan who'd gotten the entire dorm hooked on *Survivor.* Before anyone could figure out how it had occurred, all the girls were obsessed with the participants and their lives. It became as important as mealtimes to learn who'd been voted off and who'd won that week's challenges.

For no particular reason, Shelly thought of Aunt Milly's wedding dress—which seemed to have become her own private challenge. Sighing, she dropped her share of the bill and a tip on the table. "I'll see you Tuesday, then."

"Right. And, Shelly, don't look so worried. No enchanted wedding dress is going to interfere with your life—unless you allow it to."

Easy for Jill to say, since it wasn't *her* life and *her* great-aunt's wedding dress. Nevertheless, her advice was sound. Aunt Milly might have had some fanciful dream about Shelly's marrying a tall man with blue eyes, but that didn't mean it was going to happen, especially when Shelly was so determined that it wouldn't.

"You're absolutely right," she said emphatically. "I know I keep saying that, but…well, I seem to need reminding. So, thanks. Again." With a final wave, she wandered out of the restaurant, barely noticing the colorful shop windows as she passed them. As Jill had pointed out, Aunt Milly meant well, but the letter and the wedding dress shouldn't be taken too seriously.

Shelly knew exactly what kind of man she'd fall in love with, and he wouldn't bear any resemblance to

Mark Brady. He'd be unconventional, and fervent about life, and as passionate as she was herself. Naturally, he'd appreciate her work and take pride in his own. He'd be a free spirit, like her. She'd prefer a man with gumption, too—someone who possessed initiative. It'd be nice if he was a little better at organizational skills than she was, but that wasn't a requirement.

With marriage so prominent in her mind, Shelly found herself standing in front of a jeweler's display window, studying a large assortment of wedding bands. She noticed one ring that stood out from the rest: three small rows of diamond chips, bracketed on each side by a thin band of gold. The ring was striking in its simplicity, its uncontrived beauty.

For the longest moment Shelly stared at the rings as she wove whimsical dreams around the happy bride and the tall groom. *Tall groom.* Her thoughts came to a skidding halt.

What on earth had come over her? She didn't know, but whatever it was, she didn't like it. Self-consciously she glanced around, fearful that someone was watching her. Well, a very specific someone, to be honest. Someone who definitely shouldn't see her gazing with open longing at a collection of absurdly high-priced wedding rings. Mark Brady.

With a sense of urgency, Shelly hurried toward the mall exit. It was all she could do to keep from breaking into a run. No matter how fast she walked, however, she couldn't shake the feeling that *he* was there, watching her. Twice she whirled around, convinced she'd see Mark Brady strolling behind her, sneering and making contemptuous remarks.

He wasn't there.

With profound relief, she arrived at the parking lot and located her car. She finally felt herself relax as she neared her apartment building. Once she'd parked her car, Shelly stopped in the lobby to collect her mail. As soon as she opened the small box, Mrs. Livingston's head poked out her door.

"Good afternoon, Shelly," she chirped, smiling at her expectantly.

It took Shelly a moment to realize that Mrs. L. must have been waiting to hear about the contents of her package.

"It's a lovely day," Shelly said conversationally, sorting through her mail. Two bills, a flyer and something from the Internal Revenue Service. The way her luck had been going, it was probably an audit notice. A quick inspection revealed exactly that. She closed her eyes and groaned inwardly.

"A lovely day indeed," Mrs. Livingston echoed cheerfully.

Muttering under her breath, Shelly stuffed the IRS notice back inside the envelope. When she looked up, she saw that the older woman was now standing in the hallway.

"I suppose you're wondering about the package," Shelly said resignedly, tucking her mail inside her purse. "It was a gift from my aunt Milly."

"Something from the past, I guess?" Mrs. Livingston asked.

"Why…yes. How'd you know?"

"I'd take whatever it is very, very seriously if I were you," Mrs. Livingston continued in a solemn voice. "Wizard wouldn't go anywhere near that box. Think what you want, but my cat's always had a sixth sense when it comes to this sort of thing."

"It's a dress, Mrs. L.," Shelly explained, hiding behind a false smile. "How am I supposed to take a dress seriously?" It was exactly what she'd vowed *not* to do.

Mrs. Livingston opened her apartment door and scooped the large black-and-white cat into her arms. "That I wouldn't know," she returned, her eyes narrowed. "All I can tell you is that Wizard felt skittish around that package. You don't suppose there's…magic in it, do you?"

Somehow Shelly managed a reply, although she felt certain it was unintelligible. Taking the stairs two at a time, she dashed into her apartment, leaning breathlessly against the door. Even Mrs. Livingston's cat knew there was something strange about Aunt Milly's wedding dress!

When Jill arrived late Tuesday afternoon, Shelly was ready and waiting for her, brightly wrapped baby gift in hand. She was eager to get out and socialize—eager to get out, period. Anything to escape another phone call from her mother, who'd recently heard from Aunt Milly.

Now Faith Hansen was calling daily for updates on the romantic prospects in her daughter's life.

"Well?" Jill demanded as she entered the apartment. "Are you going to show it to me?"

"Show what to you?"

Jill gave her a look that seemed to question her intelligence. "The wedding dress, of course."

For several hours Shelly had succeeded in putting the dress out of her mind. "No," she said forcefully. "I want to forget about the whole thing."

"Met any tall blue-eyed men lately?" Jill couldn't resist asking.

"None," Shelly answered shortly. Checking her watch, she noted that they were early but suggested they leave, anyway. "Shall we go?"

"We've got lots of time," Jill countered, moving toward Shelly's bedroom. "Come on, it isn't going to hurt to let me look at the dress."

"Oh, all right," Shelly conceded ungraciously. Leading the way, she opened the closet door and reached into the back of the closet.

She brought out the lace-and-satin gown, holding it up for Jill's inspection. She'd hardly looked at the dress the day she'd received it, and now she was almost shocked by how beautiful it actually was.

The laughter drained from Jill's dark brown eyes as she stared at the gown. "Oh, Shelly, it's…lovely." She gently touched the Elizabethan sleeve and ran her finger along the delicate layer of pearls that decorated the cuff.

The high neckline was also trimmed with an intricate design of pearls. "I don't know what I expected," Jill said in an awed whisper, "but certainly nothing as beautiful as this."

Shelly nodded wordlessly. The dress was far more exquisite than she'd realized. Her heart swelled with sudden emotion, and to her dismay, tears filled her eyes as she thought about the old Scottish woman who had so lovingly constructed the gown. Each pearl had been sewn into place by hand. She thought of her aunt Milly, as tall and statuesque as Shelly herself, wearing the dress. Then she recalled her uncle John, such a determined man, so wise and sensible. Shelly thought fondly of those two, who'd been so completely different, yet had loved each other so well….

For a moment neither she nor Jill spoke. "Have you tried it on?" Jill finally asked.

Shelly shook her head adamantly, not wanting her friend to know how emotional she'd become. "Heavens, no, but you can if you want."

"I don't think I could resist if I were you," Jill whispered, obviously affected by the dress, too. "Just seeing it…makes me wish I was a bride myself."

"There's always Ralph," Shelly teased. Jill had been dating Ralph, a computer programmer, for several months, but Shelly couldn't understand what her friend saw in him.

Jill threw her an irritated look. "The dress is for you, not me."

"But I don't want it," Shelly insisted, though she was no longer sure what she felt. Not since she'd really examined the dress and allowed herself to remember the wonder of John and Milly's romance.

"You're sure you don't mind?" Jill asked, slipping off her shoes. "I mean, if you'd rather I didn't try it on, I'll understand."

"No, feel free." Shelly strove for a flippant air. "As far as I'm concerned, the dress is nothing but bad luck. It arrived on Friday the thirteenth. The next day I had that minor accident on the mall escalator. Now I'm being audited by the IRS."

It was as if Jill didn't hear. "I doubt it'll fit," she said as she cautiously removed the gown from the padded hanger. "I'm a good five inches shorter than you and heavier on top."

"Maybe the dress was meant for you in the first place," Shelly ventured. Perhaps Aunt Milly had been confused and it was Jill she'd viewed in her dream. After all, Milly's eyes weren't what they used to be….

"Does your mother know?" Jill asked as she stepped into the dress. She raised it over her hips and turned around to let Shelly fasten the buttons that ran down the back.

"That's another thing," Shelly moaned. "Mom's been calling me every day since I got the dress, wanting to know if I've met anyone special yet."

"What did you tell her?" Jill asked, looking at Shelly over her shoulder.

"What's there to tell?" she asked irritably.

"Well, you might have mentioned Mark."

"Mark," Shelly repeated. She shrugged elaborately. "I haven't given him a thought in days." Not strictly true, but she'd been *trying* not to think about him. Even if he was interested in her—and he'd made very clear that he wasn't—she couldn't imagine two more ill-suited people. "I haven't seen him since Saturday and I doubt I'll ever see him again."

"You're sure of that?"

"Positive."

"Well, what do you think?" Jill asked next, pirouetting slowly in front of her. "My hair's a mess and I've got hardly any makeup on, but…"

Shelly studied her friend and sighed audibly. Never had she seen Jill look lovelier. It was as if the dress had been made for her. "Absolutely enchanting. It fits like a dream."

"I feel like I *am* dreaming," Jill admitted softly. "Here," she said, turning around, "undo me before I start longing for a husband and 2.5 children."

"Don't forget the house with the white picket fence," Shelly teased, unfastening the buttons.

Jill slipped out of the dress. "Your turn," she said as she laid it carefully across the bed. "If it fits me, then it can't possibly fit you. You've got the perfect excuse to send it back to your aunt Milly."

"I…don't know." Shelly bit her lip. She felt an inexplicable urge to keep the dress, and at the same time she would've willingly returned it to her aunt. Even while she hesitated, Shelly found herself undressing. She couldn't explain her sudden eagerness to try on the wedding gown any more than she could fathom its growing emotional appeal.

The dress slid easily over her hips. She turned around so Jill could secure the back, then glanced at the mirror, expecting to find the skirt miles too short. It would have to be in order to fit Jill as perfectly as it had.

"Shelly," Jill whispered, then cupped her hand over her mouth. "My goodness…you look beautiful…really beautiful."

That was what Shelly had felt the instant she'd seen her friend in the dress. "Something's wrong," she said once she found her voice. "Something's very wrong."

"No," Jill countered, "it's very right. It's as if the dress was made for you."

"Then answer me this," Shelly whispered. "How is it possible for the same dress to fit two women who wear totally different sizes?"

Five

Shelly struggled to open the door of the Internal Revenue office, her arms weighed down with a huge box stuffed full of receipts and records for the audit. By bracing the box against the wall with her knee, she freed one hand to open the door. For the first time ever, she'd completed her tax return early—all by herself, too—and *this* was her reward. She grumbled righteously and bit her lip, more in anxiety than annoyance.

She'd just managed to grasp the door handle, when the door unexpectedly opened and she staggered into the room, nearly colliding with an end table. She did a quick pirouette, convinced she'd ruined a new pair of panty hose. With a heartfelt sigh, she set her box of records on the floor and sank into the first available chair, neatly arranging her unaccustomed skirt around her knees. Only then did she bother to look around. There was one other person in the large reception area.

Shelly's heart did a nosedive, landing in the pit of her

stomach. The man who'd opened the door for her, the man sitting in this very waiting room, was none other than Mark Brady—the man she'd hoped to avoid for the rest of her natural life. She gave an involuntary gasp.

Mark was leafing through the dog-eared pages of a magazine when he happened to glance her way. The automatic smile faded from his face, and his eyes narrowed as if he strongly suspected Shelly had purposely arranged this meeting.

"What are you doing here?" Shelly demanded.

"I might ask you the same thing."

"I didn't follow you here, if that's what you're implying!"

"Listen, Ms….Hansen, I really couldn't care less." With that he returned to his magazine, but he raised his head again a moment later. "*You're* the person who blurted out to everyone within hearing distance that you weren't marrying me. As if I'd even asked! As if I even *knew* you!"

Shelly felt the heat rising up her neck and offered the first excuse she could think of. "I…was distraught."

"Obviously," he muttered from behind his magazine.

A few minutes of strained silence passed. Shelly shifted uncomfortably in her chair, checking her watch approximately every ten seconds. She was early for her appointment, but if this was where promptness got you, she'd prefer to be late.

"All right, I apologize," Shelly said when she couldn't tolerate the silence any longer. "What I said was ridiculous and…and out of turn—"

"Out of turn," Mark echoed, throwing the magazine down on the table. "I repeat—I don't even know you."

"I realize that."

He inhaled deeply, which drew her attention to his broad, muscular chest. She saw that he was as meticulously dressed as he'd been at their first encounter. His dark suit and silk tie, however conventional, added a touch of sophistication to his natural good looks.

"If there's anyone to blame for this it's Aunt Milly," Shelly said, more to herself than him.

"Aunt Milly?" Mark repeated, sounding unsure. He eyed her warily.

She'd said this much; she might as well launch into the whole ludicrous tale.

"Actually, it has more to do with the wedding dress than with my aunt Milly, although by now the two of them are inseparable in my mind. I don't usually dabble in this sort of thing, but I'm beginning to think there might be something supernatural about that silly dress, after all."

"Supernatural?"

"Magic, if you prefer."

"Magic in a wedding dress?" Mark gazed hopefully at the door that led to the inner offices of Internal Revenue, as though he was anxious to be called away.

"It's unbelievable, but the dress fits both Jill and me, which is virtually impossible. You saw Jill—she's the friend I was having lunch with last Saturday. I know we were halfway across the room from you, but you couldn't help noticing how much shorter she is than I am. We're completely different sizes."

Mark hurriedly reached for the magazine as if he wanted to shut her out before she said anything else.

"I know it seems crazy. I don't like this any better than you do, but I'm afraid you're the one Aunt Milly mentioned in her letter." Well, it was only fair to tell him that.

Mark glanced in her direction again, blue eyes suspicious. "Your aunt Milly mentioned me in a letter?"

"Not by name—but she said she had a clear vision of me in the wedding dress and I was standing with a tall man. She also referred to blue eyes. You're tall and you have blue eyes and the legend says I'm going to marry the first man I meet after receiving the dress."

"And I just happened to be that man?"

"Yes," Shelly cried. "*Now* do you understand why I was so disturbed when we met?"

"Not entirely," Mark said after a moment.

Shelly sighed loudly. How obtuse could the man be? "You're tall, aren't you? And you have blue eyes."

He flipped intently through the magazine, not looking at her as he spoke. "I really don't care what the letter said, nor am I concerned about this wedding dress you keep bringing up."

"Of course you don't care," Shelly said indignantly. "Why should you? It must all seem quite absurd to you. And I'm aware that I'm overreacting, but I do have a tendency to get emotional. If it helps any, I want you to know I'm happy with my life just the way it is. I don't want to get married—to anyone." When she'd finished, she drew in a deep breath and began leafing idly through a magazine, doing her utmost to ignore him.

Silence returned. Silences had always bothered Shelly. It was as if she felt personally responsible for filling them. "If you want something to be grateful about, you can thank your lucky stars I didn't mention you to my mother."

"Your mother," Mark repeated. "Does she know about Aunt Milly sending you this…dress?"

"Of course she does," Shelly answered, closing the magazine. "She's phoned me every day since she heard, because she thinks I'm going to meet that special some-one any minute."

"And you didn't say anything about me?"

"How could I? The instant I do that, she'll be calling the caterers."

"I see." The edges of his mouth lifted as though he was beginning to find the situation amusing. "She be-lieves in the power of this dress, too?"

"Unfortunately, yes. You have to understand where my mother stands on the issue of marriage," Shelly con-tinued, undaunted.

"I'm not sure I want to," Mark muttered under his breath.

Shelly disregarded his comment. "By age twenty-eight—my age now, coincidentally—Mom had been married for eight years and already had three children. She's convinced I'm letting the best years of my life slip away. There's nothing I can say to make her believe differently."

"Then I'll add my gratitude that you didn't mention me."

Mollified, Shelly nodded, then glanced at her watch. Her meeting was in ten minutes and she was nervous, since this was the first time she'd done her own taxes. She should have known there'd be a problem.

"I take it you're here for an audit?" Mark asked.

She nodded again, studying her tax return, sure she'd be in jail by nightfall without even understanding what she'd done wrong.

"Relax."

"How can I?"

"Have you knowingly hidden something from the government? Lied about the income you received, or claimed expenditures you've never made?"

"Oh, no!"

"Then you don't have anything to worry about."

"I don't?" Shelly stared at him, envying his confidence. She'd been restless for days, worrying about this meeting. If it wasn't the wedding dress giving her nightmares, it was the audit.

"Don't volunteer any information unless they ask for it."

"All right."

"Did you prepare your own tax return?"

"Well, yes. It didn't seem that complicated, and well, this sounds silly but Jill bet me I couldn't do it. So I did.

Back in February. You see, numbers tend to confuse me and I decided to accept the challenge, and…" She realized she was chattering, something she did when she was nervous. Forcing herself to stay quiet, she scanned her return for the hundredth time, wondering what she could have possibly done wrong.

"Do you want me to look it over for you?"

Shelly was surprised by his generosity. "If you wouldn't mind. Are you being audited yourself?"

Mark smiled and shook his head. "A client of mine is."

"Oh."

He crossed the room and sat next to her. When Shelly handed him her tax return, he quickly ran down the row of figures, then asked her several questions.

"I've got everything right here," she assured him, gesturing toward the carton she'd lugged in with her. "I really am careful about saving everything I should."

Mark gestured at the large cardboard box. "This is all for one year?"

"No," she admitted sheepishly. "I brought along everything I had for the past six years. I mean, it made sense at the time."

"That really wasn't necessary."

"I'd rather be safe than sorry," Shelly said with a shrug. She watched Mark as he scrutinized her return. At such close range, she saw that his eyes were even bluer than she'd thought. *Blue as the sky on a bright July afternoon…* Her heart felt heavy in her chest, and hard as she tried, she couldn't keep herself from staring.

Mark handed back her return. "Everything looks fine. I don't think you'll have a problem."

It was astonishing how relieved she felt at hearing that. No, at hearing that from *him*. Mark smiled at her and Shelly found herself responding readily with a smile of her own. The fluttery sensation returned to her stomach. She knew her eyes were wide and questioning and although she tried to look away, she couldn't do it.

Surprise mingled with gentleness on his face, as if he were seeing her for the first time, really seeing her. He liked what he saw—Shelly could read that in his eyes. Slowly his gaze traveled over her features, and she felt her pulse speed up. The letter she'd received from Aunt Milly flitted through her mind, but instead of dismissing the memory, she wondered, *Could there really be something to all this?*

Mark was the one to break eye contact. He stood abruptly and hurried back to his seat. "I don't think you have to worry."

"Yes, you told me."

"I mean about your aunt Milly's wedding dress."

"I don't have to worry?" Shelly repeated. She wasn't sure she understood.

"Not with me, at any rate."

"I don't quite follow…." If he was even half-aware of the way her heart was clamoring as they gazed into each other's eyes, he wouldn't be nearly as confident.

"I'm engaged."

"Engaged?" Shelly felt as though someone had slugged her in the stomach. Her first reaction was anger. "You couldn't have mentioned this sooner?" she snapped.

"It's not official yet. Janice hasn't picked out a diamond. Nor have we discussed our plans with her family."

The irritation faded, swallowed by an overwhelming sense of relief. "Engaged," she murmured, reminding herself that she really had no interest in marriage. And this proved there was no such thing as a "magic" wedding dress. If Mark was involved with Janice, he wouldn't be free to marry her. It was that simple. Shelly leaped to her feet and started to pace.

"Are you all right?" Mark asked. "You're looking pale."

She nodded and pressed her hands to her cheeks, which suddenly felt hot. "I'm so relieved," she whispered hoarsely. "You have no idea how relieved I am. You're engaged… My goodness, I feel like I've got a new lease on life."

"As I explained," Mark said, frowning, "it isn't official yet."

"That's okay. You're committed to someone else and that's all that matters. However—" she forced a smile "—you might have said something sooner and saved me all this anxiety."

"You did ask that day at the mall, but I was more concerned with avoiding a scene than revealing the personal details of my life."

"I'm sorry about that."

"No problem."

Shelly settled back in the chair and crossed her legs, hoping to strike a relaxed pose. She even managed to skim a couple of magazines, although she barely knew what she was reading.

Finally, the receptionist opened the door and called her name. Eager to get this over with, Shelly stood, picking up the large box she'd brought with her. She paused on her way out of the reception area and turned to Mark. "I wish you and Janice every happiness," she said formally.

"Thank you," he answered, then grinned. "Same to you and whatever, uh, lucky guy the wedding dress finds you."

Six

She should be happy, Shelly told herself early the following morning. Not only had she survived the audit—in fact she'd come away with an unexpected refund—but she'd learned that Mark was practically engaged.

Yes, she should be dancing in the streets, singing in the aisles... Instead she'd been struggling with a strange melancholy ever since their last encounter. She seemed to have lost her usual vitality, her sense of fun.

Now it was Saturday, and for once she had no looming deadlines, no appointments, no pressing errands. Remembering the exhilaration and solace she'd felt when she recorded an ocean storm sequence recently, Shelly decided to see if she could recapture some of those feelings. She headed over to Long Beach, a resort town on the Washington coastline. The sky was clear and almost cloudless; the sun was bright and pleasantly warm—a perfect spring day. Once she drove onto the freeway, the miles sped past and two hours later she was standing on the sandy beach with the breeze riffling her long hair.

She walked around for a while, enjoying the sights and sounds—the chirping of the sea gulls, the salty spray of the Pacific Ocean and the scent of wind and sea. She was satisfied with her beach DVD and started to work out plans for a whole series—the ocean in different seasons, different moods. That would be something special, she thought, something unique.

She wandered down the beach, kicking at the sand with the toes of her running shoes. Tucking her fingertips in the pockets of her jeans, she breathed in the vivid freshness around her. After an hour or so, she made her way back to the concession stands, where she bought a hot dog and a cold drink.

Then, just because it looked like fun, she rented a moped.

She sped along the shore, thrilled with the sensation of freedom, reveling in the solitude and the roar of pounding surf.

The wind tossed her hair about her face until it was a confusion of curls. Shelly laughed aloud and listened as the galloping breeze carried off the sound.

Her motorized bike rushed forward, spitting sand in its wake. She felt reckless with exhilaration, as though there was nothing she couldn't do. It was that kind of afternoon. That kind of day.

When she least expected it, someone else on a moped raced past her. Shelly hadn't encountered anyone during her ride and this person took her by surprise. She glanced quickly over her shoulder, astonished by how far she'd traveled. The only other person she could see was the one who'd passed her.

To her surprise, the rider did an abrupt turnaround and headed back in her direction. With the sun in her eyes and the wind pelting her, Shelly slowed to a crawl and shaded her eyes with one hand.

It wasn't until he was nearly beside her that Shelly recognized the other rider.

Mark Brady.

She was so shocked that she allowed the engine to die, her feet dropping to the sand to maintain her balance. Mark appeared equally shocked. He braked abruptly.

"Shelly?" He seemed not to believe it was her.

Shelly shook her head and blinked a couple of times just to make sure she wasn't fantasizing. She certainly hadn't expected to encounter Mark Brady on a beach two hours out of Seattle. Mr. Conservative riding a moped! This time, though, he wasn't wearing a dark suit. He didn't have his briefcase with him, either. And he looked even handsomer than usual in worn jeans and a University of Washington sweatshirt.

"Mark?" She couldn't prevent the astonishment from creeping into her voice.

"What are you doing here?"

She heard the hostility in his tone and answered him coolly. "The same thing as you, apparently." She pushed the hair from her face, and the wind promptly blew it back.

Mark's blue eyes narrowed suspiciously. "You didn't happen to follow me, did you?"

"Follow you?" she repeated indignantly. She'd rarely been more insulted. "Follow you!" she said again, starting her moped and revving the engine. "May I remind you that I was on the beach first? If anyone was doing any following, it was *you* following me." She was breathless by the time she finished. "In fact, you're the last person I'd follow anywhere!"

Mark scowled at her. "The feeling's mutual. I'm not in the mood for another story about your aunt Martha's damn wedding dress, either."

Shelly felt an unexpected flash of pain. "I was having a perfectly wonderful afternoon until you arrived," she said stiffly.

"I was having a good time myself," he muttered.

"Then I suggest we go our separate ways and forget we ever met."

Mark looked as if he was about to say something else, but Shelly was in no frame of mind to listen. She twisted the accelerator on the handlebar of her moped and took off down the beach. Although she knew she was being unreasonable, she was furious. Furious at the surge of joy she'd felt when she recognized him. Furious at Mark, because he didn't seem even a little pleased to see her. She bit her lower lip, remembering the comment he'd made about not wanting to hear any more about her "damn wedding dress." Now, that was just rude, she told herself righteously. She could *never* be interested in a man who was not only conventional but rude.

Squinting, Shelly hunched her shoulders against the wind, in a hurry now to return to the boardwalk. She hadn't meant to go nearly this far.

The wet, compact sand made for smooth, fast riding and Shelly stayed close to the water's edge in an effort to outdistance Mark. Not that he was likely to chase her, but she wanted to avoid any possibility of another embarrassing encounter.

Then it happened.

A large wave came in, sneaking its way up the sand, creating a thin, glistening sheen. Shelly hardly noticed as her front tire ripped through the water, spraying it out on both sides. Then the moped's front wheel dipped precariously. One minute she was sailing down the beach at breakneck speed and the next she was cartwheeling over her handlebars.

She landed heavily in a patch of wet sand, too paralyzed with shock to know if she was hurt or not.

Before she could move, Mark was crouching at her side. "Shelly? Are you all right?"

"I...don't know." Carefully she flexed one arm and then the other. Sitting up, she tested each leg and didn't feel pain there, either. Apparently she'd survived the experience unscathed.

"You crazy fool!" he yelled, leaping to his feet. "What are you trying to do, kill yourself?"

"Ah…" It was painful to breathe, otherwise she would've answered him.

"Can you imagine what I thought when I saw you flying through the air like that?"

"Good riddance?" she suggested.

Mark closed his eyes and shook his head. "I'm in no mood for your jokes. Here, let me help you up." He moved behind her, sliding his arms around her waist and gently raising her.

"I'm fine," she protested the instant his arms surrounded her. The blood rushed to her head, but Shelly didn't know if that was because of her tumble or because Mark was holding her. Even when she was on her feet, he didn't release her.

"Are you sure you're not hurt?"

Shelly nodded, not trusting her voice. "I'm less confident about the moped, though." Her bike seemed to be in worse shape than she was.

"It doesn't look good to me, either," Mark said. He finally dropped his arms and retrieved the moped, which was lying on its side, the waves lapping over it. There were regular hissing sounds as the cold water splashed against the heated muffler. Steam rose from the engine.

Mark did his best to start the bike, but to no avail. "I'm afraid it's hopelessly wet. It won't start now until it's had a chance to dry. A mechanic should check it over to be sure nothing's wrong."

Shelly agreed. There was no help for it; she was going to have to walk the bike back to the rental shop.

No small feat when she considered she was about three miles down the beach.

"Thank you very much for stopping," she said a bit primly. "But as you can see I'm not hurt...."

"What do you think you're doing?" Mark asked as she began pushing the moped. It made for slow progress; the bulky machine was far more difficult to transport under her own power than she'd expected. At this rate, she'd be lucky to return it by nightfall.

"I'm taking the bike back to the place where I rented it."

"That's ridiculous."

"Do you have any better ideas?" she asked in a reasonable tone of voice. "I don't understand what you're doing here in the first place," she said, sounding far calmer than she felt. "You should be with Janet."

"Who?" he demanded. He tried to take the moped away from her and push it himself, but she wouldn't let go.

"The woman you're going to marry. Remember?"

"Her name is Janice and as I said before, the engagement's unofficial."

"That doesn't answer my question. You should be with her on a beautiful spring day like this."

Mark frowned. "Janice couldn't get away. She had an important meeting with a client—she's a lawyer. Listen, quit being so stubborn, I'm stronger than you. Let me push the bike."

Shelly hesitated; his offer was tempting. She hadn't gone more than a few feet and already her side ached.

She pressed one hand against her hip and straightened, her decision made. "Thanks, but no thanks," she answered flatly. "By the way, it's Aunt Milly who sent me the wedding dress, not Aunt Martha, so if we're going to get names straight, let's start there."

Mark rolled his eyes skyward, as though he'd reached the end of his limited patience. "Fine, I'll apologize for what I said back there. I didn't mean to insult you."

"I didn't follow you," she said.

"I know, but I didn't follow you, either."

Shelly nodded, deciding she believed him.

"Then how do you explain that we've inadvertently bumped into each other twice in the last week?" Mark asked. "The odds of that happening have got to be phenomenal."

"I know it sounds crazy, but...I'm afraid it's the dress," Shelly mumbled.

"The wedding dress?" Mark repeated.

"I'm really embarrassed about all this. I'm not sure I believe any of it myself. And I do apologize, especially since there's been an apparent mix-up...."

"Why's that?" Mark asked.

"Well...because you're involved with Janice. I'm sure the two of you are a perfect match and you'll have a marvelous life together."

"What makes you assume that?"

His question caught her off guard. "Well, because... didn't you just tell me you're about to become officially engaged?"

"Yes," he muttered.

Although she was reluctant to admit it, Shelly found pushing the moped extremely taxing, so she stopped to rest for a moment. "Listen," she said a little breathlessly, "there's no need for you to walk with me. Why don't you just go on ahead?"

"There most definitely is a need," Mark answered sharply. He didn't seem too pleased with her suggestion. "I'm not going to desert you now."

"Oh, Mark, honestly, you don't have to be such a gentleman."

"You don't like gentlemen?"

"Of course I do—but it's one of the reasons you and I would never get along for any length of time. You're very sweet, don't get me wrong, but I don't need anyone to rescue me."

"Forgive me for saying so, but you *do* appear to need rescuing." The look he gave her implied that he was referring to more than the moped.

"I was the one foolish enough to get the engine wet," she said brightly, ignoring his comment. "So I should be the one to deal with the consequences."

Mark waited a moment, as if debating whether to continue arguing. "Fine, if that's the way you feel," he said finally, straddling his moped and starting the engine, which roared to life with sickening ease. "I hope you don't tire out too quickly."

"I'll be okay," she said, hardly able to believe he was actually going to abandon her.

"I hope you're right about that," he said, revving the engine.

"You...you could let someone know," she ventured. Maybe the rental agency would send someone out with a truck to find her.

"I'll see what I can do," he agreed, then grinning broadly, took off at top speed down the beach.

Although she'd made the suggestion that he go on without her, Shelly had assumed he wouldn't take it seriously. She'd said it more for the sake of dignity, of preserving her pride. She'd been enjoying his company, enjoying the banter between them.

As he vanished into the distance, Shelly squared her shoulders, determined to manage on her own—particularly since she didn't have any choice. She'd been dragging her moped along for perhaps ten minutes when she noticed another moped racing toward her. It didn't take her long to identify the rider, with his lithe, muscular build, as Mark. She picked up her pace, unreasonably pleased that he'd decided to return. He slowed as he approached her.

"Still eager to be rid of me?"

"No," she admitted, smiling half in relief, half in pleasure. "Can't you tell when a woman means something and when she's just being polite?"

"I guess not." He smiled back, apparently in a jovial mood. "Rest," he said, parking his own moped and taking hers. "A truck will be along any minute."

Shelly sank gratefully down on the lush sand. Mark

lowered himself onto the beach beside her. She plucked several blades of grass and began weaving them industriously together. That way, she wouldn't have to look at him.

"Are you always this stubborn?" he asked.

"Yes," she said quietly, giving him a shy smile. Shelly couldn't remember being shy in her life. But something about Mark made her feel shaky inside, and oddly weak. An unfamiliar sensation, but she dared not analyze it, dared not examine it too closely. She turned away from him and closed her eyes, trying to picture Janice, the woman he was going to marry. Despite her usually creative imagination, Shelly couldn't seem to visualize her.

"Shelly, what's wrong?"

"Wrong?"

"It's not like you to be so quiet."

She grinned. They were barely more than acquaintances, and he already knew her. "Nothing."

"I think there must be." His finger against the side of her face guided her eyes toward him. Their lips were so close. Shelly's breath seemed to be caught in her throat as she stared helplessly into the bluest eyes she'd ever seen....

His forehead touched hers, then he angled his face, brushing her cheek. Shelly knew she should break away, but she couldn't make herself do it. Gently, deliberately, he pressed his mouth to hers, his lips warm and moist.

Shelly moaned at the shock of sensation. Her eyes drifted shut as his mouth moved hungrily over hers, and soon their arms were wrapped tightly around each other, their bodies straining close.

The sound of the approaching truck intruded into their private world and broke them apart. Mark's eyes met hers, then he scowled and glanced away. But Shelly didn't know whether he was angry with her or with himself. Probably her.

Seven

"Hey," Shelly said reassuringly, "don't look so concerned. It was just an ordinary, run-of-the-mill kiss." She stood and brushed the wet sand from her jeans. "Besides, it didn't mean anything."

Mark's scowl darkened. "Didn't mean anything?" he echoed.

"Of course it didn't! I mean, we were both wondering what it would be like, don't you think? Good grief, we seem to be running into each other every other day and it's only logical that we'd want to, you know, experiment."

"In other words, you think the kiss was just a means of satisfying our mutual curiosity?"

"Sure. All this nonsense about the wedding dress overcame our common sense, and we succumbed to temptation." Thank goodness Mark seemed to understand her rambling. Shelly's knees were shaking. It was a wonder she could still stand upright. Although she'd tried to minimize the effects of his kiss, it left her feeling as though she'd never been kissed before. Her entire body had been overwhelmed by a feeling of *rightness*. Now all she felt was the crushing weight of confusion. She shouldn't be feeling any of these things for Mark. A CPA! An almost-engaged CPA, to boot.

"And was your curiosity satisfied?" he asked. His blue eyes probed.

"Uh…yes. And yours?"

"Yes," he muttered, but he was frowning again.

The kid from the rental agency leaped out of the truck and loaded Shelly's moped into the back. "You're not supposed to get the engine wet," he scolded. "It's in the rental agreement. You'll have to pay a fine."

Shelly nodded. She didn't have an excuse; she doubted the agency would accept her trying to escape Mark as a legitimate reason for damaging one of their vehicles.

Mark drove his moped, while Shelly got into the pickup's cab and rode silently down the long stretch of beach.

Shelly went to the office to deal with her fine and was surprised to find Mark waiting for her when she'd finished. "You hungry?" he asked in an offhand invitation.

"Uh…" She would've thought he'd be anxious to see the last of her.

"Good," he said immediately, not giving her a chance to reply. He grasped her elbow firmly as he led her to a nearby fish-and-chips stand. Shelly couldn't recall any other time a man had taken her elbow. Her first reaction was to object to what she considered an outdated gesture but she was surprised to find it oddly comforting, even pleasant.

They ordered their fish and chips, then carried the small baskets to a picnic table.

"I should've paid for my own," she said once they were seated, feeling vaguely guilty that he'd paid for both meals. Janice might be the jealous type, and Shelly didn't want her to hear about this.

His eyes met hers, steady and direct. "When I ask you to join me, I pick up the bill."

Any argument she had vanished before it reached her lips.

After that, Shelly concentrated on her fish and chips, which were fresh and absolutely delicious. Mark seemed equally preoccupied with his meal.

"What brought you to the beach today?" Shelly asked, finishing the last few French fries in her basket. Perhaps if they could determine what had brought them both to a lonely stretch of beach two hours from Seattle, they might be able to figure out how they'd happened upon each other once more.

"I have a beach house here. After tax time I generally try to get away for a few days. I like to come down here and relax."

"I had no idea." She found it inordinately important that he understand she hadn't somehow managed to stalk him across the state. Their meeting was pure coincidence…again.

"Don't worry about it, Shelly. You couldn't possibly

have known about the beach house or that I intended to be here today. I didn't know it myself until this morning."

Shelly suddenly wished Mark hadn't kissed her. Everything was becoming far too complicated.

"You're very talented," he told her out of the blue. "I bought one of your DVDs the other day."

"How'd you know what I do?" Shelly felt flustered by his praise; she was at a complete loss to understand why it meant so much to her.

"I saw it on the income tax form and I was curious about your work."

"Curiosity seems to have gotten us both into trouble," she said.

Mark grinned, a shameless, irresistible grin. The kind of grin that makes a woman forget all sorts of things. Like the fact that he was practically engaged. And that he was a tall, blue-eyed stranger who, according to Aunt Milly's letter, would soon become her husband....

Shelly scrambled to her feet, hurrying toward the beach. Mark followed.

"You shouldn't look at me like that," she said, her voice soft and bewildered.

"You said it was just a kiss. Was it?"

"Yes," she lied boldly. "How could it be anything more?"

"You tell me."

Shelly had no answers to give him.

"While you're at it, explain why we keep bumping into each other or why I can't stop thinking about you."

"You can't?" She hadn't been able to stop thinking about him, either, but she wasn't ready to admit it.

"No." He stood behind her, his hands caressing her shoulders. Leisurely he stroked the length of her arms. His touch was so light that she thought she was imagining it, and she felt both excited and afraid.

He turned her around and gazed at her lips. "If that was just a run-of-the-mill kiss, then why do I feel the need to do it again?"

"I don't know."

His lips brushed hers. Briefly, with a whisper-soft touch, as though he was testing her response. Shelly closed her eyes and moaned. She didn't want to feel any of this. They were so far apart, such different people. Besides, *he* was involved with another woman and *she* was involved with her career.

When the kiss ended and he slowly released her, it was all Shelly could do to keep from sinking to the sand. "I have...to get back to Seattle," she managed to say, backing away from him. She turned and took four or five wobbly steps before she realized she was headed toward the Pacific Ocean.

"Shelly?"

"Yes?"

"Seattle is due north. If you continue going west, you'll eventually end up in Hawaii."

"Oh, yeah, right," she mumbled, reversing her direction, eager now to escape.

* * *

The first person Shelly called when she got home was Jill. "Can you come over?" she asked without preamble. She couldn't keep the panic out of her voice.

"Sure. What's wrong?"

"I saw Mark again."

"And?"

"Let me put it like this. We kissed and I haven't stopped trembling since."

Jill's romantic sigh came over the receiver. "This I've got to hear. I'll be there in ten minutes."

Actually it was closer to seven. Shelly had begun pacing the moment she got off the phone. She'd checked her watch repeatedly, waiting desperately for a dose of Jill's good sense.

"Shelly," Jill said, smiling as she breezed into the apartment, "what happened to your hair?"

Shelly smoothed down her curls. "I was at Long Beach."

"That's where you saw Mark? That's kind of a coincidence, isn't it?"

"I saw him earlier in the week, too…. Remember I told you I was being audited by the IRS? Lo and behold, guess who was in their waiting room when I arrived?"

"I don't need to be a rocket scientist to figure that one out. Mark Brady!"

"Right." Shelly rubbed her damp palms along her jeans in agitation. They, at least, had finally dried.

"And?"

Shelly groaned. "Can't you see what's happening? This is the third time we've been thrown together in the past few days. I'd never seen the man before, and all of a sudden he's around every corner. Then the wedding dress fit. It fit you…and it fits me."

"I agree that's all rather odd, but I wouldn't put too much stock in it, if I were you."

"Put too much stock in it… Listen, Jill, no man's ever made me feel the way Mark does—all weak inside and, I don't know, special somehow. To be perfectly honest, I don't like it." She closed her eyes, hoping to chase away the memory of his touch, but it did no good. "You want to know the real kicker?" she asked abruptly, turning to face her friend. "He's engaged."

"Engaged," Jill echoed, her voice as startled as her expression.

"He keeps insisting it's not official yet. Nevertheless he's involved with someone else."

"But it was you he kissed," Jill pointed out.

"Don't remind me." Shelly covered her eyes with both hands. "I don't mind telling you, I find this whole thing unnerving."

"Obviously. Here," Jill said, directing Shelly toward the kitchen. "Now sit down. I'll make us some tea, then we can try to reason this out. Honestly, Shell, I don't think I've ever seen you so upset."

"I'm not upset!" she cried. "I'm confused. There's a big difference. I'm…I'm trapped." Despite all logic to the contrary, she couldn't help fearing that the entire course of her life was about to change because her aunt Milly had fallen asleep watching *Dr. Phil* one day and had some nonsensical dream.

"Trapped?" Jill said. "Aren't you being a bit dramatic?"

"I don't know anymore." Shelly rested her elbows on the table, buried her face in her hands and breathed in deeply. She had a tendency to become emotional, especially over family issues; she realized that. But this was different. This was scary.

"Calm down," Jill advised. "Once you think it through in a rational manner, you'll realize there's a perfectly ordinary explanation for everything."

Jill's serenity lent Shelly some badly needed confidence. "All right, you explain it."

"I can't," Jill admitted matter-of-factly, pouring boiling water into Shelly's teapot. "I'm not even going to try. My advice to you—once again—is to quit taking all of this so seriously. If a relationship develops between you and Mark, just enjoy it—provided the other woman's out of the picture, of course! But forget about that dress."

"Easy for you to say."

"That's true," Jill agreed. "But you're going to have to do it for your own peace of mind."

Shelly knew good advice when she heard it. "You're right. I'm leaping into the deep end unnecessarily."

"A dress can't make you do anything you don't want to do."

Shelly always counted on her friend's levelheadedness. Although Jill had given her basically the same advice several days earlier, Shelly needed to hear it again.

Jill prepared two cups of tea and carried them to the table. "Are you going to be all right now?"

Shelly nodded. "Of course. I just needed a friend to remind me that I was overreacting." She took a sip of tea, surprised by how much it revived her. "You're still planning to see *Jersey Boys* with me tomorrow afternoon, aren't you?"

The recent Broadway hit was showing locally, and Shelly and Jill had purchased their tickets several weeks earlier.

"That's not tomorrow, is it?" Jill looked stricken, her teacup poised midway to her mouth.

"Jill…"

"I promised I'd work for Sharon Belmont. She's got some family thing she has to attend. She was desperate and I completely forgot about the play. Oh, dear, you'll have to go without me."

"You're sure you can't get out of it?" Shelly couldn't help feeling disappointed.

"I'm sure. I'm really sorry, Shell."

Although frustrated that Jill couldn't come with her, Shelly decided to go to the theater alone. She wasn't pleased about it and, given her proclivity for running into Mark Brady, she didn't feel entirely convinced that this wasn't another attempt by the fates to regulate their lives.

However, if she stayed home, she'd be missing a won-

derful show. Not only that, she'd be giving in to a neb-
ulous and irrational fear, something she refused to do.

The following afternoon, Shelly dressed carefully, in
the type of conservative outfit her mother would have
approved of. Mark, too, would approve of her rose-colored
linen dress with its matching jacket…. The minute the
thought flashed through her head, she rejected it.

She was on her way out the door when her phone
rang. For a split second she toyed with the idea of not
answering. More than likely it was her mother, checking
in to see if Shelly had met a prospective husband yet.
Her calls had become more frequent and more urgent
since Aunt Milly's dress had arrived.

But years of habit prompted her to reach for the phone.

"Shelly." Mark's voice came over the line. "I was
about to leave for the afternoon's performance of *Jersey
Boys*. Since we seem to have this tendency to run into
each other everywhere we go, I thought I should probably clear it with you. If you're going to be there, I'll
go another time."

Eight

"Actually I was planning to see it this afternoon myself," Shelly admitted hesitantly. "Jill had to cancel at the last minute."

"It seems Janice can't attend, either."

Hearing the other woman's name, the woman Mark loved, had a curious and unexpected effect on Shelly. Her heart sank, and she felt a sharp pang of disappointment. She rebounded quickly, however, forcing a lightness into her voice, a blitheness she didn't feel. "Mark, there's no need for you to miss the show. I'll call the ticket office and see about an exchange."

"No, I will," Mark said.

"That's ridiculous. Jill really wanted to see this musical and—"

"Would it really be so terrible if we both attended the same performance?"

"Uh…" The question caught Shelly unprepared. Mark was the one who'd suggested they avoid each other.

"What could it possibly hurt? You have your ticket and I have mine. It'd be absurd to let them go to waste because we're afraid of seeing each other again, don't you think?"

Forming a single, coherent thought seemed beyond Shelly at that moment. After her conversation with Jill the day before, followed by the pep talk she'd given herself, she'd recovered a degree of composure. Now, all of a sudden, she wasn't sure of anything.

"I don't think it should matter," she said finally, although it *did* matter.

"Good. Enjoy the show."

"You, too."

The theater was within walking distance of her apartment building, and Shelly left as soon as she'd finished talking to Mark. He was right. Just because they each had tickets to the same play was no reason for either of them to be penalized.

So Mark was going to see *Jersey Boys*. It wasn't the sort of production she would've thought he'd enjoy. But the man was full of surprises. Riding mopeds on the beach, kissing so spectacularly, and now this…

Shelly's mind was full of Mark as she hurried down the steep hill on Cherry Street. The theater was only a block away when she saw him. Her pulse soared and she didn't know if she should smile and wave or simply ignore him.

She didn't need to do either. He stood on the sidewalk, waiting for her.

"You're late," he said, glancing at his watch. "But then you traditionally are." His grin was wide and welcoming. "I can't see any reason not to watch the play together," he went on. "What do you say?"

"You're sure?"

"Positive." He offered her his arm, and she reflected that it was the kind of old-fashioned courtesy she expected from Mark.

The usher seated them and smiled constantly as if to say they were a handsome couple. Shelly was tempted to explain that Mark was engaged to someone else; luckily she managed to hold her tongue. Minutes after they'd settled into their seats, the curtain rose.

The musical was as lively and as good as the reviews claimed, and Shelly enjoyed herself thoroughly. Throughout the performance, however, she was all too aware of Mark sitting next to her. She found herself wondering if he was equally aware of her. She also found herself wondering how long it would be before they "bumped" into each other again—and hoped it was soon.

By the end of the show, Shelly felt inspired and full of enthusiasm, eager to start a new project of her own. As she and Mark left the theater, she talked excitedly about her idea for the "ocean moods" series. He asked a few questions and even suggested some shots. Before she realized it, they were several blocks past the theater, headed in the opposite direction from her apartment. Shelly paused and glanced around.

"There's an excellent Chinese restaurant in this

neighborhood," was all Mark said. Without giving her the opportunity to decline, he gently guided her toward the place he'd mentioned.

It was early for dinner, and they were seated immediately. Although they'd been talking comfortably during their walk, Shelly suddenly felt self-conscious. She played with her linen napkin, smoothing it across her lap.

"I'm not a big fan of musicals, so I hadn't expected to like the show as much as I did," he said after a while.

In that case, Shelly considered it a bit odd that he'd ordered tickets for this production, but perhaps he'd gotten them because Janice had wanted to see *Jersey Boys*.

"It's a little frightening the way we keep running across each other, isn't it?" she ventured.

"I can see how *you'd* find it disconcerting," Mark answered.

"You don't?"

Mark shrugged. "I haven't given it much thought."

"I'll admit all these…coincidences do throw me," she said, tracing the outline of a fire-breathing dragon on the menu cover. "But I'm learning to deal with it."

"So you feel you've been caught in something beyond your control?" Mark surprised her by asking.

Shelly lifted her gaze to his, struck by the intensity she read in his eyes. "No, not really. Well…a little, maybe. Do you?"

"It wasn't *my* aunt Milly who had the dream."

Shelly smiled and dropped her gaze. "No, but as my friend Jill reminded me recently, no sixty-year-old dress

is going to dictate my life. Or yours," she felt obliged
to add. Then she understood why he'd asked the question. "You must feel overwhelmed. All of a sudden I've
been thrust into your life. There's no escaping me, is
there?" she said wryly. "Every time you turn around,
there I am."

"Are you going to stand up and tell everyone in the
restaurant that you refuse to marry me?"

"No!" Shelly was shocked by his remark until she remembered she'd done exactly that the first time they met.

"If you can resist public declarations, then I think I
can bear up under the pressure."

Shelly ignored his mild sarcasm. "I'm not interested
in marriage yet," she told him solemnly—just in case
he'd forgotten. "I'm satisfied with my life. And I'm too
busy for a husband and family."

She hadn't noticed how forcefully she was speaking
until she saw several people at other tables glancing in
her direction. Instantly she lowered her voice. "Sorry,
my views on marriage seem to be more fervent than I
realized. But I'm not about to let either my mother or
my aunt Milly determine when I decide to settle down
and marry."

"Personally, I can't see you ever settling down,"
Mark said with a small grin. "You don't have to worry.
When you're ready, you'll know it."

"Did you?" She hadn't meant to bring up Janice, but
it seemed wise to remind him—and her—that there was
someone else in his life.

Mark raised one shoulder casually. "More or less. I took a good, long look at my life and discovered I'd already achieved several of my professional goals. It was time to invest my energy in developing the personal aspects—marriage, children and the like."

Mark talked about marriage as if it were the next chapter in a book he was reading or part of a connect-the-dots picture. Shelly couldn't stop herself from frowning.

"You have a problem with that?"

"Not a problem, exactly. I happen to think of marriage a bit differently, that's all."

"In what way?"

He seemed genuinely interested, otherwise she would've kept her opinions to herself. "People should fall in love," she said slowly. "I don't think it's necessary or even possible to plan for that. Love can be unexpected—it can take a couple by surprise, knock them both off their feet."

"You make falling in love sound like an accident—like tripping on the stairs or something."

Shelly smiled. "In some ways, I think that's how it should be. Marriage is one of the most important decisions in anyone's life, so it should be a *deeply felt* decision. It should feel inevitable. It's the union of two lives, after all. So you can't simply check your watch and announce 'it's time.'" She was suddenly concerned that she'd spoken out of turn and might have offended him, but one quick glance assured her that wasn't the case.

Mark leaned forward. "I would never have guessed it," he said.

"Guessed what?" She was beginning to feel a little foolish now.

"That a woman who gives the impression of being a scatterbrain is really quite reflective. Beneath those glow-in-the-dark sweatshirts lies a very romantic heart."

"I seem to get emotional about certain things," she responded, studying the menu, eager to change the subject. "I really like hot-and-sour soup. Have you ever tried it?"

Their conversation over dinner remained light and amusing. Shelly noticed that Mark avoided any more discussion of a personal nature, as did she.

After they'd finished their dinner and Mark had paid the bill, they strolled leisurely back toward the theater. Mark offered to drive her home when they reached his parked car, but Shelly declined. Her apartment was only a couple of blocks north and she preferred to walk.

Walk and think. Their time together had given her plenty to think about.

"Thank you for dinner," she said as he unlocked the car.

"You're welcome," he answered. "Well, good night for now," he said, grinning. "I suspect I'll be seeing you soon."

She grinned back. "Probably within a day or two. Maybe we should synchronize our schedules," she teased.

"That wouldn't bother you, would it? If we ran into each other, I mean."

"Oh, no. What about you?" She hated the way her voice rose expectantly with the question. She certainly wasn't *bothered* by the prospect of seeing him again. In fact, she was downright eager to see what tricks fate would play on them next.

Mark's eyes found hers then, and he slowly pocketed his car keys. His look was so potent, so full of emotion, that Shelly took a step in retreat. "I had a wonderful afternoon, a wonderful evening. Thanks again," she said nervously.

Mark didn't say a word as he continued to gaze at her.

"The play was great, wasn't it? And dinner…fabulous." Shelly's throat seemed to close as Mark stepped onto the curb and walked toward her.

The whole world came to an abrupt halt when she realized he intended to kiss her. *Not again,* her mind shouted. *Please hurry,* her heart sang.

Her heart tripped wildly as Mark lowered his head, his mouth seeking hers. Despite the fierce battle inside her, Shelly had to admit how much she wanted this kiss. If for no other reason, she told herself, than to prove that the first time had been a fluke.

Only it happened again. But this kiss was a hundred times more compelling than the first one they'd shared. A hundred times more exciting.

Shelly wanted to cry out at the unfairness of it all. If a man's kiss was going to affect her like this, why did it have to be Mark Brady's?

He broke away from her reluctantly, his warm breath fanning her cheek. His eyes were filled with questions, filled with surprise. Shelly wasn't sure what her own eyes were saying to him. She didn't even want to know.

"Take care," he whispered as he turned away.

Shelly stayed home from work on Monday. She wasn't sick, just puzzled and confused. Nothing about her relationship with Mark made sense. He was everything she *didn't* want in a man—and everything she did.

Shelly didn't realize how despondent she was until she found herself standing barefoot in front of her closet, carrying on a conversation with Aunt Milly's wedding dress.

"I'll have you know I had a perfectly good life until you got here," she muttered. "Now my whole world's been turned upside down." She slammed the door shut, then jerked it open. "No wonder Mrs. Livingston's cat wouldn't go near you. You're *dangerous*."

Nine

"The show was great," Shelly told Jill over coffee Wednesday afternoon. She'd stopped off at PayRite, hoping Jill could get away for lunch. "Even Mark—"

"Mark?" Jill's coffee cup hit the saucer with a clang. "He went to see *Jersey Boys?*"

Shelly nodded sheepishly. "I guess I forgot to mention I ran into him, didn't I? Actually he called me first and since we both had plans to attend the same performance, we decided to go together."

"Is there anything else you haven't told me?" Jill's eyes narrowed astutely.

Shelly tried to hide her uneasiness behind a relaxed shrug, but how well she succeeded in fooling Jill remained to be seen. "We had dinner afterward…as friends. It didn't mean anything. I did tell you he's engaged, didn't I?"

"*Unofficially* engaged." Jill was studying her closely and Shelly felt uneasy under her scrutiny.

"We've been friends for a long time," Jill reminded

her. "I know you, and I know there's something troubling you."

Shelly nodded. There was no point in hiding the truth from Jill. Her need to confide in a sympathetic, understanding person was the very reason for her impromptu visit to Jill's workplace. Lunch had been a convenient excuse.

"You won't believe this," Shelly said, cradling the coffee cup in both hands and keeping her gaze lowered. "I can hardly believe it myself."

"You're falling in love with Mark."

Shelly's eyes shot upward. "It's that obvious?"

"No," Jill said softly. "But you look like you're about to break into tears."

"If I wasn't so darn irritated I would. Good grief, think about it. Can you imagine two people less suited to each other? Mark is so…so responsible…"

"So are you."

"Not in the same way," Shelly argued. "He's so sincere and—"

"Shelly, so are you."

"Perhaps, but I'm such a scatterbrain." She grimaced as she remembered that was the very word Mark had used. "I'm disorganized and always late and I like to do things my own way. You know that better than most."

"I prefer to think of you as creative."

Shelly sent Jill a smile of appreciation. "That's the reason you're my best friend. I don't mind telling you, Jill, I'm worried. Mark Brady may be the Rock of Gibraltar, but I doubt he's got an original thought in his head. Everything's done by the book or according to a schedule."

"You need someone like Mark in your life," Jill returned. "Don't look so shocked. It's true. The two of you balance each other. He needs you because you're fun and crazy and imaginative, and you need him because he knows his multiplication tables by heart and will remind you when it's time for meals."

"The problem is, Mark's the type of man who'd expect a woman to *cook* those meals."

Jill chuckled.

"If the fates are determined to match me up with a man," Shelly moaned, "couldn't it be with someone other than an accountant?"

"Apparently not."

"What really angers me is that I allowed it to happen. The first time he kissed me—"

"He *kissed* you?" Jill feigned a look of horror.

Shelly ignored it. "Yes. Twice. It's only natural—our being curious about each other, don't you think?"

"I suppose," Jill said quickly, no longer teasing. "So tell me what happened."

"Fireworks bigger than the Fourth of July. I've never experienced the feelings I do with Mark, and all because of a kiss." She paused. "Well, two kisses."

"And does Mark feel the same thing?"

"I—I can't speak for him, but I assume it's equally disturbing for him. He certainly looked as if he'd been taken by surprise."

"How do you get along with him otherwise?"

"Fine, I guess." Shelly took a sip of her coffee. "I'm sure I amuse him. But someone like Mark isn't looking for a woman to entertain him, any more than I'm looking for a man to handle my finances."

"His opinion of you has mellowed, hasn't it?" Jill asked, then answered her own question. "There was a time when he thought you were more than a little bizarre, remember?"

Shelly did, all too well. "At first I thought he was totally unexciting, but I've altered my opinion of him, too."

"So what's the problem?"

"I don't *want* to fall in love," Shelly said pointedly. "I've got bigger plans for my life than to tie myself down to a committed relationship right now."

"Then don't. It shouldn't be that difficult. Decide what you want and disregard everything else. There's no law that says you have to fall in love this minute. For that matter, no one can regulate when and who you marry, either. Not even your aunt Milly."

Jill was saying everything Shelly wanted to hear. Everything she *needed* to hear. But it didn't make any difference; her heart was already involved. If she could forget she'd ever met Mark, she would. But it was too late. She was in love with him. With Mark, who was in love with someone else. Mark, who saw love and marriage as goals to be achieved within a certain time frame. He'd probably never done anything impulsive in his life.

A relationship between them would never last. If he

wasn't smart enough to figure that out, she was. Something had to be done and soon, and Shelly knew it would be up to her to do it.

Shelly didn't have long to wait before she saw Mark again. They met at the main branch of the Seattle Public Library on Wednesday evening. She was returning ten overdue books. Six months overdue. The library had sent her three warnings, each progressively less friendly.

She was half-afraid the buzzer inside the library entrance would go off the moment she walked through the hallowed doors, and armed officers would haul her away.

"I wondered when we'd find each other again," Mark said, strolling up to her at the counter. She'd seen him almost immediately and tried to pretend she hadn't.

Shelly acknowledged him with a quick nod and ordered her heart to be still. She managed a slight smile. "Hello again," she said, drawing a checkbook out of her purse. At least she'd come prepared. The fine for the books was sure to be monstrous; in fact, it might be cheaper to buy them.

Mark set the two volumes he was borrowing on the counter. Shelly noted the titles—*Tools for Time Management* and *The State of the Language,* and groaned inwardly. To someone like her accountant friend, these books were probably easy reading. Her own tastes leaned more toward mystery and romance, with a little nonfiction thrown in.

"Have you got time for a cup of coffee?" Mark asked as she wrote out the check to pay her fine.

She was gladdened by the invitation, but knew she had to refuse it. Before he could say or do anything to change her mind, she shook her head. "Not tonight, thanks."

His smile faded as though her refusal had startled him. "You're busy?"

She nodded, smiling at the librarian as she handed over her check. The librarian smiled back. It had been a civilized exchange, Shelly thought, and her library card had't been confiscated, despite her transgressions.

"You've got a date waiting for you?"

It took Shelly a second to understand that Mark was referring to her refusal to join him for coffee.

"Not exactly." She turned away from the counter and headed toward the exit. To her surprise Mark followed her outside.

"Something's wrong," he said, standing at the top of the steps.

She stopped her descent and stood below him, looking up. Pretense had never suited Shelly; she was too innately honest to hide her feelings. "Mark, I think you're a very nice man—"

"But you don't want to marry me," he concluded for her. "I've heard that line before, remember? Actually, half the mall heard it, too."

"I've already apologized for that. It's just that...all

right, if you must know, I'm beginning to like you…
really like you, and frankly that terrifies me."

Her candid response seemed to unnerve him. He
frowned and rubbed the side of his jaw. "I know what
you mean. I'm beginning to like you, too."

"See!" she cried, raising both hands. "If we don't
take care of this now, heaven only knows what could
happen. It has the potential of ruining both our lives.
We're mature adults, aren't we?" At the moment,
though, she felt singularly lacking in maturity.

All her senses were clamoring, telling her to enjoy
their brief time together, despite the consequences. It
was what her heart wanted, but she couldn't allow her
life to be ruled by her heart. Not when it came to Mark.

"Liking each other doesn't have to be a federal
crime," he said, advancing one step toward her.

"You're right, of course, but I know myself too well.
I could easily fall in love with you, Mark." She didn't
dare admit she already had. "Before we knew it, we'd
be spending more and more time with each other. We
might even become seriously involved."

He remained suspiciously silent.

"You're a wonderful man. If my mother were to meet
you she'd be shouting from the rooftops, she'd be so
thrilled. For a while I might convince myself that we
could really make something of this relationship. I
might even consider taking cooking classes because
you're the kind of man who'd expect a woman to know
how to make a roast and mashed potatoes."

"It'd probably come in handy someday," he said.

"That's what I thought," she murmured, disheartened. "I'm not a traditional woman. I never will be. The only time I ever baked a pie I ended up throwing it in the garbage disposal—and it broke the disposal."

"A pie ruined your garbage disposal?" Mark repeated, then shook his head. "Never mind, don't bother explaining. It seems to me you're getting ahead of yourself here. You're talking as though coffee together means a lifetime commitment."

Shelly wasn't listening. "What about Janice?" she demanded. "*She's* the one you should be inviting to coffee, not me."

"What's Janice got to do with this?" he asked impatiently.

"Janice," Shelly snapped, her own temper short. "The woman you've decided to marry. Remember her? The love of your life? The woman you're unofficially engaged to marry."

"It's not unofficial anymore," Mark explained evenly.

"Oh, great, you're taking me out to dinner, kissing me and at the same time picking out engagement rings with another woman." She had to admit he'd never lied to her about his relationship with the faceless Janice. He'd been forthright about it from the beginning. But it hurt, really hurt, to learn that he was going ahead with his plans to marry Janice.

He was about to speak, but she forestalled him, struggling to force some enthusiasm into her voice. "Congratulations are in order. I wish you both the very best." With that she turned and bounded down the stairs, taking them recklessly fast.

"Shelly!"

She could hear Mark calling after her, but she ignored him, desperate to get away before the lump in her throat made it impossible to breathe. Tears had formed in her eyes and she cursed herself for being so ridiculous, for caring so much. Her vision blurred and she wiped a hand across her face, furious at her lack of control. This marriage was what she'd hoped would happen. What she wanted for Mark. *Wasn't it?*

"Shelly, for heaven's sake, will you wait?"

When she reached the bottom of the steps, Shelly moved into a side street, hoping to disappear in the crowd, praying Mark wouldn't pursue her.

She thought she'd escaped until a hand on her shoulder whirled her around.

"Shelly, please listen," Mark pleaded breathlessly, his shoulders heaving. "The engagement isn't official because there is no engagement. How could I possibly marry Janice after meeting you?"

Ten

"You broke off your engagement with Janice?" Shelly demanded furiously. Something inside, some reservoir of emotion, had burst wide-open. "You fool," she shouted. "You idiot!" Her eyes brimmed with tears, and deep in her heart she felt the stirrings of glad excitement. "That was the worst thing you could've done!"

"No," he said. "It was the smartest."

"How can you say that?" she wailed.

"Shelly?"

He reached for her as though to offer comfort, but Shelly jerked away and stepped back, freeing herself from his grasp. "Janice was perfect for you," she lamented.

"How do you know that?" he asked calmly and much too reasonably to suit Shelly. "You never met her."

"I didn't need to. I know she was right for you. You'd never have asked her to marry you if she wasn't."

"Janice is a wonderful woman and she'll make some man a good wife, but it won't be me."

"You're crazy to break off your engagement. Crazy!"

"No, I'm not," Mark returned confidently. "I'm absolutely certain I did the right thing. Do you know why?"

Shelly could only shake her head, wiping away the tears with the back of her hand. She was ecstatic—and yet she was so frightened. She loved him; she was sure of it. Then why had everything become so difficult and confused?

"What you said about love the other day changed my mind."

"You *listened* to me?" she cried in real horror. "Do I look like an expert on love? I've never been in love in my life!" Not counting what she felt for him, of course. She'd always thought love would clarify her life, not make it more complicated.

Mark paid no attention to her outburst. "You helped me understand that I was marrying Janice for the wrong reasons. I'd decided it was time to settle down. Janice had come to the same conclusion. She's thirty and figured if she was going to marry and have a family, the time was now. It wasn't a love match, and we both knew it."

"This is none of my business," Shelly said, frantically shaking her head as if to chase the words away. "I don't want to hear it."

"You *are* going to hear it," Mark insisted, clasping her elbows and gently drawing her closer. "You claimed people shouldn't plan love. It should take them by surprise, you said, and you were right. Janice and I are fond of each other, but—"

"There's nothing wrong with fond!"

His eyes widened. "No, there isn't," he agreed, "but Janice isn't a zany producer. I like spending time with you. I've come to realize there's a certain thrill in expecting the unexpected. Every minute with you is an adventure."

"A relationship between us would never last," Shelly insisted, drawing on the most sensible argument. "It would be fine for a while, but then we'd drift apart. We'd have to. In case you haven't noticed, we're nothing alike."

"Why wouldn't a relationship last?" Mark asked patiently.

"For all the reasons I listed before!" Mark was so endearing, and he was saying all the words she'd secretly longed to hear, but nothing could change the fundamental differences between them.

"So you aren't as adept in the kitchen as some women. I'm a fair cook."

"It's more than that."

"Of course it is," he concurred. "But there's nothing we can't overcome if we're willing to work together."

"You know what I think it is?" she said desperately, running her splayed fingers through her hair. "You're beginning to believe there's magic in Aunt Milly's wedding dress."

"Don't you?"

"No," she cried. "Not anymore. I did when I was a little girl...I loved the story of how Aunt Milly met Uncle John, but I'm not a child anymore, and what seemed so romantic then just seems unrealistic now."

"Shelly," Mark said in exasperation. "We don't need to do anything right away. All I'm suggesting is we give this thing between us a chance."

"There's nothing between us," she denied vehemently.

Mark's eyes narrowed. "You don't honestly believe that, do you?"

"Yes," she lied. "You're a nice guy, but—"

"If I hear any more of this nice-guy stuff I'm going to kiss you and we both know what'll happen then."

His gaze lowered to her mouth and she unconsciously moistened her lips with anticipation.

"I just might, anyway."

"No." The threat was real enough to make her retreat a couple of steps. If Mark kissed her, Shelly knew she'd be listening to her heart and not her head. And then *he'd* know… "That's what I thought." His grin was downright boyish.

"I think we should both forget we ever met," she suggested next, aware even as she said it how ludicrous she sounded. Mark Brady had indelibly marked her life and no matter how much she denied it, she'd never forget him.

"Don't you remember that you threw yourself into my arms? *You* can conveniently choose to overlook the obvious, but unfortunately that won't work for me. I'm falling in love with you, Shelly."

She opened her mouth to argue that he couldn't possibly love her—not yet, not on such short acquaintance—but he pressed his finger to her lips, silencing her.

"At first I wasn't keen on the idea," he admitted, "but

it's sort of grown on me since. I can see us ten years in the future and you know what? It's a pleasant picture. We're going to be very happy together."

"I need to think!" She placed her hands on either side of her head. Everything was happening much too quickly; she actually felt dizzy. "We'll leave it to fate...how does that sound?" she offered excitedly. It seemed like the perfect solution. "The next time we bump into each other, I'll have more of a grasp on my feelings. I'll know what we should do." She might also hibernate inside her apartment for a month, but she wasn't mentioning that.

"Nope." Mark slowly shook his head. "That won't work."

"Why not?" she asked. "We bump into each other practically every day."

"No, we don't."

He wasn't making any sense.

"*Jersey Boys* was a setup," he informed her. "I made sure we bumped into each other there."

"How? When?"

"The day at the beach I saw the ticket sticking out of your purse. Our meeting at the theater wasn't any accident."

Mark couldn't have shocked her more if he'd announced he was an alien from outer space. For the first time in recent memory, she was left speechless. "Tonight?" she asked when she could get the words out. "The library?"

"I'd decided to stop off at your apartment. I was prepared to make up some story about the wedding dress luring me into your building, but when I drove past, I saw you coming down the front steps loaded down with library books. It wasn't hard to figure out where you were headed. I found a parking space and waited for you inside."

"What about…the IRS office and the beach?" She didn't know how he'd managed *those* meetings.

Mark shook his head again and grinned. "Coincidence, unless you had anything to do with them. You didn't, did you?"

"Absolutely not," she replied indignantly.

Still grinning, he said, "I didn't really think you had."

Shelly started walking, her destination unclear. She felt too restless to continue standing there; unfortunately the one action that truly appealed to her was leaping into his arms.

Mark matched his own steps to hers.

"It's Aunt Milly's wedding dress, I know it is," Shelly mumbled under her breath. She'd tried to bring up the subject, but Mark had refused to listen. "You broke off an engagement because you believe fate's somehow thrown us together."

"No, Shelly, the dress doesn't have anything to do with how I feel," Mark said calmly.

"But you'd already decided to marry someone else!"

"I'm choosing my own destiny, which is to spend the rest of my life with you."

"You might have consulted me first. I have no intention of getting married...not for years and years."

"I'll wait."

"You can't do that," she cried. He didn't understand because he was too respectable and adorable and too much of a gentleman. The only thing that would work would be to heartlessly send him away.

She faced Mark, careful to wear just the right expression of remorse and regret. "This is all very flattering, but I don't love you. I'm sorry, Mark. You're the last person in the world I want to hurt."

For a moment Mark said nothing, then he shrugged and looked away. "You can't be any more direct than that, can you? There's no chance you'll ever fall in love with me?"

"None." Her breath fell harshly, painfully, from her lips. It shouldn't hurt this much to do the right thing. It shouldn't hurt to be noble. "You're very nice, but..."

"So you've said before."

Falteringly, as though the movement caused him pain, he lifted his hand to her face, his fingers caressing the curve of her jaw.

Until that moment, Shelly hadn't understood how fiercely proud Mark was. He could have dealt with every argument, calmed every doubt, answered every question, but there was nothing he could say when she denied all feeling for him.

"You mean it, don't you?" he asked huskily. He was standing so close that his breath warmed her face.

Shelly had schooled her features to reveal none of her

clamoring emotions. His touch, so light, so potent, seemed to clog her throat with anguish, and she couldn't speak.

"If that's what you want—" he dropped his hand abruptly "—I won't trouble you again." With those words, he turned and walked away. Before she fully realized what he intended, Mark had disappeared around a corner.

"You let him go, you idiot!" she whispered to herself. A tear escaped and she smeared it across her cheek.

Mark meant what he'd said about not bothering her. He was a man of his word. He'd never try to see her again—and if they did happen upon each other, he'd pretend he didn't know her.

He might eventually decide to marry Janice. Hadn't he admitted he was fond of the other woman?

Shelly's heart clutched painfully inside her chest. Before she could stop herself, before she could question the wisdom of her actions, she ran after Mark.

She turned the corner and was halfway down the block when she realized he wasn't anywhere to be seen. She came to a skidding halt, then whirled around, wondering how he could possibly have gotten so far in such a short time.

Mark stepped out from the side of a building, hands on his hips, a cocky, jubilant smile on his face. "What took you so long?" he asked, holding out his arms.

Shelly didn't need a second invitation to throw herself into his embrace. His mouth feasted on hers, his kiss hungry and demanding, filled with enough emotion to last a lifetime.

Shelly slid her arms around his neck and stood on her tiptoes, giving herself completely to his kiss, to his love. All that mattered was being in his arms—exactly where she was supposed to be.

"I take it this means you love me, too?" he whispered close to her ear. His voice was rough with emotion.

Shelly nodded. "I'm so afraid."

"Don't be. I'm confident enough for both of us."

"This is crazy," she said, but she couldn't have moved out of his arms for the world. Breathing deeply, she buried her face in his chest.

"But it's a good kind of crazy."

"Aunt Milly saw us together in her dream. She wrote to me about a tall, blue-eyed man."

"Who knows if it was me or not?" Mark whispered into her hair and brushed his lips over her temple. "Who cares? If fate had anything to do with me finding you or if your aunt Milly's wedding dress is responsible, I can't say. Personally, I couldn't care less. I love you, Shelly, and I believe you love me, too."

She glanced up at this man who had altered the course of her life and smiled, her heart too full for words. "I do love you," she said when she could. "An accountant! In a suit! Hardly the husband I imagined for myself."

Mark chuckled. "I would never have guessed I'd fall head over heels in love with a woman who wears the type of clothes you do—but I did."

"I love you, too," Shelly said and closed her eyes.

* * *

The morning of her wedding day, Shelly couldn't sit still. Her mother was even worse, pacing in front of her, dabbing her eyes and sniffling.

"I can't believe my baby's getting married."

Shelly had to restrain herself from reminding her dear mother that less than a month before, she'd been desperate to marry her daughter off. Thank goodness Jill was there. Without her best friend to reassure her, Shelly didn't know what she would've done. While her mother fussed with the caterers, complained to the florists and fretted about who had a key to the kitchen in the reception hall, Jill led Shelly upstairs to her childhood bedroom and helped her dress. When Shelly was finished, Jill stood back to examine her.

"Well?" Shelly asked, smoothing her hand down the antique dress, loving the feel of the satin and lace against her fingers. It was probably her imagination but now that she was wearing the dress, really wearing it, she could almost feel its magic.

Tears gathered in Jill's eyes as she stared at her friend.

"That bad?" Shelly teased.

Jill pressed her fingers to her lips. "You're beautiful," she whispered. "Mark isn't going to believe his eyes when he sees you."

"Do you really think so?" Shelly hated sounding so insecure, but she wanted everything to be perfect today. She was crazy in love—and crazy enough to give her mother free rein planning her wedding. Crazy enough to go through with a formal wedding in the first place. If it'd been up to her, they would've eloped weeks ago. But Mark had wanted a proper wedding and her mother certainly wasn't going to be cheated out of this moment. So Shelly had gone along with it.

Mark and her mother had defeated most of her ideas. She'd wanted to hire clowns to entertain at the reception, but her mother didn't seem to think that was a good idea.

Shelly had never been that fond of white wedding cake, either. She'd suggested Cherries Jubilee instead, but Mark was afraid something might catch on fire and so in the interests of safety, Shelly had agreed to a traditional cake, decorated with pink roses.

A knock sounded on her bedroom door and Jill opened it. In walked Aunt Milly, looking absolutely delighted with herself.

She introduced herself to Jill, then turned to gaze lovingly at Shelly. "So I see the dress worked."

"It worked," Shelly agreed.

"You love him?"

Shelly nodded. "Enough to eat white wedding cake."

Milly laughed softly and sat on the edge of the bed. Her hair was gray and her face wrinkled, but her eyes were still blue and clear. It was difficult to tell that she was a woman well into her eighties. She clasped both of Shelly's hands in her own.

"Nervous?"

Shelly nodded again.

"I was, too, although I knew to the bottom of my heart that I'd made the right decision in marrying John."

"I feel the same way about Mark."

Aunt Milly hugged her tightly. "You're going to be very happy, my dear."

An hour later Shelly and Mark stood at the front of a packed church with Pastor Johnson, who'd known her most of her life. He smiled warmly as he spoke a few words, then asked Shelly to repeat her vows.

Linking hands with Mark, she raised her eyes to his. Everyone else faded away. Aunt Milly. Jill. Her mother. Her long-suffering dad. Her brothers and their wives. There were only the two of them. She felt a jolt of pure joy at the love that radiated from Mark's eyes. He stood tall and proud, his gaze holding hers, the love shining through without question, shining through for her to read. Shelly knew her eyes told him the same thing.

Later, Shelly couldn't remember speaking her vows, although she was sure she did. The words came directly from her heart. Directly from Mark's.

They'd been drawn to this place and this time by forces neither fully understood. Shelly wasn't entirely sure she believed Aunt Milly's wedding dress was responsible, but as Mark had said, it didn't matter. They were there out of love. She didn't know exactly when it had happened. Perhaps that day on the beach, when Mark first kissed her. Something had happened then, something that touched them both.

The love that began as a small spark had grown and flared to life until they'd been brought here, to stand before God and family, pledging their lives to each other. To love. To cherish. All the days of their lives.

THE MAN YOU'LL MARRY

For Jenny and Kevin

One

Jill Morrison caught her breath as she stared excitedly out the airplane window. Seattle and everything familiar was quickly shrinking from view. She settled back and sighed with pure satisfaction.

This first-class seat was an unexpected gift from the airline. The booking agent had made a mistake and Jill turned out to be the beneficiary. Not a bad way to start a long-awaited vacation.

She glanced, not for the first time, at the man sitting beside her. He looked like the stereotypical business-man, typing industriously on a laptop, his brow fur-rowed with concentration. She couldn't tell exactly what he was doing, but noticed several columns of figures. He paused, and something must have troubled him, because he reached for a calculator in his briefcase and punched out a series of numbers. When he'd finished, he returned to his computer. He seemed impatient and restless, as though he begrudged the travel time. Not a good sign, in Jill's opinion, since the flight to Honolulu was scheduled to take five hours.

He wasn't the talkative sort, either. In her enthusiasm before takeoff, Jill had made a couple of attempts at light conversation, but both tries had met with minimal responses, followed by cool silence.

Great. She was stuck sitting next to this grouch for the beginning of a vacation she'd been planning for nearly two years. A vacation that Jill and her best friend, Shelly Hansen, had once dreamed of taking together. Only Shelly wasn't Shelly Hansen anymore. Her former college roommate was married now. For an entire month Shelly Hansen had been Shelly Brady.

Even after all this time, Jill had problems taking it in. For as long as Jill had known Shelly, her friend had been adamant about making her career as a producer of DVDs her highest priority. She'd vowed that men and relationships would always remain a distant second in her busy life. For years Jill had watched Shelly discourage attention from the opposite sex. From college onward, Shelly had carefully avoided any hint of commitment.

Then it had happened. Shelly met Mark Brady and the unexpected became a reality. To Shelly's way of thinking, her mother's great-aunt Millicent—known to everyone in the family as Aunt Milly—was directly responsible for her present happiness. She'd met her tax-accountant husband immediately after the elderly woman had mailed Shelly a "magic" wedding dress. The same dress Milly had worn herself more than sixty years earlier.

Both Shelly and Jill had insisted there was no such thing as magic, especially associated with a wedding dress. Magic belonged to wands or fairy godmothers, not wedding dresses. To fairy tales, not real life. They'd scoffed at the ridiculous story that went along with the gown. Both refused to believe what Aunt Milly had written in her letter; no one in her right mind, they told each other, could possibly take the sweet old woman seriously. *Marry the next man you meet?* Preposterous.

Personally, Jill had found the whole story amusing. Shelly hadn't been laughing though. Shelly, being Shelly, had overreacted, fretting and worrying, wondering if there wasn't some small chance that Milly could be right. Shelly hadn't *wanted* her to be right, but there it was—the dress arrived one day, and the next she'd fallen into Mark Brady's arms.

Literally.

The rest, as they say, is history and Jill wasn't laughing anymore. Shelly and Mark had been married in June and to all appearances were blissfully happy.

Four weeks after the wedding, Jill was flying off to Hawaii. Not the best month to visit the tropics, perhaps, but that couldn't be helped. Her budget was limited and July offered the most value for her money.

Her seatmate leaned back and sighed deeply, pinching the bridge of his nose. Whatever problem he'd encountered earlier had persisted, Jill guessed. She must have been correct, because no more than ten seconds later, he reached for his calculator again. Jill had the impression this man never stopped working; even during their meal he continued his calculations. Not a moment of their flight time was wasted. If he wasn't studying papers from his briefcase, he was typing more columns of figures into his computer.

An hour passed. A couple of times, almost against her will, she found herself watching him. Although she assumed he was somewhere in his mid-thirties, he seemed older. No, she decided, not older, but…experienced. His face managed to be pleasing to the eye despite his rugged, uneven features. She wondered fleetingly how he'd assess *her* appearance. Except he hadn't looked at her once. He seemed totally unaware that there was anyone in the seat next to him. His eyes were gray, she'd noted earlier, the color of polished steel. There was nothing soft about him.

This was obviously a man who had it all—hand-tailored suits, Italian leather shoes, gold pen and watch. She'd bet even his plastic was gold! No doubt he lived the way he flew—first class. He was the type who had all the answers, too. The type of man who didn't question his own attitudes and beliefs….

He reminded Jill of her father, long dead, long grieved. He, too, had been an influential businessman who'd held success in the palm of his hand. Adam Morrison had fought off middle age on a gym floor. Energy was his trademark and death was an eternity away. Only it was just around the corner, and he hadn't known it.

Ironic that she should be sitting next to him thirteen

years after his death. Not her father, but someone so much like him it was all Jill could do not to ask when he'd last seen his family.

He must have felt her scrutiny, because he suddenly turned and stared at her. Jill blushed guiltily, bowing her head over her book, reading it with exaggerated fervor.

"Did you like what you saw?" he asked her boldly.

"I—I don't know what you mean," she said in a small voice, moving the paperback close to her face.

For the first time since he'd taken the seat next to her, the stranger grinned. It was an odd smile, off center and unpracticed, as if he didn't often find anything to smile about.

The remainder of the flight was uneventful. Jill held her breath during the descent, until the tires bumped down on the runway in Honolulu. She wished again that Shelly was taking this trip, too. With or without her best friend, though, Jill intended to have the time of her life. She had seven glorious days to laze in the sun. Seven days to shop to her heart's content and to go sightseeing and to swim and relax and eat glorious meals.

For months Jill had dreamed of the wonders she would see and experience. Tranquil villages, orchid plantations—oh, how she loved orchids. At night, she'd stroll along lava-strewn beaches and by day there'd be canyons to explore, tumbling waterfalls and smoldering volcanoes. Hawaii was going to be a grand adventure, Jill felt sure of it.

The man beside her was on his feet the instant their

plane came to a standstill. He removed his carry-on bag from the storage compartment above the seat with an efficiency that told her he was a seasoned traveler. The smiling flight attendant handed him a garment bag as he strode off the plane.

Jill followed him, watching for directions to the baggage pickup. Her seatmate's steps were crisp and purposeful. It didn't surprise her; this was a man on the go, always in a rush to get somewhere. Meet someone. Make a deal. No time to stop and smell the orchids for her friend the grouch.

Jill lost sight of him when she purchased a lei at a concession stand. She draped the lovely garland of orchids around her neck and fingered the delicate flowers, marveling at their beauty.

Once again the reminder that adventures awaited her on this tropical island moved full sail across her heart. She wasn't the fanciful sort, nor did she possess an extravagant imagination. Not like Shelly. Yet Jill felt something deep inside her stir to life....

Shelly had become a real believer in magic, Jill mused, smiling as she bought herself a slice of fresh pineapple. For that matter, even she—ever the practical one—found herself a tiny bit susceptible to the claims of a charmed wedding dress. Just a tiny bit, though.

Jill's pulse quickened the way it did whenever she thought about what had happened between Shelly and Mark. It was simply the most romantic thing she'd ever known.

Romance had scurried past Jill several times. Currently she was dating Ralph, a computer programmer, but it was more for companionship than romance, although he'd been hinting for several months that they should start "getting serious." Jill assumed he meant marriage. Ralph was nice, and so far Jill had been able to dissuade him from discussing the future of their relationship. She didn't want to hurt his feelings, but she just wasn't interested in marrying him.

However, Jill fully intended to marry someday. There'd never been any question of that. The only question was *who*. She'd dated frequently in college, but there hadn't been anyone special. Then, when she'd been hired as a pharmacist for PayRite, a drugstore chain with several outlets in the Pacific Northwest, the opportunities to meet eligible men had dwindled dramatically.

Prospects weren't exactly crowding the horizon, but Jill had given up worrying about it. She'd done a fair job of pushing the thought of a husband and family to the far reaches of her mind—until she'd made one small mistake.

She'd tried on Aunt Milly's wedding dress.

Shelly had hung the infamous dress in the very back of her closet. Out of sight, out of mind—only it hadn't worked that way. Not a minute passed that Shelly wasn't keenly aware of the dress and its alleged powers.

On impulse, Jill had tried it on herself. To this day she didn't know what had prompted her to slip into the beautiful hand-sewn wedding dress. It was so elegant, so beautiful, with row upon row of pearls and delicate lace layered over satin.

That it fit as though it had been specifically designed for her had been as much of a surprise to Shelly as it had to Jill. Shelly had seemed almost giddy with relief, insisting her aunt had made a mistake and the dress was actually meant for Jill. But by that time, Shelly had already met Mark....

No, Aunt Milly hadn't made a mistake—the wedding dress had been meant for Shelly all along. Her marriage to Mark proved it. And really, she'd have to attribute Shelly's meeting and marrying Mark to the power of suggestion, the power of expectation—not to *magic*. She shook her head and hurried off to retrieve her luggage.

Then she headed outside, intent on grabbing a taxi. As the driver loaded her bags, she stood for a moment, savoring the warm breeze, enjoying the first sounds and sights of Hawaii. She couldn't wait to get to her hotel. Through a friend who was a travel agent, Jill had been able to book a room in one of the most exclusive places on Oahu at a ridiculously low rate.

The hotel was everything the brochure had promised and more. Jill had to pinch herself when she got to her room. The first thing she did was walk to the sliding-glass doors that led to the lanai, a balcony overlooking the swimming-pool area. Beyond that, the Pacific Ocean thundered against the sandy shore. The sight was mesmerizing, the beauty so keen, it brought tears of appreciation to Jill's eyes.

She tipped the bellhop, who'd brought up her luggage, and returned to the view. If she never went beyond this room, Jill would have been satisfied. She stood at the railing, the breeze riffling her long hair.

The hotel was U-shaped, and something—a movement, a figure—caught her eye. A man. Jill glanced across the swimming pool, across the tiki-hut roof of the bar until her gaze found what she was seeking. The grouch. In a lanai directly opposite hers. At least she thought so. He wore the same dark suit as the man with whom she'd spent five of the most uncommunicative hours of her life.

Jill didn't know what prompted her, but she waved. After a moment, he waved back. He stepped farther out onto the lanai and she knew beyond a doubt. Their rooms were in different sections of the hotel, but they were on the same floor, their lanais facing each other.

He held a cell phone to his ear, but slowly lowered it.

For several minutes they simply stared at each other. After what seemed like an embarrassingly long time, Jill tried to pull herself away and found she couldn't. Unsure why, unsure what had attracted her attention to the man in the first place, unsure of everything, Jill looked away.

A knock at the door distracted her.

"Yes?" she asked, opening her door. A bellhop in a crisp white uniform stood before her with a large wrapped box.

"This arrived by special courier for you earlier today, Ms. Morrison," he explained politely.

When he'd gone, Jill studied the package, reading the Seattle postmark and the unfamiliar block printing. She carried it to the bed, still puzzled. She had no idea who would be mailing her anything from home. Especially since she'd only left that morning.

Sitting on the edge of the bed, she unwrapped the package and lifted the lid. Her hands froze. Her heart froze. Her breath jammed in her throat. When she was able to move again, she inhaled sharply and closed her eyes.

It was Aunt Milly's wedding dress.

A letter rested on top of the tissue-wrapped dress. With trembling hands, Jill reached for it.

Dearest Jill,

Trust me, I know exactly what you're feeling. I remember my own emotions when I opened this very box and found Aunt Milly's wedding dress staring up at me. As you know, my first instinct was to run and hide. Instead I was fortunate enough to find Mark and fall in love.

I suppose you're wondering why I'm mailing this dress to you in Hawaii. Why didn't I just give it to you before you left Seattle? Good question, and if I had a reasonable answer I'd be more than happy to share it.

One thing I've learned these past few months is that there's precious little logic when it comes to understanding any of this—love, fate, the magic within Aunt Milly's wedding dress. Take my advice and don't even try to make sense of it.

I suppose I should tell you why I'm giving you the dress. I was sitting at the table one morning last week, with my first cup of coffee. I wasn't fully awake yet. My eyes were closed. Suddenly you were in my mind, standing waist-deep in blue-green water. There was a waterfall behind you and lush, beautiful plants all around. It had to be Hawaii. You looked happier than I can ever remember seeing you.

There was a man with you, and I wish I could describe him. Unfortunately, he was in shadow. Read into that whatever you will. There was a look about you, a look I've only seen once before—the day you tried on the wedding gown. You were radiant.

I talked to Mark about it, and he seemed to feel the same way I did—that the dress was meant for you. I phoned Aunt Milly and told her. She said by all means to make you its next recipient.

I should probably have given you the dress then, but something held me back. Nothing I can put into words, but a feeling that it would be too soon. So I'm sending it to you now.

My wish for you, Jill, is that you find someone to love. Someone as wonderful as Mark. Of the two of us, you've always been the sensible one. You believed in logic and common sense. But you also believed in love, long before I did. I was the skeptic there. Something tells me the man you'll marry is just as cynical as I once was. You're going to have to teach him about love, the same way Mark's taught me.

Call me as soon as you get back. I'll be waiting to hear what happens. In my heart I already know it's going to be wonderful.

Love,
Shelly

Jill read the letter twice. Her pulse quickened as her eyes lifted and involuntarily returned to the lanai directly across from her own.

The frantic pace of her heart slowed to normal.

The grouch was gone.

Jill recalled Aunt Milly's letter to Shelly. "When you receive this dress," she'd written, "the first man you meet is the man you'll marry."

So it wasn't the grouch, it was someone else. Not that she really believed in any of this. Still, her knees went unaccountably weak with relief.

After unpacking her clothes, Jill showered and lay down for a few minutes. She hadn't intended to fall asleep, but when she awoke, a rosy dusk had settled. Flickering fires from the bamboo poles that surrounded the pool sent shadows dancing on her walls.

She'd seen him, Jill realized. While she slept. Her hero, her predestined husband. But try as she might, she couldn't bring him into clear focus. Naturally it was her imagination. Fanciful thinking. Dreams gone wild. Jill reminded herself stoutly that she didn't believe in the power of the wedding dress any more than she believed in the Easter Bunny. But it was nice to fantasize now and then, to pretend.

Unquestionably, there was a certain amount of anticipation created by the delivery of the wedding dress and Shelly's letter. But unlike her friend, Jill didn't expect anything to come of this. Jill's feet were firmly planted on the ground. She wasn't as whimsical as Shelly, nor was she as easily influenced.

True, at twenty-eight, Jill was more than ready to marry and settle down. She knew she wanted children eventually, too. But when it came to finding the man of her dreams, she'd prefer to do it the old trial-and-error way. She didn't need a magic wedding dress guiding her toward him!

Initially, Shelly had had many of the same thoughts herself, Jill remembered, but she'd married the first man she'd met after the dress arrived.

The first man you meet. She was thinking about that while she changed into a light cotton dress and sandals. She was still thinking about it as she rode the elevator down to the lobby to have a look around.

There must have been something in the air. Maybe it was because she was on vacation and feeling free of her usual routines and restraints; Jill didn't know. But for some reason she found herself glancing around, wondering which man it might be.

The hotel was full of possibilities. A distinguished gentleman sauntered past. An ambassador perhaps? Or a politician? Hmm, that might be nice.

Nah, she countered silently, laughing at herself. She wasn't interested in politics. Furthermore she didn't see herself as an ambassador's wife. She'd probably say the wrong thing to the wrong person and inadvertently cause an international incident.

A guy who looked like a rock star strolled her way next. Now, there was an interesting prospect, although Jill had a minor problem picturing herself married to a man who wore his hair longer than she did. He was cute, though. A definite possibility—*if* she took Shelly's letter seriously.

A doctor would be ideal, Jill decided. With her medical background, they were sure to have a lot in common. She scanned the lobby area, searching for someone who looked as if he'd feel at home with a stethoscope around his neck.

No luck. Nor, for that matter, did she seem to be generating any interest herself. She might as well be invisible. So much for that! These speculations were all in fun anyway….

Swallowing an urge to laugh, she headed out the back of the hotel toward the pristine beach. A lazy evening stroll among swaying palms sounded just the thing.

She walked toward the ocean, removed her shoes and held them by the straps as she wandered ankle-deep into the delightfully warm water. She wasn't paying much attention to where she was going, thinking, instead, about her hopes for a family of her own. Thinking about the few truly happy memories she had of her father. The Christmas when she was five and a camping trip two years later. A picnic, once. But by the time she was eight, his success had overtaken him. It wasn't that he didn't love her or her mother, she supposed, but—

"I wouldn't go out much farther if I were you," a deep male voice called from behind her.

Jill's pulse soared at the unexpectedness of the intrusion. She saw the silhouette of a man leaning against a palm tree. In the darkness she couldn't make out his features, yet he seemed vaguely familiar.

"I won't," she said, trying to see who'd spoken. Whoever it was stayed stubbornly in the shadows of the tree.

From the distance Jill noted that he had the physique of an athlete. She happened to appreciate wide, powerful shoulders on a man. She stepped closer, attempting to get a better look at him without being obvious. Although his features remained hidden, his chin was tilted at a confident angle.

She'd always found confidence an appealing trait in a man....

"I wondered if you were planning to go swimming at night. Only a fool would do that."

Jill bristled. She had no intention of swimming. For one thing, she wasn't dressed for it. Before she could defend herself, however, he continued, "You look like one of those helpless romantics who can't resist testing the water. Let me guess—this is your first visit to the islands?"

Jill nodded. She'd ventured far enough onto the beach to actually see him now. Her heart sank—no wonder he'd seemed familiar. No wonder he was insulting. For the second time in a twenty-four-hour period she'd happened upon the grouch.

"I don't suppose you took time to eat dinner, either."

"I…had something earlier. On the plane." That had been one of the benefits of her unexpected move to first class.

"I was there, remember?" He snickered softly. "Plastic food."

Jill didn't agree—she'd enjoyed it—but she wasn't going to argue. "I don't know what concern it is of yours," she said.

"None," he admitted, shrugging.

"Then my going without dinner shouldn't bother you." She bristled again at the intense way he was studying her. His mouth had twisted into a faint smile, and he seemed amused by her.

"Thank you for your advice," she said stiffly, turning away from him and heading back toward the water.

"You're not wearing your lei."

Jill's fingers automatically went to her neck as she stopped. She'd left it in her room when she changed clothes.

"Allow me." He stepped forward, removed the one

from his own neck and draped it around hers. Since this was her first visit to the islands, Jill didn't know if giving someone a lei had any symbolism attached to it. She didn't really want that kind of connection with him. Just in case.

"Thank you." She hoped she sounded adequately grateful.

"I might have saved your life, you know."

That was a ridiculous comment. "How?"

"You could've drowned."

Jill couldn't help it. She laughed. "Not very likely. I had no intention of swimming."

"You can't trust the tides here. Even this close to shore, the waves are capable of jerking your feet right out from under you. You might easily have been swept out to sea."

"That's absurd."

"Perhaps," he agreed, amicably enough. "But I was hoping you'd realize you're in my debt."

Ah, now they were getting somewhere. This man wasn't given to generosity. She'd bet a month's wages that he'd initiated the conversation for his own purposes. He'd had plenty of time on their flight from Seattle to advise her about swimming.

No, he was after something.

"What is it you want?" she asked bluntly.

He grinned that cocky, unused smile of his and nodded. Apparently this was high praise of her finely honed intuitive skills.

"Nothing much. I was hoping you'd attend a small business dinner with me."

"Tonight?"

He nodded again. "You did mention you hadn't eaten."

"Yes, but…"

"It'll only take an hour or so of your time." He sounded impatient, as if he'd expected her to agree to his scheme without question.

"I don't even know who you are. Why would I want to attend a dinner party with you? I'm Jill Morrison, by the way."

"Jordan Wilcox," he said abruptly. "All right, if you must know, I need a woman to come with me so I won't be forced to offend someone I can't afford to alienate."

"Then don't."

"He's not the one I'm worried about. It's his daughter. She's apparently set her sights on me and doesn't seem capable of taking a hint."

"Well, then, it sounds as though you've got yourself a problem." Privately Jill wondered at the woman's taste.

He frowned, shoving his hands into the pockets of his dinner jacket. He'd changed clothes, too, but he hadn't substituted something more casual for his business suit. Quite the reverse. But then, that shouldn't have surprised her. It was always business, never pleasure, with people like him.

"I don't know what it is about you women," he said plaintively. "Can't you tell when a man's not interested?"

"Not always." Jill was beginning to feel a bit smug.

She swung her shoes at her side. "In other words, you need me as a bodyguard."

Clearly he didn't approve of her terminology, but he let it pass. "Something like that."

"Do I have to pretend to be madly in love with you?"

"Good heavens, no."

Jill hesitated. "I'm not sure I brought anything appropriate to wear."

He reached inside his pocket and pulled out a thick wad of cash. He peeled away several hundred-dollar bills and stuffed them in her hand. "Buy yourself something. The shop in the hotel's still open."

Two

"I'll pay for the dress myself," Jill insisted for the tenth time. She couldn't believe she'd agreed to attend this dinner party with Jordan Wilcox. Not only didn't she know the man, she didn't even like him.

"I'll pay for the dress," he said, also for the tenth time. "It's the least I can do."

They were in the ultraexpensive dress shop located off the hotel lobby. Jill was shifting judiciously through the rack of evening gowns. Most were outrageously overpriced. She found a simple one she thought might flatter her petite build, ran her hand down the sleeve until she reached the white tag, then sighed. The price was higher than any of the others. Grumbling under her breath, she dropped the sleeve and continued her search.

Jordan glanced impatiently at his watch. "What's wrong with this one?" He held up an elegant cocktail dress. It was made of dark green silk, with a draped bodice and a slim skirt. Lovely indeed, but hardly worth a week's salary.

"Nothing's wrong with it," she answered absently as she flipped through the row of dresses.

"Then buy it."

Jill glared at him. "I can't afford eight hundred dollars for a dress I'll probably wear once."

"I can," he returned from between clenched teeth.

"I *won't* allow you to pay for my dress."

"The party's in thirty minutes," he reminded her sharply.

"All right, all right."

He sighed with relief and put out a hand for the dress. Jill stopped him.

"Obviously nothing here is going to work. I'll check what I brought with me. Maybe what I have is more suitable than I thought."

Groaning, he followed her to the elevator. "Wait in the hall," she said as she unlocked her door. She wasn't about to let a strange man into her room. She stood by the closet and rooted through the few dresses she'd unpacked that afternoon. The only suitable one was an antique-white sleeveless dress with large gold buttons down the front. It wasn't exactly what one would wear to an elegant dinner party, but it was passable.

She raced to the door and held it up for Jordan. "Will this do?"

The poor man looked exasperated. "How do I know?"

Leaving the door open, Jill ran back to her closet.

"The only other dress I have is Aunt Milly's wedding gown," she muttered.

"You packed a wedding dress?" His gray eyes lit up with amusement. It seemed an effort not to laugh out loud. "You apparently have high hopes for this vacation."

"I didn't bring it with me," she informed him primly, sorry she'd even mentioned it. "A friend had it delivered."

"You're getting married?"

"No. I— Oh, I don't have time to explain."

Jordan eyed her as if he had plenty of questions, but wasn't sure he wanted to ask them.

"Wear the one you showed me, then," he said testily. "I'm sure it'll be fine."

"All right, I will." By now Jill regretted agreeing to attend the dinner party. "I'll be ready in five minutes." She closed the door again, but not before she got a glimpse of the surprised look on Jordan's face. It wasn't until she'd slipped out of her sundress that she realized he probably wasn't accustomed to women who left him waiting in the hallway while they changed clothes.

Although she knew Jordan was impatient, Jill took an extra few minutes to freshen her makeup and run a brush through her shoulder-length brown hair. Using a gold clip, she pinned it up in a simple chignon. Despite herself, she couldn't help feeling excited about this small adventure. There was no telling whom she might meet tonight.

Drawing in a deep breath to calm herself, she

smoothed the skirt of her dress, then walked slowly to the door. Jordan was waiting for her, his back against the opposite wall. He straightened when she appeared.

"Do I look okay?"

His gaze narrowed assessingly. His scrutiny made Jill uncomfortable, and she held herself stiffly. At last he nodded.

"You look fine," was all he said.

Jill heaved a sigh of relief, returned to her room to retrieve her purse and then joined Jordan.

The dinner party, as he'd explained earlier, was in a private room in one of the hotel's restaurants. Jordan led the way to the elevator, his pace urgent.

"You'd better tell me what you want me to do," she said.

"Do?" he repeated with a frown. "Just do whatever you women do to let one another know a certain man is off-limits, and make sure Suzi understands." He hesitated. "Only do it without fawning all over me."

"I wouldn't dream of it," Jill said, gazing up at him in mock adoration and fluttering her lashes.

Jordan's frown deepened. "None of that, either."

"Of what?"

"That thing with the eyes." He motioned with his hand, looking annoyed.

"Should I know something about who's attending the party?"

"Not really," he said impatiently.

"What about you?" He shot her a puzzled look, and Jill elaborated. "If I'm your date, it makes sense I'd know who you are—something beyond your name, I mean—and what you do."

"I suppose it does." He buried his hands in his pockets. "I'm the CEO for a large development company based in Seattle. Simply put, we develop projects, gather together the financing, arrange for the construction, and then once the project's completed, we sell."

"That sounds interesting." If you thrived on tension and pressure, that is.

"It can be," was his only response. He looked her over once more, but his glance revealed neither approval nor reproach.

"I didn't like you when we first met." Jill wasn't sure why she felt obliged to tell him this. In fact, she still didn't like him, although she had to admit he was a very attractive man indeed. "When I sat next to you during the flight, I thought you were very unfriendly," she continued.

"I take it your opinion of me hasn't changed?" He cocked one brow with the question, as if to suggest her answer wouldn't trouble him one way or the other.

Jill ignored him. "You don't like women very much, do you?"

"They have their uses."

He said it in such a belittling, negative way that Jill felt a flash of hot color invade her cheeks. She turned to look at him, feeling almost sorry for a man who had everything yet seemed so empty inside. "What's made you so cynical?"

He glanced at her again, a bit scornfully. "Life."

Jill didn't know what to make of that response, but luckily the elevator arrived just then.

"Is there anything else I should know before we get there?" she asked once they were inside. Her role, Jill understood, was to protect him from an associate's daughter. She had no idea how she was supposed to manage that, but she'd think of something when the time came.

"Nothing important." He paused, frowning. "I'm afraid the two of us might arouse some curiosity, though."

"Why's that?"

"I don't generally associate with...innocents."

"Innocents?" He made her sound like one of the preschool crowd. No one she'd ever known could insult her with less effort. "I am over twenty-one, in case you didn't realize it."

He laughed outright at that, and Jill stiffened, regretting—probably not for the last time—that she'd actually agreed to this.

"I think you're wonderful, too," she said sarcastically.

"So you told me before."

The elevator arrived at the top floor of the hotel, where the restaurant was located. Jordan spoke briefly to the maître d', who led them to the dinner party.

Jill glanced around the simple, elegant room, and her heart did a tiny somersault. All the guests were executive types, the men in dark suits, the women in sophisticated dresses that could all have been bought at the little boutique downstairs. Everyone had an aura of prosperity and power.

Jill's breath came in shallow gasps. She was miles out of her league. These people had money, real money, whereas she'd spent months just saving for this vacation. Her money was invested in panty hose and frozen dinners, not property and office towers and massive stock portfolios.

Jordan must have felt her unease, because he turned to her and smiled briefly. "You'll be fine."

It astonished Jill that three little words from him could give her an immeasurable boost of confidence. She smiled and drew herself up as tall as her five-foot-three-inch frame would allow.

Waiters carried trays of delicate hors d'oeuvres and narrow etched-glass flutes filled with sparkling, golden champagne. Jill reached for a glass and took her first sip, widening her eyes in surprise. Never had she tasted anything better.

"This is excellent."

"It should be, at three hundred dollars a bottle."

Before Jill could comment, an older, distinguished-looking gentleman detached himself from a younger colleague and made his way across the room toward them. He looked close to sixty, but could have stepped off the pages of *Gentlemen's Quarterly*.

"Jordan," he said in a hearty voice, extending his hand, "I'm delighted you could make it."

"I am, too."

"I trust your flight was uneventful."

Jordan's gaze briefly met Jill's. "It was fine. I'd like you to meet Jill Morrison. Jill, Dean Lundquist."

"Hello," she said pleasantly, giving him her hand.

"Delighted," Dean said again, turning to smile at her. He held her hand considerably longer than good manners required. Jill had the impression she was being carefully inspected and did her utmost to appear composed.

Finally, he released her and nodded toward the entrance. "If you'll both excuse me for a moment, Nicholson's just arrived."

"Of course," Jordan agreed politely.

Jill waited until Dean Lundquist was out of ear-shot. Then she leaned toward Jordan and whispered, "Suzi's dad?"

Jordan made a wry face. "Smart girl."

Not really, since few other men would have had cause to inspect her so closely, but Jill didn't discount the compliment. She wasn't likely to receive that many, at least not from Jordan.

"Who was that standing with him?" She inclined her head in the direction of a tall, good-looking young man. Something about him didn't seem quite right. Nothing she could put her finger on, but it was a feeling she couldn't shake.

"That's Dean, Junior," Jordan explained.

Jill noticed the way Jordan's mouth thinned and the thoughtful, preoccupied look that came into his eyes. "He's being groomed by Daddy to take my place."

"Junior?" Jill studied the younger man a second time. "I don't think you'll have much of a problem."

"Why's that?"

She shrugged, not sure why she felt so confident of that. "I can't picture you losing at anything."

His gaze swept her warmly. "I have no intention of giving Junior the opportunity, but I'm going to have a real fight on my hands soon."

"Just a minute," Jill said. "If Suzi is Dean Senior's daughter, then wouldn't a marriage between you two secure your position?" It wouldn't exactly be a love match, but she couldn't envision Jordan marrying for something as commonplace as love.

Jordan gave her a quick, unreadable look. "It'd help, but unfortunately I'm not the marrying kind."

Jill had guessed as much. She doubted there was time in his busy schedule for love or commitment, just for work, work, work. Complete one project and start another. She knew the pattern.

Jill couldn't imagine falling in love with someone like Jordan. And she couldn't picture Jordan in love at all. As he'd said, he wasn't the marrying kind.

"Jordan." A woman's shrill voice sent a chill up Jill's spine as a beautiful blonde hurried past her and straight into Jordan's unsuspecting arms, locking him in a tight embrace.

"This must be Suzi," Jill said conversationally from behind the woman who was squeezing Jordan for all she was worth.

Jordan's irate eyes found hers. "Do something!" he mouthed.

Jill was enjoying the scene far too much to interrupt Suzi's passionate greeting. While Jordan was occupied, Jill took an hors d'oeuvre from a nearby silver platter. Whatever it was tasted divine, and she automatically reached for two more. She hadn't recognized how hungry she was. Not until she was on her third cracker did she realize she was sampling caviar.

"Oh, darling, I didn't think you'd ever get here," Suzi said breathlessly. Her pretty blue eyes filled with something close to hero worship as she gazed up at Jordan. "Whatever took you so long? Didn't you know I'd been waiting hours and hours for you?"

"Suzi," Jordan said stiffly, disentangling himself from the blonde's embrace. He straightened the cuffs of his shirt. "I'd like you to meet Jill Morrison, my date. Jill, this is Suzi Lundquist."

"Hello," Jill said before helping herself to yet another cracker. Jordan's look told her this was not the time to discover a taste for Russian caviar.

Suzi's big blue eyes widened incredulously. She really was lovely, but one glimpse and Jill understood Jordan's reluctance. Suzi was very young, early twenties at most, and terribly vulnerable. She had to admire his tactic of putting the girl off without being unnecessarily rude.

Jordan had made Dean Lundquist's daughter sound like a vamp. Jill disagreed. Suzi might be a vamp-in-training, but right now she was only young and head-strong.

"You're Jordan's date?" Suzi asked, fluttering her incredible lashes—which were almost long enough to cause a draft, Jill decided.

She smiled and nodded. "We're very good friends, aren't we, Jordan?" She slipped her arm in his and looked up at him, ever so sweetly.

"But I thought—I hoped…" Suzi turned to Jordan, who'd edged himself closer to Jill, draping his arm across her shoulders as though they'd been an item for quite some time.

"Yes?"

Suzi glanced from Jordan to Jill and then back to Jordan. Tears brimmed in her bright blue eyes. "I thought there was something special between us…."

"I'm sorry, Suzi," he said gently.

"But Daddy seemed to think…" She left the rest unsaid as she slowly backed away. After three short steps, she turned and dashed out of the room. Jill popped another cracker in her mouth.

Several people were looking in their direction, although Jordan seemed unaware of it. Jill, however, keenly felt the interested glances. Not exactly a comfortable feeling, especially when one's mouth was full of caviar.

After an awkward moment, conversation resumed, and Jill was able to swallow. "That was dreadful," she muttered. "I feel sorry for the poor girl."

"Frankly, so do I. But she'll get over it." He turned

toward Jill. "A lot of help *you* were," he grumbled. "You were stuffing down crackers like there was no tomorrow."

"This is the first time I've tasted caviar. I didn't know it was so good."

"I didn't bring you along to appraise the hors d'oeuvres."

"I served my purpose," Jill countered. "But I'm not happy about it. She's not a bad kid."

"Believe me," Jordan insisted, his face tightening, "she *will* get over it. She'll pout for a while, but in the end she'll realize we did her a favor."

"I still don't like it."

Now that her mission was accomplished, Jill felt free to examine the room. She wandered around a bit, sipping her champagne. The young man playing the piano caught her attention. He was good. Very good. After five years of lessons herself, Jill knew talent when she heard it. She walked over to the baby grand to compliment the pianist, and they chatted briefly about music until she saw Jordan looking for her. Jill excused herself; their meal was about to be served.

Dinner was delicious. Jill was seated beside Jordan, who was busy carrying on a conversation with a stately-looking gentleman on his other side. The man on her right, a distinguished gentleman in his mid-sixties, introduced himself as Andrew Howard. Although he didn't acknowledge it in so many words, Jill knew he was the president of Howard Pharmaceuticals, now retired. Jill pointed out that PayRite Pharmacy, where she worked, carried a number of his company's medications, and the two of them were quickly engaged in a lengthy conversation. By the time dessert was served Jill felt as comfortable with Mr. Howard as if she'd known him all her life.

Following a glass of brandy, Jordan seemed ready to leave.

"Thank you so much," she told Mr. Howard as she slid back her chair. "I enjoyed our conversation immensely."

He stood with her and clasped her hand warmly. "I did, too. If you don't mind, I'd like to keep in touch."

Jill smiled. "I'd enjoy that. And thank you for the invitation."

Then she and Jordan exchanged good-nights with her dinner companion and headed for the elevator. Jordan didn't speak until they were inside.

"What was all that with Howard?"

"Nothing. He invited me out to see his home. Apparently it's something of a showplace."

"He's a bit old for you, don't you think?"

Jill gave him an incredulous look. "Don't be ridiculous. He assumed you and I knew each other. He just wanted me to feel welcome." She didn't mention that Jordan had spent the entire dinner talking with a business associate. He seemed to have all but forgotten she was with him.

"Howard invited you to his home?"

"Us, actually. You can make your excuses if you want, but I'd really like to take him up on his offer."

"Andrew Howard and my father were good friends.

My father passed away several years back, and Howard likes to keep track of the projects I'm involved with. He's gone in on the occasional deal."

"He's a sweet man. Did you know he lost his only son to cancer? It's the reason his company's done so much in the field of cancer research. His son's death changed his life."

"I had no idea." Jordan was obviously astounded that he'd known Andrew Howard for so many years and hadn't realized he'd lost a child. "You learned this over dinner?"

"Good grief, dinner lasted nearly two hours." She sighed deeply and pressed her hands to her stomach. "I'm stuffed. I'll never sleep unless I walk off some of this food."

"It would've helped if you hadn't eaten half the hors d'oeuvres all by yourself."

Jill decided to ignore that comment.

"Do you mind if I join you?" Jordan surprised her by asking.

"Not in the least, as long as you promise not to make any more remarks about hors d'oeuvres. *Or* lecture me about the dangers of swimming at night."

Jordan grinned. "You've got yourself a deal."

They walked through the lobby and out of the hotel toward the beach. The surf thundered against the shore, slapping the sand, then retreating. Jill found the rhythmic sounds relaxing.

"What sort of project do you have planned for Hawaii?" she asked after a few minutes.

"A shopping complex."

Although he'd answered her question, his expression was preoccupied. "Why the frown?" she asked.

He shot a quick glance her way. "The Lundquists seem to have some sort of hidden agenda," he said.

"You said Daddy's grooming Junior to take your place," Jill prompted.

"It looks like I'm headed for a proxy fight, which is an expensive and costly proposition for everyone involved. For now, I have the controlling interest, but by no means do I have control."

"This trip to Hawaii?"

"Is strictly business. I just wish I knew what's going on behind my back."

"Good luck with it." This was a world far removed from Jill's.

"Thanks." He grinned and suddenly seemed to leave his worries behind.

They strolled for several minutes in companionable silence. The breeze was warm, the moon full and bright, and the rhythm of the ocean waves went on and on.

"I suppose I should go back," Jill said reluctantly. She had a full day planned, beginning first thing in the morning, and although she didn't feel the least bit tired, she knew she should get some sleep.

"Me, too."

They altered their meandering course in the direction of the hotel, their shoes sinking into the moist sand.

"Thanks for your help with Suzi Lundquist."

"Anytime. Just say the word and I'll be there, especially if there's caviar involved." She felt guilty, however, about the young and vulnerable Suzi. Jordan had been gentle with her; nevertheless, Jill's sympathy went out to the girl. "I feel kind of bad for Suzi."

Jordan sighed. "The girl just won't take no for an answer."

"Do you?"

"What do you mean?"

Jill stopped a moment to collect her thoughts. "I don't understand finance, but it seems to me that you'd never get anywhere if you quit at the first stumbling block. Suzi takes after her father and brother. She saw what she wanted and went after it. Rather an admirable trait, I guess. I suspect you haven't seen the last of her."

"Probably not, but I won't be here for more than a few days. I should be able to avoid her during that time."

"Good luck," she said again. She hesitated when they reached the pathway, bordered by vivid flowering shrubs, that led to the huge lighted swimming pool.

Jordan grinned. "I have a feeling I'm going to need it."

The night couldn't have been more perfect. It seemed such a shame to waste these romantic moments, but Jill finally forced herself to murmur goodnight.

"Here," Jordan said just as she did.

Jill was startled when he presented her with a single lavender orchid. "What's this for?"

"In appreciation for all your help."

"Actually, I should be the one thanking you. I had a wonderful evening." It sure beat sitting in front of her television and ordering dinner from room service, which was what she'd planned. She held the flower under her nose and breathed in its delicate scent.

"Enjoy your stay in Hawaii."

"Thank you, I will." Her itinerary was full nearly every day. "I might even see you...around the hotel."

"Don't count on it. I'm headed back to Seattle in two days."

"Goodbye, then."

"Goodbye."

Neither moved. Jill didn't understand why. They'd said their good-nights—there seemed nothing left to say. It was time to leave. Time for her to return to her room and sleep off the effects of an exceptionally long day.

She made a decisive movement, but before she could turn away, his hand at her shoulder stopped her. Jill's troubled eyes met his. "Jordan?"

He caught her chin, his touch light but firm.

"Yes?" she whispered, her heart in her throat.

"Nothing." He dropped his hand.

Jill was about to turn away again when he stepped toward her, took her by the shoulders and kissed her. Jill had certainly been kissed before, and the experience had always been pleasant, if a bit predictable.

Not this time.

Exciting, unfamiliar sensations raced through her.

Jordan's mouth caressed hers with practiced ease while his hands roved her back, moving slowly, confidently.

Jill was breathless and weak when he finally broke away. He stared down at her with a perplexed look, as if he'd shocked himself by kissing her. As if he didn't know what had come over him.

Jill didn't know, either. There was a sinking feeling in the pit of her stomach, and then she remembered something Shelly had told her—the overwhelming sensation she'd experienced the first time Mark had kissed her. From that moment on, Shelly had known her fate was sealed.

Jill had never felt anything that even came close to what she'd just felt in Jordan's arms. Was it possible? *Could* there be something magical about Aunt Milly's wedding dress? Jill didn't know. She didn't want to find out, either.

"Jill?"

"Oh, no," she moaned as she looked up at him.

"Oh, no," Jordan echoed, apparently amused. "I'll admit women have reacted when I've kissed them, but no one's ever said that."

She barely heard him.

"What's wrong?"

"The dress…" Jill stopped herself in time.

"What dress?"

Jill knew she wasn't making any sense. The whole thing was ridiculous. Unbelievable.

"What dress?" he repeated.

"You wouldn't understand." She had no intention of explaining it to him. She could just imagine what someone like Jordan Wilcox would say when he heard about Aunt Milly's wedding dress.

Three

Jill glared at Jordan. He had no idea how devastating she'd found his kiss. And the worst of it was, *she* had no idea why she was feeling this way.

"Jill?" he said, eyeing her suspiciously. "What does my kissing you have to do with a dress?"

She squeezed her eyes shut, then opened them. "It doesn't have anything to do with it," she blurted without thinking, then quickly corrected herself. "It's got everything to do with it." She knew she was overreacting, but she couldn't seem to help herself. All he'd done was kiss her! There was no reason to behave like a fool. She had a good excuse, however. It had been a long and unusual day compounded by Shelly's letter and the arrival of the wedding dress. Who *wouldn't* be flustered? Who wouldn't be confused—especially in light of Shelly's experience?

"You're not being too clear," Jordan told her.

"I know. I'm sorry."

"What dress are you talking about?" he asked patiently. "Could you explain yourself?"

Jill didn't see how that was possible. Jordan wouldn't understand. Not only that, he was cynical and scornful. The man who placed power and profit above all else would laugh at something as absurd as the story about the wedding dress.

She drew in an unsteady breath. "There's nothing I can say."

"Was my kiss so repugnant to you?" It didn't appear that he was going to graciously drop the matter, not when his male ego was on the line.

Forcing her voice to sound carefree, Jill placed a hand on his shoulder and looked him square in the eye. "I'd think a man of your experience would be accustomed to having women crumple at his feet."

"Don't be ridiculous." His habitual frown snapped into place.

"I'm not," she said. Best to keep Jordan in the dark, otherwise he might misread her intentions. Besides, he wouldn't be any more enthusiastic about a romance between them than she was. "The kiss was very nice," she admitted grudgingly.

"And that's bad?" He rubbed a frustrated hand along his blunt, determined-looking jaw. "Perhaps you'll feel better once you're back in your room."

Jill nodded eagerly. "Thank you. For dinner," she added, remembering her manners.

"Thank you for joining me. It was…a pleasure meeting you."

"You, too."

"I probably won't see you again."

"That's right," she agreed resolutely. No reason to tempt fate. She was beginning to like him and that could be dangerous. "You'll be gone in a couple of days, won't you? I'm here for the week." She retreated a couple of steps. "Have a safe trip home, and don't work too hard."

They parted then, but before she walked into the hotel, Jill turned back to see Jordan strolling in the opposite direction, away from her.

Jill awoke late the following morning. It was rare for her to sleep past eight-thirty, even on weekends. The tour bus wasn't scheduled to leave the hotel until ten, so she took her time showering and dressing. Breakfast consisted of coffee, an English muffin and slices of fresh pineapple, which she ate leisurely on her lanai, savoring the morning sunlight.

Out of curiosity, she glanced over at Jordan's room to see if the drapes were open. They were. From what she could discern, he was sitting at a table near the window, talking on his phone and working with his computer.

Business. Business. Business.

The man lived and breathed it, just like her father had. And, in the end, it had killed him.

Dismissing Jordan from her thoughts, she collected

her purse and hurried down to the lobby, where she was meeting the tour group.

The sightseeing expedition proved excellent. Jill visited Pearl Harbor and the U.S.S. *Arizona* memorial and a huge shopping mall, returning to the hotel by three o'clock.

Her room was cool and inviting. Jill took a few minutes to examine the souvenirs she'd purchased, a shell lei and several colorful T-shirts. Then, with a good portion of the day still left to enjoy, she decided to spend the remaining afternoon hours lazing around the pool. Once again she glanced over at Jordan's room, her action almost involuntary. And once again she saw that he was on the phone. Jill wondered if he'd been talking since morning.

Changing into her bathing suit, a modest one-piece in a—what else—Hawaiian print, she carried her beach bag, complete with three different kinds of sunscreen, down to the swimming pool. With a large straw hat perched on her head and sunglasses protecting her eyes, she stretched out on a chaise longue to absorb the sun.

She hadn't been there more than fifteen minutes when a waiter approached carrying a dome-covered platter and a glass of champagne. "Ms. Morrison?"

"Yes?" Jill sat up abruptly, knocking her hat askew. "I…I didn't order anything," she said uncertainly as she reached up to straighten her hat.

"This was sent compliments of Mr. Wilcox."

"Oh." Jill wasn't sure what to say. She twisted around and, shading her eyes with her hand, looked up. Jordan was standing on his lanai. She waved, and he returned the gesture.

"If that will be all?" the waiter murmured, stepping away.

"Yes… Oh, just a moment." Jill scrambled in her beach bag for a tip, which she handed to the young man. He smiled his appreciation.

Curious, she balanced the glass of champagne as she lifted the lid—and nearly laughed out loud. Inside was a large array of crackers topped with caviar. She glanced up at Jordan a second time and blew him a kiss.

Something must have distracted him then. He turned away, and when Jill saw him again a few minutes later, he was pacing the lanai, phone in hand. She was convinced he'd completely forgotten about her. It was ironic, she mused, and really rather sad; here he was in paradise and he'd hardly ventured beyond his hotel room.

Jill drank her champagne and savored a few of the caviar-laden crackers, then decided she couldn't stand his attitude a minute longer. Packing up her things, she looped the towel around her neck and picked up the platter in one hand, her beach bag in the other. After that, she headed back inside the hotel. She knew she was breaking her promise to herself by seeking him out, but she couldn't stop herself.

Muttering under her breath, she took the elevator up to Jordan's floor, calculated which room was his and knocked boldly on the door.

A long moment passed before the door finally

opened. Jordan, still talking on his phone, gestured her inside. He didn't so much as pause in his conversation, tossing dollar figures around as casually as other people talked about the weather.

Jill sat on the edge of his bed and crossed her legs, swinging her foot impatiently as Jordan strode back and forth across the carpet, seemingly oblivious to her presence.

"Listen, Rick, something's come up," he said, darting a look in her direction. "Give me a call in five minutes. Sure, sure, no problem. Five minutes. See if you can contact Raymond, get these numbers to him and call me back." He disconnected the line without a word of farewell, then glanced at Jill.

"Hello," he said.

"Hi," she returned, holding out the platter to offer him an hors d'oeuvre.

"No, thanks."

She took one herself and chewed it slowly. She could almost feel his irritation.

"Something I can do for you?"

"Yes," she stated calmly. "Sit down a minute."

"Sit down?"

She nodded, motioning toward the table. "I have a story to tell you."

"A story?" He didn't seem particularly charmed by the idea.

"Yes, and I promise it won't take longer than five minutes," she added pointedly.

He was obviously relieved that she intended to keep this short. "Go on."

"As I've mentioned before, I don't know a lot about the world of high finance. But I'm well aware that time has skyrocketed in value. I also realize that the value of any commodity depends on its availability."

"Does this story have a point?"

"Actually I haven't got to the story yet, but I will soon," she announced cheerfully.

"Can you do it in—" he paused to check his watch "—two and a half minutes?"

"I'll hurry," she promised, and drew a deep breath. "I was nine when my mother signed me up for piano lessons. I could hardly wait. The other kids dreaded having to practice, but not me. From the time I was in kindergarten, I loved to pound away at the old upright in our living room. My heart and soul went into making music. It was probably no coincidence that one of the first pieces I learned was 'Heart and Soul.' I hammered out those notes like machine-gun blasts. I overemphasized each crescendo, cherished each lingering note. Van Cliburn couldn't have finished a piece with more pizzazz than I did. My hands would fly into the air, then flutter gently to my lap."

"I noticed you standing by the piano at the dinner party. Are you a musician?"

"Nope. For all my theatrical talents, I had one serious shortcoming. I could never master the caesura—the rest."

"The rest?"

"You know, that little zigzag thingamajig on sheet music that instructs the player to do nothing."

"Nothing," he repeated slowly.

"My impatience was a disappointment to my mother. I'm sure I frustrated my piano teacher no end. As hard as she tried, she couldn't make me understand that music was always sweeter and more compelling after a rest."

"I see." His hands were buried deep in his pockets as he studied her.

If Jordan was as much like her father as she suspected, she doubted he really did understand. But she'd told him what she'd come to say. Mission accomplished. There wasn't any other reason to stay, so she got briskly to her feet and scooped up her beach bag.

"That's it?"

"That's it. Thank you for the caviar. It was a delightful surprise." With that she moved toward the door. "Just remember what I said about the rest," she said, glancing over her shoulder.

The phone pealed sharply and Jill grimaced. "Goodbye," she mouthed, grasping the doorknob.

The phone rang again. "Goodbye." Jordan hesitated. "Jill?"

"Yes?" The way he said her name seemed so urgent. She whirled around, hope surging in her heart. Perhaps he didn't intend to answer the phone!

It rang a third time, and Jordan's eyes, dark gray, smoky with indecision, traveled from Jill to the telephone.

"Yes?" she repeated.

"Nothing," he said harshly, reaching for the phone. "Thanks for the story."

"You're welcome." With nothing left to say, Jill walked out of his room and closed the door. Even before the lock slid into place she heard Jordan rhyming off lists of figures.

Her room felt less welcoming than when she'd returned earlier. Jill slipped out of her swimsuit and showered. She was vain enough to check her reflection in the mirror, hoping to have enhanced the slight tan she'd managed to achieve between Seattle's infamous June cloudbursts. It didn't look as though her sojourn in the tropics had done anything but add a not-so-fetching touch of pink across her shoulders.

She dressed in a thick terry robe supplied by the hotel and had just wrapped a towel around her wet hair when her phone rang.

"Hello," she said, breathlessly, sinking onto her bed. Her stomach knotted with anticipation.

"Jill Morrison?"

"Yes." It wasn't Jordan. But the voice sounded vaguely familiar, although she couldn't immediately place it.

"Andrew Howard. I sat next to you at the dinner party last night."

"Yes, of course." Her voice rose with pleasure. She'd thoroughly enjoyed her chat with the older man. "How are you?"

He chuckled. "I'm fine. I tried to phone earlier, but you were out and I didn't leave a message."

"I went on a tour this morning."

"Ah, that explains it. I realize it's rather short notice, but are you free for dinner tonight?"

Jill didn't hesitate. "Yes, I am."

"Good, good. Could you join me around eight?"

"Eight would be perfect." Normally Jill dined much earlier, but she wasn't hungry yet, thanks to an expensive snack, compliments of Jordan Wilcox.

"Wonderful." Mr. Howard seemed genuinely pleased. "I'll have a car waiting for you and Wilcox out front at seven-thirty."

And Wilcox. She'd almost missed the words. So Jordan had accepted Mr. Howard's invitation. Perhaps she'd been too critical; perhaps he'd understood the point of her story, after all, and was willing to put business aside for one evening. Perhaps he was as eager to spend time with her as she was with him.

"I wondered if you'd be here," Jordan announced when they met in the lobby at the appointed time. He didn't exactly greet her with open enthusiasm, but Jill comforted herself with the observation that Jordan wasn't one to reveal his emotions.

"I wouldn't miss this for the world," he added. That was when she remembered he was hoping to interest the older man in his shopping-mall project. Dinner, for Jordan, would be a golden opportunity to conduct business, elicit Mr. Howard's support and gain the financial backing he needed for the project.

Jill couldn't help feeling disappointed. "I'll do my best not to interrupt your sales pitch," she said sarcastically.

"My sales pitch?" he echoed, then grinned, apparently amused by her assumption. "You don't have to worry. Howard doesn't want in on this project, which is fine. He just likes to keep tabs on me, especially since Dad died. He seems to think I need a mentor, or at least some kind of paternal adviser."

"Do you?"

Jordan shrugged. "There've been one or two occasions when I've appreciated his wisdom. I don't need him holding my hand, but I have sometimes looked to him for advice."

Remembering her dinner conversation with the older man, Jill said, "In some ways, Mr. Howard must think of you as a son."

"I doubt that." Jordan scowled. "I've known him all this time and not once did he ever mention he'd lost a son."

"It was almost thirty years ago, and as I told you, it's the reason his company's done so much cancer research. Howard Pharmaceuticals makes several of the leading cancer-fighting drugs." When Andrew Howard had told her about his son's death, a tear had come to his eye. Although Jeff Howard had succumbed to childhood leukemia a long time ago, his father still grieved. Andrew had become a widower a few years later, and he'd never fully recovered from the double blow. Jill was deeply touched by his story. During their conversation, she'd shared a little of the pain she'd felt at her own father's death, something she rarely did, even with her mother or her closest friend.

"What shocks me," Jordan continued, "is that I've worked on different projects with him over the years. We've also kept in touch socially. And not once, *not once,* did he mention a son."

"Perhaps there was never a reason."

Jordan dismissed that idea with a shake of his head.

"Mr. Howard's a sweet man. I really like him," Jill asserted.

"Sweet? Andrew Howard?" Jordan grinned, his eyes bright with humor. "I've known alligators with more agreeable personalities."

"Apparently there's more to your friend than you realized."

"My friend," Jordan repeated. "Funny, I'd always thought of him as my father's friend, not mine. But you're right—he *is* my friend and— Oh, here's the car." With a hand on her arm, he escorted her outside.

A tall, uniformed driver stepped from the long white limousine. "Ms. Morrison and Mr. Wilcox?" he asked crisply.

Jordan nodded, and the chauffeur ceremoniously opened the back door for them. Soon they were heading out of the city toward the island's opposite coast.

"Do you still play the piano?" Jordan asked unexpectedly.

"Every so often, when the mood strikes me," Jill told him a bit ruefully. "Not as much as I'd like."

"I take it you still haven't conquered the caesura?"

"Not yet, but I'm learning." She wasn't sure what had prompted his question, then decided to ask one of her own. "What about you? Do you think you might be interested in learning to play the piano?"

Jordan shook his head adamantly. "Unfortunately, I've never had much interest in that sort of thing."

Jill sighed and looked away.

Nearly thirty minutes passed before they reached Andrew Howard's oceanside estate. Jill suspected it was the longest Jordan had gone without a business conversation since he'd registered at the hotel.

Her heart pounded as they approached the beautifully landscaped grounds. A security guard pushed a button that opened a huge wrought-iron gate. They drove down a private road, nearly a mile long and bordered on each side by rolling green lawns and tropical flower beds. At the end stood a sprawling stone house.

No sooner had the car stopped than Mr. Howard hurried out of the house, grinning broadly.

"Welcome, welcome!" He greeted them expansively, holding out his arms to Jill.

In a spontaneous display of affection, she hugged him and kissed his cheek. "Thank you so much for inviting us."

"The pleasure's all mine. Come inside. Everything's ready and waiting." After exchanging a hearty handshake with Jordan, Mr. Howard led the way into his home.

Jill had been impressed with the outside, but the

beauty of the interior overwhelmed her. The entry was tiled in white marble and illuminated by a sparkling crystal chandelier. Huge crystal vases of vivid pink and purple hibiscus added color and life. From there, Mr. Howard escorted them into a massive living room with floor-to-ceiling windows that overlooked the Pacific. Frothing waves crashed against the shore, bathed in the fire of an island sunset.

"This is so lovely," Jill breathed in awe.

"I knew you'd appreciate it." Mr. Howard reached for a bell, which he rang once. Almost immediately the house-keeper appeared, carrying a tray of glasses and bottles of white and red wine, sherry and assorted aperitifs.

They were sipping their drinks when the same woman reappeared. "Mr. Wilcox, there's a phone call for you."

It was all Jill could do not to gnash her teeth. The man was never free, the phone cord wrapped around his neck more tightly than a hangman's noose.

"Excuse me, please," Jordan said as he left the room, his step brisk.

Jill looked away, refusing to watch him go.

"How do you feel about that young man?" Mr. Howard asked bluntly when Jordan was gone.

"We met only recently. I—I don't have any feelings for him one way or the other."

"Well, then, what do you think of him?"

Jill stared down at her wine. "He works too hard."

Sighing, the old man nodded and rubbed his eyes. "He reminds me of myself more than thirty years ago.

Sometimes I'd like to take him by the shoulders and shake some sense into him, but I doubt it'd do much good. That boy's too stubborn to listen. Unfortunately, he's a lot like his father."

Knowing so little of Jordan and his background, Jill was eager to learn what she could. At the same time, a saner part of her insisted she was better off not hearing this. The more she knew, the greater her chances of caring.

Nevertheless, Jill found herself asking curiously, "What made Jordan the way he is?"

"To begin with, his parents divorced when he was young. It was a sad situation." Andrew leaned forward and clasped his wineglass with both hands. "It was plain as the nose on your face that James and Donna Wilcox were in love. But, somehow, bitterness replaced the love, and their son became a weapon they used against each other."

"Oh, how sad." Just as she'd feared, Jill felt herself sympathizing with Jordan.

"They both married other people, and Jordan seemed to remind his parents of their earlier unhappiness. He was sent to the best boarding schools, but there was precious little love in his life. Before he died, James tried to build a relationship with his son, but..." He shrugged. "And to the best of my knowledge his mother hasn't seen him since he was a teenager. I'm afraid he's had very little experience of real love, the kind that gives life meaning. Oh, there've been women, plenty of them, but never one who could teach him how to love and bring joy into his life—until now." He paused and looked pointedly at Jill.

"As I said before, I've only known Jordan for a short time."

"Be patient with him," Mr. Howard continued, as though Jill hadn't spoken. "Jordan's talented, don't get me wrong—the boy's got a way of pulling a deal together that amazes just about everyone—but there are times when he seems to forget about human values, like compassion. And the ability to enjoy what you have."

Jill wasn't sure how to respond.

"Frankly, I was beginning to lose faith in him," Mr. Howard said, grinning sheepishly. "He can be hard and unforgiving. You've given me the first ray of hope."

Jill took a big swallow of wine.

"He needs you. Your warmth, your gentleness, your love."

Jill wanted to weep with frustration. Andrew Howard was telling her exactly what she didn't want to hear. "I think you're mistaken," she murmured.

He chuckled. "I doubt that, but I'm an old man, so indulge me, will you?"

"Of course, but—"

"There's a reason you've come into his life," he said, gazing intently at her. "A very important reason." Andrew closed his eyes. "I feel this more profoundly than I've felt anything in a long while. He needs you, Jill."

"No...I'm sure he doesn't." Jill realized she was beginning to sound desperate, but she couldn't help it.

The old man's eyes opened slowly and he smiled. "And I'm just as sure he does." He would have continued, but Jordan returned to the room then.

From the marinated-shrimp appetizer to the home-made mango-and-pineapple ice cream, dinner was one of the most delectable, elegant meals Jill had ever tasted. They lingered over coffee, followed by a glass of smooth brandy. By the end of the evening, Jill felt mellow and warm, a dangerous sensation. Jordan had been wonderful company—witty, charming, fun. He seemed more relaxed, too. Apparently the phone call had brought good news; it was the only thing to which she could attribute his cheerfulness.

"I can't thank you enough," she told Andrew when the limousine arrived to drive her and Jordan back to the hotel. "It was a lovely evening."

The older man hugged Jill and whispered close to her ear, "Remember what I said." Breaking away, he extended his hand, gripping Jordan's elbow. "It was good of you to come."

"I'll be in touch soon," Jordan promised.

"I'll look forward to hearing from you. Let me know what happens with this shopping-mall project."

"I will," Jordan said.

The car was cool and inviting in the warm night. Before she realized it, Jill found her head resting on Jordan's broad shoulder. "Oh, sorry," she mumbled through a yawn.

"Are you sleepy?"

She smiled softly to herself, too tired to fight the power of attraction—and exhaustion. "Maybe a little. Wine makes me sleepy."

Jordan pressed her head against his shoulder and held her there. His hand gently stroked her hair. "Do you mind telling me what went on between you and Howard while I was on the phone?"

Jill went stock-still. "Uh, nothing. What makes you ask?" She decided it was best to pretend she didn't know what he was talking about.

"Then why was Howard wearing a silly grin every time he looked at me?" Jordan demanded.

"I—I don't know. You'll have to ask him." She tried to straighten, but Jordan wouldn't allow it. After a moment she gave up, too relaxed to put up much of a struggle.

"I swear there was a twinkle in his eye from the moment I returned after my phone call. It was like I'd been left out of a joke."

"I'm sure you're wrong."

Jordan seemed to ponder that. "I doubt it," he said.

"Hmm." She felt sleepy, and leaning against Jordan was strangely comforting.

"I've been thinking about what you said this afternoon," he told her a few minutes later. His mouth was against her ear, and although she might have been mistaken, she thought his lips lightly brushed her cheek.

"My sad but true tale," she whispered on the end of another yawn.

"About your trouble with the musical rest."

"Ah, yes, the rest."

"I'm flying back to Seattle tomorrow," Jordan said abruptly.

Jill nodded, feeling inexplicably sad, then surprised by the intensity of her reaction. With Jordan in Seattle, they wouldn't be bumping into each other at every turn. Wouldn't be arguing, bantering—or kissing. With Jordan in Seattle, she wouldn't confuse him with the legacy behind Aunt Milly's dress. "Well...I hope you have a good flight."

"I have a meeting Tuesday morning. It would be impossible to cancel at this late date, but I was able to change my flight."

"You changed your flight?" Jill prayed he wouldn't hear the breathless catch in her voice.

"I don't have to be at the airport until evening."

"When?" It shouldn't make any difference to her, yet she found herself wanting to know. Needing to know.

"Eight."

Jill was much too dazed to calculate the time difference, but she knew it meant he'd arrive in Seattle in the early morning. He'd be exhausted. Not exactly the best way to show up at a high-powered meeting.

"I was thinking," Jordan continued. "I've been to Hawaii a number of times but other than meetings or dinner engagements, I haven't seen much of the islands. I've never explored them."

"That's a pity," she said, meaning it.

"And," he went on, "it seemed to me that sightseeing wouldn't be nearly as much fun alone."

"I enjoyed myself this morning." Her effort to refute him was feeble at best.

His fingers were entwined in her hair. "Will you come with me, Jill?" he asked, his voice a husky whisper. "Share the day with me. Let's discover Hawaii together."

Four

"I can't" was Jill's immediate response. She'd already lowered her guard—enough to be snuggling in his arms. So much for her resolve not to get involved with Jordan Wilcox, she thought with dismay. So much for steering a wide course around the man.

"Why not?" Jordan asked with the directness she'd come to expect from him.

"I've...m-made plans," she stammered. Even now, she could feel herself weakening. With his arm around her and her head nestled against his shoulder it was difficult to refuse him.

"Cancel them."

How arrogant of him to assume she should abandon her plans because the almighty businessman was willing to grant her some of his valuable time.

"I'm afraid I can't do that," she answered coolly, her determination reinforced. She'd already paid for the rental car as part of her vacation package, she rationalized, and she wasn't about to let that money go to waste.

"Why not?" He sounded surprised.

Isn't being with him what you really want? The question stole into her mind, and Jill wanted to scream out her response. A resounding NO. Jordan Wilcox frightened her. It was all too easy to envision them together, strolling hand in hand along sun-drenched beaches. He'd kissed her that first time, that only time, on the beach, and the memory stubbornly refused to go away.

"Jill?"

At the softness in his voice, she involuntarily raised her eyes to his. Jill hadn't expected to see tenderness in Jordan, but she did now, and it was nearly her undoing. Her feelings for him were changing, and she found herself more strongly attracted than ever. She remembered when she'd first seen him, the way she'd been convinced there was nothing gentle in him. He'd seemed so hard, so untouchable. Yet, right now, at this very moment, he'd made himself vulnerable to her. *For* her.

"You're trembling," he said, running his hands down her arms. "What's wrong?"

"Nothing," she denied quickly, breathlessly. "I'm…a little tired. It's been a long day."

"That's what you said last night when I kissed you. Remember? You started mumbling some nonsense about a dress, then you went stiff as a board on me."

"Nothing's wrong," she insisted, breaking away from

him. She straightened and lowered her hand to her skirt, smoothing away imaginary creases.

"I don't buy that, Jill. Something's bothering you."

She wished he hadn't mentioned the dress, because it brought to mind, uninvited and unwanted, Aunt Milly's wedding dress, which was hanging in her hotel-room closet.

"You'd be shaking, too, if you knew the things I did," she exclaimed, instantly regretting the impulse.

"What are you afraid of?"

She stared out the window, then slowly her lower lip began to quiver with the effort to restrain her laughter. She was actually frightened of a silly dress! She wasn't afraid to fall in love; she just didn't want it to be with Jordan.

"For a woman who drags a wedding dress on vacation with her, you're not doing very much to encourage romance."

"I did not bring that dress with me!"

"It was in the room when you arrived? Someone left it behind?"

"Not exactly. Shelly did. She, uh, enjoys a good laugh. She mailed it to me."

"It never occurred to me that you might be engaged," he said slowly. "You're not, are you?"

"No." But according to her friend, she soon would be.

"Who's Shelly?"

"My best friend," Jill explained, "or at least she used to be." Then, impulsively, her heart racing, she added, "Listen, Jordan, I think you have a lot of potential in the husband category, but I can't fall in love with you. I just can't."

A stunned silence followed her announcement.

He cocked his eyebrows. "Aren't you taking a bit too much for granted here? I asked you to explore the island with me, not bear my children."

She'd done it again, blurted out something totally illogical. Worse, she couldn't make herself stop. Children were a subject near and dear to her heart.

"That's another thing," she wailed. "I bet you don't even like children. No, I can't go with you tomorrow. Please don't ask me to…because it's so hard to say no." It must be the wine, Jill decided; she was saying far more than she should.

Jordan relaxed against the leather upholstery and crossed his long legs. "All right, if you'd rather not go, I'm certainly not going to force you."

His easy acceptance astonished her. She glanced at him out of the corner of her eye, feeling almost disappointed that he wasn't trying to persuade her.

Something was drastically, dangerously wrong with her. She was beginning to like Jordan, really like him. Yet she couldn't allow this attraction to continue. She couldn't allow herself to fall in love with a man so much like her father. Because she knew what that meant, what kind of life it led to, what kind of unhappiness it caused.

When the limousine stopped in front of the hotel, it was all Jill could do to wait for the chauffeur to climb out of the driver's seat, walk around the car and open the door for her.

She hurried inside the lobby, needing to breathe in the fresh air of reason. Wait for sanity to catch up with her heart.

She reached the elevators and pushed the button, holding her thumb in place, hoping that would hurry it along.

"Next time, keep your little anecdotes to yourself," Jordan said sharply from behind her. Then he walked leisurely across the lobby.

Keep her little anecdotes to herself? The temptation to rush after him and demand an explanation was strong, but Jill made herself resist it.

Not until she was in the elevator did she understand. This entire discussion had arisen because she'd told him her story about the caesura and her lack of musical talent. And now he was turning her own disclosure against her! Righteous anger began to build in her heart.

But by the time Jill was in her room and ready for bed, she felt wretched. Jordan had asked her to spend a day with him, and she'd reacted as if he'd insulted her.

The way she'd gone on and on about his potential as a husband was bad enough, but then she'd dragged the subject of children into their conversation. That mortified her even more. The wine could be blamed for only so much.

She cringed, too, as she recalled what Andrew

Howard had said, the faith he'd placed in her. Jordan needed her, he'd said, apparently convinced that Jordan would never experience love if she didn't teach him. She hated disappointing Andrew, and yet…and yet…

It didn't surprise Jill that she slept poorly. By morning she wasn't feeling any enthusiasm at all about picking up her rental car or sightseeing on the north shore.

She reviewed the room-service menu, ordered coffee and toast, then stared at the phone for several minutes before conceding there was one thing she still had to do. Anxious to get it over with, Jill rang through to Jordan's room.

"Hello," he answered gruffly on the first ring. He was definitely a man who never ventured far from his phone.

"Hello," she said with uncharacteristic meekness. "I'm…calling to apologize."

"Are you sorry enough to change your mind and spend the day with me?"

Jill hesitated. "I've already paid for a rental car."

"Great, then I won't need to get one."

Jill closed her eyes. She knew what she was going to say, had known it the night before. In the same heartbeat, she realized she'd regret it later. "Yes," she whispered. "If you still want me to join you, I'll meet you in the lobby in half an hour."

"Twenty minutes."

She groaned. "Fine, twenty minutes, then."

Despite her misgivings, Jill's spirits lifted immediately. "One day won't hurt anything," she said out loud.

What could possibly happen in so short a time? Certainly nothing earth-shattering. Nothing of consequence.

Who was she kidding? Not herself, Jill admitted.

She thought she understood why moths ventured close to the fire, enticed by the light and the warmth. Against her will, Jordan was drawing her dangerously close. She knew even as she came nearer that she was going to get burned. And yet she didn't walk away.

He was waiting for her when she stepped out of the elevator and into the lobby. He stood there grinning, his look almost boyish. This was the first time she'd seen him without a business suit. Instead, he wore white slacks and a pale blue shirt with the sleeves rolled up.

"You ready?" he asked, taking her beach bag from her.

"One question." Her heart was pounding because she had no right to ask.

"Sure." His eyes held hers.

"Your cell phone—do you have it?"

Jordan nodded and pulled a tiny phone from his shirt pocket.

Jill stared at it for a moment, feeling the tension work its way down her back. Jordan's cell phone reminded her of the pager her father had always carried. Always. All family outings, which were few and far between, had been subject to outside interference. Early in life, Jill had received a clear message: business was more important to her father than she was. In fact, almost everything had seemed more significant than spending time with the people who loved him.

Jordan must have read the look in her eyes because he said, "I'll leave it in my room," and then promptly strolled to the elevator. Stunned, Jill watched as he stepped inside. Bit by bit, her muscles began to relax.

While he was gone, Jill filled out the paperwork for the rental car. She was waiting outside by the economy model when Jordan appeared. He paused, staring at it with narrowed eyes as if he wasn't sure the car would make it to the end of the street, let alone around the island.

"I'm on a limited budget," Jill explained, hiding a smile. The car suited her petite frame perfectly, but for a man of Jordan's stature it was like...like stuffing a rag doll inside a pickle jar, Jill thought, enjoying the whimsical comparison.

"You're positive this thing runs?" he muttered under his breath as he climbed into the driver's seat. His long legs were cramped below the steering wheel, his head practically touching the roof.

Jill nodded. She remembered reading that this particular model got exceptionally good gas mileage—but then it should, with an engine only a little bigger than a lawnmower's.

To prove her right, the car roared to life with a flick of the key.

"Where are we going?" Jill asked once they'd merged with the flow of traffic on the busy thoroughfare by the hotel.

"The airport."

"The airport?" she repeated, struggling to hide her

disappointment. "I thought your flight didn't leave until eight."

"Mine doesn't, but ours takes off in half an hour."

"Ours?" What about the sugarcane fields and watching the workers harvest pineapple? Surely he didn't intend for them to miss that. "Where is this plane taking us?"

"Hawaii," he announced casually. "The island of. Do you know how to scuba dive?"

"No." Her voice was oddly breathless and high-pitched. She might have spent the past twenty-odd years in Seattle—practically surrounded by water—but she wasn't all that comfortable *under* it.

"How about snorkeling?"

"Ah…" She jerked her thumb over her shoulder. "There are pineapple fields on the other side of this island. I assumed you'd want to see those."

"Another visit, perhaps. I'd like to try my hand at marlin fishing, too, but we don't have enough time today."

"Snorkeling," Jill said as though she'd never heard the word before. "Well…it might be fun." In her guide-book Jill remembered reading about green beaches of crushed olivine crystals and black sands of soft lava. These were sights she couldn't expect to find anywhere else. However, she wasn't sure she wanted to view them through a rubber mask.

A small private plane was ready for them when they arrived at Honolulu Airport. The pilot, who apparently knew Jordan, greeted them cordially. After brief intro-ductions and a few minutes' chat, they were on their way.

Another car, considerably larger than the one Jill had rented, was waiting for them on the island of Hawaii. A large, white wicker picnic basket sat in the middle of the backseat.

"I hope you're hungry."

"Not yet."

"You will be," Jordan promised.

He drove for half an hour or so, until they reached a deserted inlet with a magnificent waterfall. He parked the car, then got out and opened the trunk. Inside was everything they'd need for snorkeling in the crystal-clear aquamarine waters.

Never having done this before, Jill was uncertain of the procedure. Jordan patiently answered her questions and waded into the water with her. He paused when they were waist-deep, gave her detailed instructions, then clasped her hand. His touch lent her confidence, and soon she was investigating an undersea world of breathtaking beauty. Swimming out of the inlet, they came upon a reef, with colorful fish slipping in and out of white coral caverns. After what seemed like only minutes, Jordan steered them back toward the inlet and shore.

"I don't think I've ever seen anything more beautiful," she breathed, pushing the mask from her face.

"I don't think I have, either," he agreed as they emerged from the water.

While Jill ran a comb through her hair and put on a shirt to protect her shoulders from the sun, Jordan brought out their lunch.

He spread the blanket in the shade of a palm tree. Jill knelt down beside him and opened the basket. Inside were generous crab-salad sandwiches, fresh slices of papaya and pineapple and thick chocolate-chip cookies. She removed two cold cans of soda and handed one to Jordan.

They ate, then napped with a cool, gentle breeze whisking over them.

Jill awoke before Jordan. He was asleep on his back with his hand thrown carelessly across his face, shading his eyes from the glare of the sun. His features were more relaxed than she'd ever seen them. Jill studied him for several minutes, her heart aching for the man she'd loved so long ago. Her father. The man she'd never really had a chance to know. In some ways, Jordan was so much like her father it pained her to be with him, and at the same time it thrilled her. Not only because in learning about Jordan she was discovering a part of her past, of herself, but because she'd rarely felt so *alive* in anyone's company.

As she recognized this truth, a heaviness settled over her. She didn't *want* to fall in love with him. She was so afraid her life would mirror her mother's. Elaine Morrison had grown embittered. She'd been a young woman when her husband died, but she'd never remarried; instead she'd closed herself off, not wanting to risk the kind of pain that loving Jill's father had brought her.

Sitting up, Jill shoved her now-dry hair away from her face. She wrapped her arms around her bent legs and pressed her forehead to her knees, gulping in breath after breath.

"Jill?" His voice was soft. Husky.

"You shouldn't have left your pager behind, after all," she told him, her voice tight. "Or your phone." Without them, he was a handsome, compelling man who appealed to all her senses. Without them, she was defenseless against his charm.

"Why not?"

"Because I like you too much."

"That's a problem?"

"Yes!" she cried. "Don't you understand?"

"Obviously not," he said with such tenderness she wanted to jump to her feet and yell at him to stop. "Maybe you'd better explain it to me," he added.

"I can't," she whispered, keeping her head lowered. "You'd never believe me. I don't blame you—I wouldn't believe me, either."

Jordan frowned. "Does this have something to do with your reaction the first time I kissed you?"

"The only time!"

"That's about to change."

Her head shot up at the casual way in which he said it, as though kissing her was a foregone conclusion.

He was right.

His kiss was gentle. Jill resisted, unwilling to give him her heart, knowing what became of women who loved men like this. Men like Jordan Wilcox.

Their kiss now was much more potent than that first night. His touch somehow transcended the sensual. Jill could think of no other words to describe it. His fingers brushed her temple. His lips moved across her face, grazing her chin, her cheek, her eyes. She moaned, not from pleasure, but from fear, from a pain that reached deep inside her.

"Oh, no…"

"It's happening again, isn't it?" he whispered.

She nodded. "Can you feel it?"

"Yes. I did the other time, too."

Her eyes drifted slowly open. "I can't love you."

"So you've told me. More than once."

"It isn't personal." She tried to break free without being obvious about it, but Jordan held her firmly in his embrace.

"Tell me what's upsetting you so much."

"I can't." Looking into the distance, she focused on the smoky-blue outline of a mountain. Anything to avoid gazing at Jordan.

"You're involved with someone else, aren't you?"

It would be so easy to lie to him. To tell him about Ralph as though the friendship they shared was one of blazing passion, but she found she couldn't do it.

"No," she wailed, "but I wish I was."

"Why?" he demanded gruffly.

"What about you?" she countered. "Why did you seek out my company? Why'd you ask me to attend the dinner party with you? Surely there was someone else, someone more suitable."

"I'll admit that kissing you is a…unique experience," he confessed.

"But I've been rude."

"Actually, more amusing than rude."

"But why?" she asked again. "What is it about me that interests you? We're about as different as two people can get. We're strangers—strangers with nothing in common."

Jordan was frowning, his eyes revealing his own lack of understanding. "I don't know."

"See what I mean?" She spoke as if it were the jury's final decree. "The whole thing is a farce. You kiss me and…and I feel a certain…feeling."

"So do I. And it's something I can't explain. But I've seen electrical storms that unleash less energy than we did when we kissed."

Suddenly Jill found it nearly impossible to breathe. Jordan couldn't be affected by the wedding dress and its so-called magic—could he? Jill swore the minute she arrived in Seattle she was returning it to Shelly and Mark. She wasn't taking any chances.

"You remind me of my father," Jill said, refusing to meet his eyes. Even talking about Adam Morrison was painful to her. "He was always in a hurry to get somewhere, to meet someone, to make a deal. We took a family vacation when I was ten. My dad, my mom and me. We saw California in one day, Disneyland in an hour. Do you get the picture?" She didn't wait for a response. "He died of a heart attack when I was fifteen. We were wealthy by a lot of people's standards, and after his death my mother didn't have to work. We had no financial worries at all. And yet we would've been happier with far less money if it meant my father was still alive."

An awkward moment passed. When Jordan didn't comment, Jill glanced at him. "You don't have anything to say?"

"Not really, other than to point out that I'm not your father."

"But you're exactly like him! I recognized it the first minute I saw you." She leaped to her feet, grabbed her towel and crammed it into her beach bag.

Jordan reluctantly stood, and while she shook the sand off the blanket and folded it, he loaded their snorkeling gear into the trunk of the car.

They were both quiet during the drive back to the airport, the silence strained and unnatural. A couple of times, Jill looked in Jordan's direction. The hardness was back. The tightness in his jaw, the harsh, almost grim expression...

Jill could well imagine what he'd be like in a board meeting. No wonder he didn't seem too concerned about the threat of a takeover. He would withstand that, and a whole lot more, in the years to come. But at what price? Power demanded sacrifice; prestige didn't come cheap. There was a cost, and Jill could only speculate what it would be for Jordan. His health? His happiness?

She found it intolerable to think about. Words burned in her heart. Words of caution. Words of appeal, but he wouldn't listen to her any more than her father had heeded her mother's tearful pleas.

As the airport came into view, Jill knew she couldn't

let their day end on such an unhappy note. "I did have a wonderful time. Thank you."

"Mmm," he replied, his gaze focused on the road ahead.

Jill stared at him. "That's it?"

"What else do you want me to say?" His voice was crisp and emotionless.

"Like, I don't know, that you enjoyed yourself, too."

"It was interesting."

"Interesting?" Jill repeated.

They'd had a marvelous adventure! Not only that, he'd actually *relaxed*. The lines of fatigue around his eyes were gone. She'd bet a month's wages that this was the first afternoon nap he'd had in years. Possibly decades. It was probably the longest stretch of time he'd been away from a telephone in his adult life.

And all he'd say was that their day had been "interesting"?

"What about the kissing?" she demanded. "Was *that* interesting?"

"Very."

Jill seethed silently. "It was…interesting for me, too."

"So you said."

Jill tucked a long strand of hair behind her ear. "I was only being honest with you."

"I admit it was a fresh approach. Do you generally discuss marriage and children with a man on a first date?"

Color exploded in her cheeks, and she looked uncomfortably away. "No, but you were different…and it wasn't an approach."

"Excuse me, that's right, you were being honest." The cold sarcasm in his voice kept her from even trying to explain.

They'd almost reached the airport when she spoke again. "Would you do me one small favor?" She nearly choked on the pride she had to swallow.

"What?"

"Would you… The next time you see Mr. Howard, would you tell him something for me? Would you tell him I'm sorry?" He'd be disappointed in her, but Jill couldn't risk her own happiness because a dear man with a romantic heart believed she was Jordan Wilcox's one chance at finding love.

Jordan stopped the car abruptly and turned to glare at her. "You want me to apologize to Howard?"

"Please."

"Sorry," he said without a pause. "You'll have to do that yourself."

Five

Four days later, Jill stepped off the plane at Sea-Tac Airport in Seattle. Her skin glowed with a golden tan, accentuated by the bold pink flower print of her new sundress. She hadn't expected anyone to meet her, but was pleasantly surprised to see Shelly and Mark. Shelly waved excitedly when she located Jill in the baggage claim area.

"Welcome home," Shelly said as she rushed forward, exuberantly throwing her arms around Jill. "How was Hawaii? My goodness, your tan is gorgeous. You must've spent *hours* in the sun."

"Hawaii was wonderful." A slight exaggeration. She'd hardly slept since Jordan's departure.

"Tell me everything," Shelly insisted, taking Jill's hands. "I'm dying to find out who you met after we mailed you the wedding dress."

"Honey," Mark chided gently, "give her a chance to breathe."

"Are you with someone?" Shelly asked, looking around expectantly. "I mean, you know, you're not married, are you?"

"I'm not even close to being married," Jill informed her friend dryly.

Mark took charge of the beach bag Jill had brought home with her, stuffed full of souvenirs and everything she couldn't fit into her suitcase. She removed one of the three leis she was wearing and looped it around Shelly's neck. "Here, my gift to you."

"Oh, Jill, it's beautiful. Thank you," Shelly said, fingering the fragrant lei of pink orchids. As they walked toward the appropriate carousel, Shelly slipped her arm through Jill's. "I can't wait a second longer. Tell me what happened after the dress arrived. I want to hear every detail."

Jill had been dreading this moment, but she hadn't thought she'd face it quite so soon. "I'm afraid I'm going to have to return the dress."

Shelly stared at her as if she hadn't heard correctly. "Pardon?"

"I didn't meet anyone."

"You mean to tell me you spent seven days in Hawaii and you didn't speak to a single man?" Shelly asked incredulously.

"Not exactly."

"Aha! So there was someone."

Jill tried not to groan. "Sort of."

Shelly smiled, sliding one arm around her husband's waist. "The plot thickens."

"I met him briefly the first day. Actually I don't think he counts...."

"Why wouldn't he count?" Shelly asked.

"We sat next to each other on the plane, so technically we met *before* I got the wedding dress. I'm sure he's not the one." Jill had decided to play along with her friend's theory, pretend to take it more seriously than she did. Logical objections, like this mistake in timing, *should* convince Shelly—but probably wouldn't.

"In fact," she continued, "I've been thinking about that dress lately, and I'm convinced you and your aunt Milly are wrong—it's not for me. It never was."

"But it fit you. Remember?"

Jill didn't need to be reminded. "That was a fluke. I'm sure if I were to try it on now, it wouldn't."

"Then try it on! Prove me wrong."

"Here?" Jill laughed.

"When you get home. Right now, just tell me about this guy you met. You keep trying to avoid the subject."

"There's nothing to tell," Jill insisted, sorry she'd said anything. She'd tried for the past few days to push every thought of Jordan from her mind, with little success. He'd haunted her remaining time on the islands, refusing to leave her alone. If she did sleep, he invaded her dreams.

"Start with his name," Shelly said. "Surely you know his name."

"Jordan Wilcox, but—"

"Jordan Wilcox," Mark repeated. "He doesn't happen to be a developer, does he?"

"He does something along those lines."

Mark released a low whistle. "He's one of the big boys."

"Big boys," Shelly echoed disparagingly. "Be more specific. Do you mean he's tall?"

"No." Mark's smiling eyes briefly met Jill's. "Although he is. I mean he's a well-known corporate giant. I've met him a few times. If I understand it correctly, he puts together commercial projects, finds backers for them, works with the designer and the builders, and when the project's complete, he sells. He's made millions in the last few years."

"He was in Hawaii to put together financial backing for a shopping mall," Jill explained.

"Well," Shelly said, eyeing her closely, "what did you think of him?"

"What was there to think? I sat next to him on the plane and we stayed in the same hotel, but that was about it." It was best not to mention the other incidents; Shelly would put far too much stock in a couple of dinners and a day on the beach. Heaven help Jill if Shelly ever found out they'd exchanged a few kisses!

"I'm sure he's the one," Shelly announced gleefully. Her eyes fairly sparkled with delight. "I can *feel* it. He's our man."

"No, he isn't," Jill argued, knowing it was futile, yet compelled to try. "I already told you—I met him *before* the dress arrived. Besides, we have absolutely nothing in common."

"Do Mark and I?" Shelly glanced lovingly at her husband. "And I'm crazy about him."

At first, Jill had wondered what Mark, a tax consultant with orderly habits and a closetful of suits, could possibly have in common with her zany, creative, unconventional friend. The answer was simple. Nothing. But that hadn't stopped them from falling in love. Jill couldn't be in the same room with them without sensing the powerful attraction they felt for each other.

However, there was little similarity between Shelly's marriage to Mark and Jill's relationship with Jordan. What she'd learned from her father's life—and death—was the value of balance. Although her career mattered to her, it didn't define her life or occupy every minute of her time.

"In this case I think Jill might be right," Mark said, his voice thoughtful.

"He's the one," Shelly said for the second time.

"I've met him," Mark went on to say. "He's cold and unemotional. If he does have a heart, it was frozen a long time ago."

"So?" Ever optimistic, Shelly refused to listen. "Jill's perfect for him, then. She's warm and gentle and caring."

At the moment Jill didn't feel any of those things. Listening to Mark describe Jordan, she had to fight the urge to defend him, to tell them what Andrew Howard had told her. Yes, Jordan was everything Mark said, but there was another side to him, one Jill had briefly encountered. One that was so appealing it had frightened her into running away, which was exactly what she'd done that day on the beach. He'd kissed her and she'd known immediately, intuitively, that she'd never be the same. But knowing it didn't alter her resolve. She couldn't love him because the price would be too high. He would give her all the things she craved, but eventually she'd end up like her mother, lonely and bitter.

"I just can't imagine Jordan Wilcox married," Mark concluded.

"I can," Shelly interrupted with unflinching enthusiasm. "To Jill."

"Shelly," Mark said, grinning indulgently, "listen to reason."

"When has falling in love ever been reasonable?" She fired the question at her husband, who merely shrugged, then turned back to Jill. "Did you tell him about Aunt Milly's wedding dress?"

"Good heavens, no!"

"All the better. I'll bet you really threw the guy for a loop. Was he on this flight?"

"No, he returned four days ago."

"Four days ago?" Shelly asked suspiciously. "There's something you're not telling us. Come on, Jill, fess up. You did a whole lot more than sit next to him on the plane. And Mark and I want to know what."

"Uh…" Jill was tired from the flight and her resistance was low. Under normal circumstances she would've sidestepped the issue. "It isn't like it sounds," she said weakly. "We talked, that's all."

"Did you kiss?" The question came out in a soft whisper. "The first time Mark kissed me was when I knew. If you and Jordan kissed, there wouldn't be any doubt in your mind. You'd know."

Sooner or later Shelly would worm it out of her. By telling the truth now, Jill thought she might be able to avoid a lengthy inquisition later. "All right, fine. We did kiss. A couple of times."

Even Mark seemed surprised by that.

"See?" Shelly cried triumphantly. "And what happened?"

Jill heaved an exaggerated sigh. "Nothing. I want to return the wedding dress."

"Sorry," Shelly said, her eyes flashing with excitement, "it's nonreturnable."

"I don't plan on ever seeing him again," Jill said adamantly. She'd more or less told Jordan that, too. He was in full agreement; he wanted nothing to do with her, either. "I insist you take back the wedding dress," Jill said. Shelly and Mark's eyes met. Slowly they smiled, as if sharing a private joke.

But in Jill's opinion, there was nothing to smile about.

The first person Jill called when she got home was her mother. Their conversation was friendly, and she was relieved to find Elaine less vague and self-absorbed than she'd been recently. Jill told a few anecdotes, described the island and the hotel, but avoided telling her mother about Jordan.

She was strangely reluctant to call Ralph, even though she knew he was waiting to hear from her. He was terribly nice, but unfortunately she found him...a bit dull. She put off calling; two days later, he called her, leaving a message.

They'd kissed a few times, and the kisses were pleasant enough, but for her there wasn't any spark. When Jordan took her in his arms it felt like a forest fire compared to the placid warmth she experienced with Ralph.

Jordan. Forgetting him hadn't become any easier. Jill had assumed that once she was home, surrounded by everything that was familiar and comfortable, she'd be able to put their brief interlude behind her.

It hadn't happened.

Wednesday afternoon, Jill returned home from work, put water on for tea and began reading the paper. Normally she didn't glance at the financial section. She wasn't sure why she did now. Skimming the headlines, she idly folded back the page—and saw Jordan's name. It seemed to leap out at her.

Jill's heart slowed, then vaulted into action as she read the article. He'd done it. The paper was reporting Jordan's latest coup. His company had reached an agreement with a land-management outfit in Hawaii, and construction on the shopping mall would begin within the next three months.

He must be pleased. Although he hadn't said much, Jill knew Jordan had wanted this project to fly. A hundred questions bombarded her. Had he heard from

Andrew Howard? Had the older man joined forces with Jordan, after all? Had he asked Jordan about her, and if so, what had Jordan told him?

Jill had thought of writing Mr. Howard a note, but she didn't have his address. She didn't have Jordan's, either; however, it was a simple matter of checking the Internet for his company's address.

Before she could determine the wisdom of her actions, she scribbled a few lines of congratulation, addressed the envelope, and the next morning, mailed the card. She had no idea if it would even reach him.

Two days later when Jill came home from work, she noticed a long luxury car parked in front of her apartment building. Other than giving it an inquisitive glance, she didn't pay any attention. She was shuffling through her purse, searching for her keys, when she heard someone approach from behind.

She turned her head to see—and nearly dropped her purse. It was Jordan. He looked very much as he had the first time she'd met him. Cynical and hard. Detached and unemotional. His smoky gray eyes scanned her, but there was nothing to indicate that he was glad to see her, or if he'd spared her a moment's thought since they'd parted. Nothing but cool indifference.

"Hello, Jill."

She was so flustered that the newspaper, which she'd tucked under her arm, fell to the floor. Stooping, she retrieved it, then clutched it against her chest as she straightened. "Jordan."

"I got your note."

"I—I wanted you to know how happy I was for you."

He was staring pointedly at her door.

"Um, would you like to come inside?" she asked, unlatching the door with fumbling fingers. "I'll make some tea if you like. Or coffee…" She hadn't expected this, nor was she emotionally prepared for seeing him. She'd figured he'd read the card and then drop it in his wastebasket.

"Tea sounds fine."

"I'll just be a minute," she said as she hurried into the kitchen. Her heart was rampaging, pounding against her ribs. "Make yourself at home," she called out, holding the teakettle under the faucet.

"You have a nice place," he said, standing in the doorway between the kitchen and the living room.

"Thank you. I've lived here for three years." She didn't know why she'd told him that. It didn't matter to him how long she'd lived there.

"Why'd you send me the card?" he asked while she was setting out cups and saucers.

She didn't feel comfortable using her everyday mugs; she had a couple of lovely china cups her mother had given her and decided on those instead. She paused at his question, frowning slightly. "To congratulate you."

"The *real* reason."

"That was the real reason. This shopping mall was important to you and I was happy to read that everything came together. I knew you worked hard to make it

happen. That was the only reason I sent you the note."
Her cheeks heated at his implication. He seemed to
believe something she hadn't intended—or had she?

"Andrew Howard decided to invest in the project at the
last minute. It was his support that made the difference."

Jill nodded. "I was hoping he would."

"I have you to thank for that."

Nothing in his expression suggested he was grateful
for any assistance she might unwittingly have given him.
His features remained cold and hard. The man who'd
spent that day on the beach with her wasn't the harsh, un-
relenting businessman who stood before her now.

"If I played any part in Mr. Howard's decision, I'm
sure it was small."

"He seemed quite taken with you."

"I was quite taken with him, too."

A flicker of emotion passed through Jordan's eyes, one
so fleeting, so transitory, she was sure she'd imagined it.

"I'd like to thank you, if you'd let me," he said.

She was dropping tea bags into her best ceramic
teapot. "Thank me? You already have."

"I was thinking more along the lines of dinner."

Jill's first thought was that she didn't have anything
appropriate to wear. Not to an elegant restaurant, and of
course she couldn't imagine Jordan dining anywhere
else. He wasn't the kind of man who ate in a burger joint.

"Unless you already have plans…"

He was offering her an escape, and his eyes seemed
to challenge her to take it.

"No," she said, almost gasping. Jill wasn't sure why she accepted so readily, why she didn't even consider declining. "I don't have anything planned for tonight."

"Is there a particular place you'd like to go?"

She shook her head. "You choose."

Jill felt suddenly light-headed with happiness and anticipation. Trying to keep her voice steady, she added, "I'll need to change clothes, but that shouldn't take long."

He looked at her skirt and blouse as if he hadn't noticed them before. "You look fine just the way you are," he said, dismissing her concern.

The kettle whistled and Jill removed it from the burner, pouring the scalding water into the teapot. "This should steep for a few minutes." She backed out of the kitchen, irrationally fearing that he'd disappear if she let him out of her sight.

She chose the same outfit she'd worn on the trip home—the Hawaiian print shirt with the hot pink flowers. Narrow black pants set it off nicely, as did the shell lei she'd purchased the first day she'd gone touring. Then she freshened her makeup and brushed her hair.

Jordan had poured the tea and was adding sugar to his cup when she entered the kitchen. His gaze didn't waver or change in any way, yet she could tell he liked her choice.

The phone rang. Jill darted a look at it, willing it to stop. She sighed and went over to check call display.

Shelly.

"Hello, Shelly." She hoped her voice didn't convey her lack of enthusiasm.

"How are you? I haven't heard a word from you since you got home. Are you all right? I've been worried. You generally phone once or twice a week, and it's not like you to—"

"I'm fine."

"You're sure?"

"Positive."

"You seem preoccupied. Am I catching you at a bad time? Is Ralph there? Maybe he'll take the hint and go home. Honestly, Jill, I don't know why you continue to see that guy. I mean, he's nice, but he's about as romantic as mold."

"Uh, I have company."

"Company," Shelly echoed. "Who? No, let me guess. Jordan Wilcox!"

"You got it."

"Talk to you later. Bye." The drone of the disconnected line sounded in her ear so fast that Jill was left holding the receiver for several seconds before she realized her friend had hung up.

No sooner had Jill replaced it than the phone rang again. She looked at call display, cast an apologetic glance toward Jordan and snatched up the receiver. "Hello, Shelly."

"I want it understood that you're to give me a full report later."

"Shelly!"

"And don't you dare try to return that wedding dress. He's the one, Jill. Quit fighting it. I'll let you go now, but just remember, I want details, so be prepared." She hung up as quickly as she had the first time.

"That was my best friend."

"Shelly?"

"She's married to Mark Brady." Jill waited, wondering if Jordan would recognize the name.

"Mark Brady." He spoke slowly, as though saying it aloud would jar his memory. "Is Mark a tax consultant? I seem to recall hearing something about him not long ago. Isn't he the head of his own firm?"

"That's Mark." Jill nearly told him how Shelly and Mark had met, but stopped herself just in time. Jordan knew about the wedding dress—though not, of course, its significance—because Jill had inadvertently let it slip that first night.

"And Mark's married to your best friend?"

"That's right." She took a sip of her tea. "When I said I'd met you, Mark knew who you were right away."

"So you mentioned me." He seemed pleasantly surprised.

He could have no idea how much he'd been in her thoughts during the past two weeks. She'd tried, heaven knew she'd tried, to push every memory of him from her mind. But it hadn't worked. She couldn't explain it, but somehow nothing was the same anymore.

"You ready?" he asked after a moment.

Jill nodded and carried their empty cups to the sink. Then Jordan led her to his car, opening the door and ushering her inside. When he joined her, he pulled out his ever-present cell phone…and turned it off.

"You don't need to do that on my account," she told him.

"I'm not," he said, his smile tight, almost a grimace. "I'm doing it for me." With that he started the engine.

Jill had no idea where they were going. He took the freeway and headed north, exiting into the downtown area of Seattle. There were any number of four-star restaurants within a five-block area. Jill was curious, but she didn't ask. She'd know soon enough.

When Jordan drove into the underground garage of a luxury skyscraper, Jill was momentarily surprised. But then, several of the office complexes housed world-class restaurants.

"I didn't know there was a restaurant here," she said conversationally.

"There isn't."

"Oh."

"I live in the penthouse."

"Oh."

"Unless you object?"

"No…no, that's fine."

"I phoned earlier and asked my cook to prepare dinner for two."

"You have a cook?" Oddly, that fact astounded her, although she supposed it shouldn't have, considering his wealth.

He smiled, his first genuine smile since he'd shown up at her door. "You're easily impressed."

He talked as though *everyone* employed a cook, and Jill couldn't help laughing.

They rode a private elevator thirty floors up to the penthouse suite. The view of Puget Sound that greeted Jill as the doors glided open was breathtaking.

"This is beautiful," she whispered, stepping out. She followed him through his living room, past a white leather sectional sofa and a glass-and-chrome coffee table that held a small abstract sculpture. She wasn't too knowledgeable when it came to works of art, but this looked valuable.

"That's a Davis Stanford piece," Jordan said matter-of-factly.

Jill nodded, hoping he wouldn't guess how ignorant she was.

"White wine?"

"Please." Jill couldn't take her eyes off the view. The waterways of Puget Sound were dotted with white-and-green ferries. The islands—Bainbridge, Whidbey and Vashon—were jewellike against the backdrop of the Olympic Mountains.

"Nothing like Hawaii, is it?" Jordan asked as he handed her a long-stemmed wineglass.

"No, but just as beautiful in its own way."

"I'm going back to Oahu next week."

"So soon?" Jill was envious.

"It's another short trip. Two or three days at most."

"Perhaps you'll get a chance to go snorkeling again."

Jordan shook his head. "I won't have time for any underwater adventures this trip," he told her.

Jill perched on the edge of the sofa, staring down at her wine. "I don't think I'll ever be able to separate you from my time in Oahu," she said softly. "The rest of my week seemed so…empty."

"I know what you mean."

Her heartbeat quickened as his gaze strayed to her mouth. He sat beside her and removed the wine goblet from her unresisting hand. Next his fingers curved around her neck, ever so lightly, brushing aside her hair. His eyes held hers as if he expected resistance. Then slowly, giving her ample opportunity to pull away if she wished, he lowered his mouth to hers.

Jill moaned in anticipation, instinctively moving closer. Common sense shouted in alarm, but she refused to listen. Just once she wanted to know what it was like to be kissed with real passion—to be cherished by a man. Just once she wanted to know what it meant to be adored. Her heart filled with delirious joy. Her hands slid up his chest to his shoulders as she clung to him. He kissed her again, small, nibbling kisses, as though he was afraid of frightening her with the strength of his need. But he must have sensed her receptiveness, because he deepened the kiss.

Suddenly it came to her. The same thing that had happened to Shelly was now happening to her. The phenomenon Aunt Milly had experienced sixty-five years earlier was coming to pass a third time.

The wedding dress.

Abruptly, she broke off the kiss. Panting, she sprang to her feet. Her eyes were wide and incredulous as she gazed down at a surprised Jordan.

"It's you!" she cried. "It really is you."

Six

"What do you mean, it's me?" Jordan demanded. When she didn't answer, he asked, "What's wrong, Jill?"

"Everything," she cried, shaking her head.

"I hurt you?"

"No," she whispered, "no." She sobbed quietly as she wrung her hands. "I don't know what to do."

"Why do you have to do anything?"

"Because...oh, you wouldn't understand." Worse, she couldn't tell him. Every time he looked at her, she became more and more convinced that Shelly had been right. Jordan Wilcox was her future.

But she *couldn't* fall in love with him, because she knew what would happen to her if she did—she'd become like her mother, lonely, bitter and unhappy. If she was going to marry, she wanted a man who was safe and sensible. A man like...Ralph. Yet the thought of spending the rest of her life with Ralph produced an even deeper sense of discontent.

"I'm not an unreasonable man," Jordan said. Then he added, "Well, generally I'm not. If there's a problem you can tell me."

"It's not supposed to be a problem. According to Shelly and her aunt Milly, it's a blessing. I know I'm talking in riddles, but…there's no way you'd understand!"

"Try me."

"I can't. I'm sorry, I just can't."

"But it has something to do with my kissing you?"

She stared at him blankly. "No. Yes."

"You seem rather uncertain about this. Perhaps we should try it again…."

"That isn't necessary." But even as she spoke, Jordan was reaching for her, pulling her onto his lap. Jill willingly surrendered to his embrace, greeting his kiss with a muffled groan of welcome, a sigh of defeat. His arms held her close, and not for the first time, Jill was stunned by the effect he had on her. It left her feeling both unnerved and overwhelmed.

"Better?" he asked in a remarkably steady voice.

Unable to answer, Jill closed her eyes, then nodded. Better, yes. And worse. Every time he touched her, it confirmed what she feared most.

"I thought so." He seemed reassured, but that did nothing to comfort Jill. For weeks she'd played a silly game of denial. They'd met, and from that moment on, nothing had been the same.

She didn't, couldn't, believe in the power of the wedding dress; she scoffed at the implausibility of its legend. Yet even Mr. Howard, who'd never heard of Aunt Milly or her dress, had felt compelled to explain Jordan's past to her, had seen Jill as his future.

She'd spent only three days with Jordan, but she knew more about him than she knew about Ralph, whom she'd been dating for months. Their day on the beach and the dinner with Andrew Howard had given her insights into Jordan's personality. Since then Jill had found it more difficult to accept what she saw on the surface—the detached, cynical male. The man who wore his I-don't-give-a-damn attitude like an elaborate mask.

Perhaps she understood him because he was so much like her father. Adam Morrison had lived for the excitement, the risks, of the big deal. He poured his life's blood into each business transaction because he'd never really acknowledged the importance of family, emotion, human values.

Jordan wouldn't, either.

Dinner was a strained affair, although Jordan made several efforts to lighten the mood. As he drove her home, Jill sensed that he wanted to say something more. Whatever it was, he left unsaid.

"Have a safe trip," she told him when he escorted her to her door. Her heart was pounding, not with excitement, but with trepidation, wondering if he planned to kiss her again.

"I'll call you when I get back," he told her. And that was all.

* * *

"I have a special fondness for this place," Shelly said as she slipped into a chair opposite Jill. They were meeting for lunch at Patrick's, a restaurant in the mall where Jill's branch of PayRite was located. Typically, she was ten minutes late. Marriage to Mark, who was habitually prompt, hadn't improved Shelly's tardiness. Jill often wondered how they managed to keep their love so strong when they were so different.

Patrick's had played a minor role in Shelly's romance with Mark. Jill recalled the Saturday she'd met her there for lunch, and how amused she'd been at Shelly's crazy story of receiving the infamous wedding dress.

The way Jill felt now—frantic, frightened, confused— was exactly the way Shelly had felt then.

"So tell me everything," Shelly said breathlessly.

"Jordan stopped by. We had dinner. He left this morning on a business trip," she explained dispassionately. "There isn't much to tell."

Shelly's hand closed around her water glass, her eyes connecting with Jill's. "Do you remember when I first met Mark?"

"I'm not likely to forget," Jill said, smiling despite her present mood.

"Anytime you or my mother or anyone else asked me about Mark, I always said there wasn't anything to tell. Remember?"

"Yes." Jill thought of how Shelly's face would become expressionless, her tone abrupt, whenever anyone mentioned Mark's name.

"Well, when I told you nothing was happening, I was stretching the truth," Shelly continued. "There was plenty going on, but nothing I felt I could share. Even with you." She raised her eyebrows. "You, my friend, have the same look I did then. A lot has taken place between you and Jordan. So much that you're frightened out of your wits. Trust me, I know."

"He kissed me again," Jill admitted.

"It was better than before?"

"Worse!"

Shelly apparently found Jill's answer humorous. She tried to hide her smile behind the menu, then lowered it to say, "Don't count on your feelings becoming any less complicated. They won't."

"He's going to be away for a few days. Thank goodness, because it gives me time to think."

"Oh, Jill," Shelly said with a sympathetic sigh, "I wish there was something I could say to help you. Why are you fighting this so hard?" She grinned sheepishly. "I fought it, too. Be smart, just accept it. Love isn't really all that terrifying once you let go of your doubts."

"Instead of talking about Jordan, why don't we order lunch?" Jill suggested a little curtly. "I'm starved."

"Me, too."

The waitress arrived at their table a moment later, and Jill ordered the split-pea soup and a turkey sandwich.

"Wait a minute," Shelly interrupted, motioning

toward the waitress. She turned to Jill. "You don't even *like* split-pea soup. You never order it." She gave Jill an odd look, then turned back to the waitress. "She'll have the clam chowder."

"Shelly!"

The waitress wrote down the order quickly, as though she feared an argument was about to erupt.

"You're more upset than I realized," Shelly said when they were alone. "Ordering split-pea soup—I can't believe it."

"It's soup, Shelly, not nuclear waste." Her friend definitely had a tendency to overreact. It drove Jill crazy, but it was the very thing that made Shelly so endearing.

"I'm going to call Jordan Wilcox myself," Shelly announced suddenly.

"You're going to *what?*" It was all Jill could do to remain in her seat.

"You heard me."

"Shelly, no! I absolutely forbid you to discuss me with Jordan. How would you have felt if I'd called Mark?"

Shelly frowned. "I'd have been furious."

"I will be, too, if you say so much as one word to Jordan about me."

Shelly paused, her eyes wide with concern. "But I'm afraid you're going to mess this up."

Nothing to fear there—Jill already had. She reached for a package of rye crisps from the bread basket, and Shelly frowned again. That was when she remembered she wasn't any fonder of rye crisps than she was of split-pea soup.

"Promise me you'll stay out of it," Jill pleaded. "Please."

"All right," Shelly muttered. "Just don't do anything stupid."

"This is a pleasant surprise," Jill's mother said as she opened the front door. Elaine Morrison was in her late fifties, slim and attractive.

"I thought I'd bring over your gift from Hawaii," Jill said, following her mother into the kitchen, where Elaine poured them each a glass of iced tea. Jill set the box of chocolate-covered macadamia nuts on the counter.

"I'm glad your vacation went so well."

Jill pulled out a bar stool and sat at the counter, trying to look relaxed when she was anything but. "I met someone while I was in Hawaii."

Her mother paused, then smiled. "I thought you might have."

"What makes you say that?"

"Oh, there's a certain look about you. Now tell me how you met, what he's like, where he's from and what he does for a living."

Jill laughed at the rapid-fire questions.

Elaine added slices of lemon to their tea and started across the kitchen, a new excitement in her step. Finally, after all these years, her mother was beginning to overcome the bitterness her husband's obsession with business had created. She was finally coming to terms not only with his death but with her grief over his neglect.

Jill was relieved and delighted by the signs of her mother's recovery, but she had to say, "Frankly, Mom, I don't think you'll like him."

Her mother looked surprised. "Why ever not?"

Jill didn't hesitate. "Because he reminds me of Daddy."

Her mother's face contorted with shock, and tears sprang to her eyes. "Jill, no! For the love of heaven, no."

"I've been giving some thought to your suggestion," Jill said to Ralph a few hours later. Her nerves were in turmoil. The clam chowder sat like a dead weight in the pit of her stomach, and her mother's dire warnings had shaken her badly.

Ralph wasn't tall and strikingly handsome like Jordan, but he was a comfortable sort of man. He made a person feel at ease. In fact, his laid-back manner was a blessed relief after the high-stress, high-energy hours she'd spent with Jordan, few though they were.

Jordan Wilcox could pull together a deal for an apartment complex before Ralph stepped out of the shower in the morning. Ralph's idea of an exhilarating evening was doing the newspaper crossword puzzle.

Everything about Jordan was complex. Everything about Ralph was uncomplicated; he was a straightforward, honest man who'd be a good husband and a loving father.

"Are you saying what I think you're saying?" Ralph prompted when she didn't immediately continue.

Jill held her water glass. "You said something not long ago about the two of us giving serious consideration to making our relationship permanent and…and I wanted you to know I was…I've been giving some thought to that."

Ralph didn't reveal any emotion. He put down his hamburger, looked at her and asked casually, "Why now?"

"Uh…I'm going to be twenty-nine soon." She managed to sound calm, although she felt anything but.

She was the biggest coward who ever lived. But what else could she do? Her mother had become nearly hysterical when Jill had told her about Jordan. Her own heart was filled with trepidation. On the one hand, there was Shelly, so confident Jordan was the man for Jill. On the other was her mother, adamant that Jill would be forever sorry if she got involved with a workaholic.

Jill was trapped in the middle, frightened and unsure.

Ralph relaxed against the red vinyl upholstery. The diner was his favorite place to eat, and he took her there every time they dined out. "So you think we should consider marriage?"

It was the subject Jill had been leading up to all evening, yet when Ralph posed the question directly, she hesitated. If only Jordan hadn't kissed her. If only he hadn't held her in his arms. And if only she hadn't spoken to her mother…

"I missed you while you were away," Ralph said, his gaze holding hers.

Jill knew this was about as close to romance as she was likely to get from Ralph. Romance was his weakest suit, dependability and steadiness his strongest. Ralph would always be there by his wife's side. He'd make the kind of father who played catch in the backyard with his son. The kind of father who'd bring his wife and daughter pretty corsages on Easter morning. He was a rock, a fortress of permanence. She wished she could fall in love with him.

Jordan might have a talent for making millions, but all the money in the world couldn't buy happiness.

"I missed you, too," Jill said softly. She'd thought of Ralph, had wondered about him. A few times, anyway. Hadn't she mailed him a postcard? Hadn't she brought him a book on volcanoes?

"I'm glad to hear that," Ralph said. Then, clearing his throat, he asked, "Jill Morrison, will you do me the honor of becoming my wife?"

The question was out now, ready for her to answer. A proposal was what she'd been hinting at all evening. Now that Ralph had asked, Jill wasn't sure what she felt. Relief? No, it wasn't even close to that. Pleasure? Yes— in a way. But not a throw-open-the-windows-and-shout kind of joy.

Joy. The word hit her like an unexpected punch. Joy was what she'd experienced the first time Jordan had taken her in his arms. A free-flowing joy and the promise of so much more.

The promise she was rejecting.

Ralph might not be the love of her life, but he'd care for her and devote his life to her. It was enough.

"Jill?"

She tried to smile, tried to look happy and excited. Ralph deserved that much. "Yes," she whispered, stretching her hand across the table. "Yes, I'll marry you."

"What do you mean you're engaged to marry Ralph?" Shelly demanded. Her voice had risen to such a high pitch that Jill held the receiver away from her ear.

"He asked me tonight and I've accepted."

"You can't *do* that!" her friend shrieked.

"Of course I can."

"What about Jordan?" Shelly asked next.

"I'd already decided not to see him again." Jill was able to keep her composure, although it wasn't easy.

"If marrying Ralph is typical of your decisions, then I'd like to suggest you talk to a mental-health professional."

Jill laughed despite herself. Her decision had been based on maintaining her sanity, not destroying it.

"I don't know what's so funny. I can't believe you'd do something like this! What about Aunt Milly's wedding dress? Doesn't that mean anything to you? Don't you care that Mark, Aunt Milly and I all felt the dress should go to you? You can't ignore it. Something dreadful might happen."

"Don't be ridiculous."

"I'm not," Shelly said resolutely. "You can't reject the man destiny has chosen for you without consequences." Shelly's voice was solemn.

"You don't know that Jordan's the man," Jill said with far more conviction than she was feeling. "We both realize a wedding dress can't dictate who I'll marry. The choice is mine—and I've chosen Ralph."

"You're honestly choosing Ralph over Jordan?" The question had an incredulous quality.

"Yes."

There was a moment's silence.

"You're scared," Shelly went on, "frightened half out of your wits because of everything you feel. I know, because I went through the same thing. Jill, please, think about this before you do something you'll regret for the rest of your life."

"I have thought about it," she insisted. She'd thought of little else since her last encounter with Jordan. Since her talk with Shelly. Since her visit to her mother's. She'd carefully weighed her options. Marrying Ralph seemed the best course.

"You have no intention of changing your mind, do you?" Shelly cried. "Do you expect me to stand by and do *nothing* while you ruin your life?"

"I'm not ruining my life. Don't be absurd." Her voice grew hard. "Naturally I'll return your aunt Milly's wedding dress and—"

"No," Shelly groaned. "Here, talk to Mark."

"Jill?" Mark came on the line. "What's the problem?"

Jill didn't want to repeat everything. She was tired and it was late and all she wanted to do was go to bed. Escape for the next eight hours and then face the world again. Jill hadn't intended to tell Shelly and Mark her news quite so soon, but there'd been a telephone message from them when she got home. She'd decided she might as well let Shelly know about her decision. Jill wasn't sure what kind of reaction she'd expected from her friends, but certainly not this.

"Just a minute," Mark said next. "Shelly's trying to tell me something."

Although Shelly had given the phone to her husband, Jill could hear her friend's frantic words as clearly as if she still held the receiver. Shelly was pleading with Mark to talk some sense into Jill, begging him to try because she hadn't been able to change Jill's mind.

"Mark," Jill called, but apparently he didn't hear her. "Mark," she tried again, louder this time.

"I'm sorry, Jill," he said politely, "but Shelly's upset, and I'm having a hard time figuring out just what the problem is. All I can make out is that you've decided not to see Jordan Wilcox again."

"I'm marrying Ralph Emery, and I don't think he'd take kindly to my dating Jordan."

Mark chuckled. "No, I don't suppose he would. Frankly, I believe the decision is yours, and yours alone. I know Jordan, I've talked to him a couple of times and I share your concerns. I can't picture him married."

"He's already married," Jill stated unemotionally, "to his job. A wife would only get in the way."

"That's probably true. What about Ralph—have I met him?"

"I don't think so," Jill returned stiffly. "He's a very nice man. Honest and hardworking. Shelly seems to think he's dull, and perhaps he is in some ways, but he...cares for me. It isn't a great love match, but we're both aware of that."

"Shelly thinks I'm dull, too, but that didn't stop her from marrying me."

Mark was so calm, so reassuring. He was exactly what Jill needed. She was so grateful she felt close to tears. "I want to do the right thing," she said, gulping in a quick breath. Her voice wavered and she bit her lower lip, blinking rapidly.

"It's difficult knowing what's right sometimes, isn't it?" Mark said quietly. "I remember how I felt the first time I met Shelly. Here was this completely bizarre woman announcing to everyone who'd listen that she refused to marry me. I hadn't even asked—didn't even know her name. Then we stumbled on each other a second time and a third, and finally I learned about Aunt Milly's wedding dress."

"What did you think when she told you?"

"That it was the most ridiculous thing I'd ever heard."

"I did, too. I still do." She wanted a husband, *but not Jordan.*

"I'm sure you'll make the right decision," Mark said confidently.

"I am, too. Thanks, Mark, I really appreciate talking to you." The more she grew to know her friend's husband, the more Jill realized how perfectly they suited each other. Mark brought balance into Shelly's life, and she'd infused his with her warmth and wit. If only she, Jill, could have met someone like Mark.

No sooner had she hung up the phone than there was a loud knock on her door. Since it was late, close to eleven, Jill was surprised.

Peering through the peephole, she gasped and drew away. Jordan Wilcox.

"I thought you were in Hawaii," she said as she opened the door.

"I was." His eyes scanned her hungrily. "This morning I had the most incredible feeling something was wrong. I tried to call, but there wasn't any answer."

"I...was out for most of the day."

He took her by the shoulders and then, before she could protest, pulled her into his arms.

"Jordan?" She'd never seen him like this, didn't understand why he seemed so disturbed.

"I just couldn't shake the feeling something was wrong with you."

"I'm fine."

"I know," he said, inhaling deeply. "Thank God you're safe."

Seven

"Of course I'm safe," Jill said, still feeling bewildered. Jordan's arms were tight around her and he buried his head in the curve of her neck, his breathing hard.

"I've never experienced anything like this before," he said, loosening his hold. His hands caressed the length of her arms as he moved back one small step. He studied her, his gaze intimate and tender. "I hope it never happens to me again." Taking her hand, he led her to the sofa.

"You're not making any sense."

"I know." He momentarily closed his eyes, then gave a deep sigh. He raised her fingers to his lips and gently kissed the back of her hand.

"It was the most unbelievable thing," he continued with a shrug. "I awoke with this feeling of impending doom. At first I tried to ignore it. But as the day wore on I couldn't shake it. All I knew was that it had something to do with you.

"I thought if I talked to you I could assure myself that

nothing was wrong and this feeling would go away. Only I couldn't get hold of you."

"I was out most of the day," she repeated unnecessarily.

Jordan rubbed a hand down his face. "I tried to phone you at home and I couldn't get an answer. I don't know your cell number. So I panicked. I booked the next flight to Seattle."

"What about your business in Hawaii?"

"I canceled one meeting and left what I could with an assistant. Everything's taken care of." He sighed once more and sagged against the back of her sofa. "I could do with a cup of coffee."

"Of course." Jill immediately stood and hurried into the kitchen, starting the coffee and assembling cups and saucers in a matter of minutes. She was arranging everything on a tray when Jordan stepped up behind her.

He slid his arms around her waist and kissed the side of her neck. "I don't know what's happening between us."

"I'm…not sure anything is."

Jordan chuckled softly, the sound a gentle caress against her skin. "I'm beginning to think you've cast a spell over me."

Jill froze. *Spell* and *magic* were words she'd rather not hear. Even the smallest hint that the wedding dress was affecting him wouldn't change what she'd done. She'd made her decision. The dress was packed away in the box Shelly had mailed her, ready to be returned.

"I've never experienced anything like this," Jordan said again, sounding almost uncertain.

Jill should have been shocked. Jordan Wilcox had probably never felt confused or doubtful about anything in his adult life. She speculated that his emotions had been buried so deep, hidden by pride for so long, that he barely recognized them anymore.

"I think I'm falling in love with you."

Jill closed her eyes. She didn't want to hear this, didn't want to deal with a declaration of love. Not now. Not when she'd settled everything in her own mind. Not when she'd reconciled herself to never seeing him again.

"That's not true," Jordan countered, turning her around and into his arms. "I can't live without you. I've known that from the first moment we kissed."

"Oh, no…"

His amused laughter filled her small kitchen. "You said the same thing that night. Remember?" The smile faded as he gazed at her upturned face. His eyes, so gray and intense, seemed to sear her with a look of such power it was all Jill could do not to cry out and break off his embrace. She glanced away, chewing nervously on her lower lip, willing him to free her, willing him to leave.

His hands cupped her face, his thumbs stroking her cheeks. "You feel it, too, don't you?" he whispered. "You have from the very first. Neither one of us can deny it."

She meant to tell him then, to blurt out that she was engaged to Ralph, but she wasn't given the chance. Before she could utter a word, before she could even begin to explain, Jordan captured her mouth with his own.

His lips were hard and desperate as they claimed possession of hers, firing her senses to life. She moaned, not from pleasure, although that was keen, but from regret.

Ralph had kissed her that night, too. Jill had tried to reassure herself their marriage would work. She'd put her heart and her soul into their good-night kiss and hadn't felt even a fraction of what she did with Jordan.

It was so unfair, so wrong. She was marrying *Ralph*, she reminded herself. But her heart, her foolish, romantic heart, refused to listen.

Nothing Jordan could say was going to change her plans, she decided, trying to think of Ralph and the commitment they'd made to each other a few hours earlier.

If only Jordan would stop kissing her. *Oh, please stop,* she begged silently as frustration brought burning tears to her eyes. If only he'd leave, walk out of her life forever so she could start forgetting.

But she had to push him out of her arms before she could push him out of her life. Yet here she was clinging to him, her arms curved around his neck. And she was holding on as though her very existence depended on it.

Jordan obviously felt none of her hesitation, none of her doubts, and soon, far too soon, Jill was returning his kisses with equal fervor. Raw emotion overwhelmed her until she was so weak she slumped against him, needing his support to remain upright. Her breath came in shallow gasps as his lips trembled against hers.

"Oh, Jill," he breathed, his voice a husky caress. "The things you do to me. I've frightened you, haven't I?"

"No." He had, but for none of the reasons he knew. She was terrified by the things he made her feel. Terrified by the rush of need and love that crowded her heart.

She hid her face in his shoulder, wanting to escape his embrace even as she submerged herself in it.

"I never knew love could be like this," Jordan said hoarsely. "I've never been in love, never experienced it before you." He rested his jaw alongside her cheek in a gesture of tenderness that moved her deeply.

Jill swallowed and blinked through a wall of tears. "Please..." She had to say something, had to let him know before he spoke again, before he convinced her to love him. She'd set her mind, her will, everything within her, to resist him and found she couldn't.

"I realize we haven't known each other long," Jordan was saying. "Yet it seems as if you've always been part of my life, always will be."

"No..."

"Yes," he countered softly, his lips grazing the side of her face. "I want to marry you, Jill. Soon. The sooner the better. I need you in my life. I need you to teach me so many things. Loving me isn't going to be easy, but—"

"No!" Abruptly she broke away from him. "Please, no." She buried her face in her hands and began to sob.

"Jill, what is it?" He tried to comfort her, tried to bring her back into his embrace, but she wouldn't let him.

"I can't marry you." The words, born of frustration and anger, were meant to be shouted, but by the time they passed her lips they were barely audible.

"Can't marry me?" Jordan repeated as though he was sure he'd misunderstood. "Why not?"

"Because…" Saying it became a nearly impossible task, but she forced herself. "Because…I'm already engaged."

She saw and felt his shock. His eyes narrowed with pain and disbelief as the color drained from his face.

"You're making it up."

"No, it's true." She held herself stiff, braced for the backlash her words would bring.

"When?" he demanded.

She heaved in a breath and squared her shoulders. "Tonight."

A shudder went through him as his eyes, dark and haunting, raked her face. Jill's throat muscles constricted at his tortured look, and she couldn't speak.

It took Jordan a moment to compose himself. But he did so with remarkable dexterity. All emotion fled from his face. For a breathless moment he just stared at her.

"I'm sure," he said finally, without any outward hint of regret, "that whoever it is will make you a far better husband than I would have."

"His name is Ralph."

Jordan grimaced, but quickly rearranged his features into a cool mask. "I wish you and…Ralph every happiness."

With that, he turned and walked out of her life. Just as she'd wanted him to…

Early the next morning, after an almost sleepless night, Jill put the infamous wedding dress in her car and drove directly to Shelly and Mark's. The curtains were open so she assumed they were up and about. Even if they weren't, she didn't care.

Keeping the wedding dress a second longer was intolerable. The sooner she was rid of it, the sooner her life would return to normal.

Jill locked her car and carried the box to the Bradys' front door. Her steps were impatient. If Shelly wasn't home, Jill swore she'd leave the wedding gown on the front steps rather than take it back to her apartment.

A few minutes passed before the door opened. Shelly stood on the other side, dressed in a long robe, her hair in disarray and one hand covering her mouth to hide a huge yawn.

"I got you out of bed?" That much was obvious, but Jill was in no state for intelligent conversation.

"I was awake," Shelly said, yawning again. "Mark had to go into the office early, but I couldn't make myself get up." She gestured Jill inside. "Come on in. I'm sure Mark made a pot of coffee. He knows I need a cup first thing in the morning."

Jill set the box down on the sofa and followed Shelly into the kitchen. Clearly her friend wasn't fully awake yet, so Jill walked over to the cupboards and collected two mugs, filling each with coffee, then bringing them to the table where Shelly was sitting.

"Oh, thanks," she mumbled. "I'm impossible until I've had my first cup."

"I seem to remember that from our college days."

"Right," Shelly said, managing a half smile. "You know all my faults. Can you believe Mark loves me in spite of the fact that I can't cook, can't tolerate mornings and am totally disorganized?"

Having seen the love in Mark's eyes when he looked at his wife, Jill could well believe it. "Yes."

"I'm glad you're here," Shelly said, resting her head on her arm, which was stretched across the kitchen table.

"You are?" It was apparent that Shelly hadn't guessed the reason for this unexpected visit, hadn't realized Jill was returning the wedding dress. Half-asleep as she was, she obviously hadn't noticed the box.

"Yes, I'm *delighted* you're here," Shelly said as her eyes drifted shut. "Mark and I had a long talk about you and Ralph. He seems to think I'm overreacting to this engagement thing. But you aren't going to marry Ralph—you know it and I know it. This engagement is a farce, even if you don't recognize that yet. Getting Ralph to propose is the only way you can deal with what's happening between you and Jordan. But you'd never go through with it. You're too honest. You won't let yourself cheat Ralph—because if you marry him, that's exactly what you'll be doing."

"He knows I'm not in love with him."

"I'm sure he does, but I'm also sure he believes that in time you'll feel differently. What he doesn't understand is that you're already in love with someone else."

A few hours earlier, Jill would have adamantly denied loving Jordan, but she couldn't any longer. Her heart burned with the intensity of her feelings. Still, it didn't change anything, didn't alter the path she'd chosen.

"Ralph doesn't know about Jordan, does he?"

"No," Jill said reluctantly. If she was forced to, she'd tell Ralph about him. Difficult as it was to admit, Shelly was right about one thing. Jill would never be able to marry Ralph unless she was completely honest with him.

Shelly straightened and took her first sip of coffee. It seemed to revive her somewhat. "I should apologize for what I said last night. I didn't mean to offend you."

"You didn't," Jill was quick to tell her.

"You frightened me."

"Why?"

"I was afraid for you, afraid you were going to ruin your life. I don't think I could stand idly by and let you do it."

"I fully intend to marry Ralph." Jill didn't know for whose benefit she was saying this—Shelly's or her own. The doubts were back, but she did her best to ignore them.

"Oh, I believe you intend to marry Ralph…now," Shelly said, "but when the time comes, I don't think it's going to happen. Neither does Mark."

"That isn't what he said when we talked." Mark had been the cool voice of reason in their impassioned discussion the night before. He'd reassured her and comforted her, and for that Jill would always be grateful.

"What he said," Shelly explained between yawns, "was that he was sure you'd make the right decision. And he is. I was, too, after he calmed me down."

"I've made my choice. There's no turning back now."

"You'll change your mind."

"Perhaps. I don't know. All I know is that I agreed to marry Ralph." No matter how hard she tried, she couldn't keep the breathless catch from her voice.

Shelly heard it, and her eyes slowly opened. "What happened?" Her gaze sharply assessed Jill, who tried not to say or do anything that would give her away.

"Tell me," she said when Jill hesitated. "You know I'll get it out of you one way or another."

Jill sighed. Hiding the truth was pointless. "Jordan came by late last night."

"I thought you said he was in Hawaii."

"He was."

"Then what was he doing at your place?"

"He said he had a feeling there was something wrong—and he flew home."

"There *is* something wrong!" Shelly cried. "You're engaged to the wrong man."

Unexpectedly, Jill felt defeated. She'd hardly slept the night before, and the tears she'd managed to suppress refused to be held back any longer. They brimmed in her eyes, spilling onto her cheeks, cool against her flushed skin.

"I'm not *engaged* to the wrong man," she said once she was able to speak coherently. "I happen to *love* the wrong one."

"If you're in love with Jordan," Shelly said, "and I believe you are, then why in heaven's name would you even consider marrying Ralph?"

It was too difficult to explain. Rather than make the effort, she merely shook her head and stood, almost toppling her chair in her eagerness to escape.

"Jill." Shelly stood, too.

"I have to go now...."

"Jill, what's wrong? My goodness, I've never seen you like this. Tell me."

Jill shook her head again and hurried into the living room. "I brought back the wedding dress. Thank your aunt Milly for me, but I can't...wear it."

"You brought back the dress?" Shelly sounded as though she was about to break into tears herself. "Oh, Jill, I wish you hadn't."

Jill didn't stay around to argue. She rushed out the front door and to her car. Her destination wasn't clear until she reached Ralph's apartment. She hadn't planned to go there and wasn't sure what had directed her there. For several minutes she sat outside, collecting her thoughts—and gathering her courage.

When she'd composed herself, blown her nose and

dried her eyes, she walked to his front door and rang the doorbell. Ralph answered, looking pleased to see her.

"Good morning. You're out and about early. I was just getting ready to leave for work."

She forced a smile. "Have you got a minute?"

He nodded. "Come on in." He paused and seemed to remember that they were now an engaged couple. He leaned forward and lightly brushed his lips across her cheek.

"I should have phoned first."

"No. I was just thinking that this afternoon might be a good time for us to look at engagement rings."

Jill guiltily dropped her gaze and her voice trembled. "That's very sweet." She could barely say the words she had to say. "I should explain...the reason I'm here—"

Ralph motioned her toward a chair. "Please, sit down."

Jill was grateful because she didn't know how much longer her legs would support her. Everything seemed so much more difficult in the light of day. She'd been so confident before, so sure she and Ralph could make a life together. Now she felt as though she were walking around in a heavy fog. Nothing was clear, and confusion greeted her at every turn.

She took a deep breath. "There's something I need to explain."

"Go ahead." Ralph sat comfortably across from her.

She was so close to the edge of the chair she was in danger of slipping off. "It's only fair you should know."

She hesitated, thinking he might say something, but when he didn't, she continued, "I met a man in Hawaii."

He nodded gravely. "I thought you must have."

His intuition surprised her. "His name… Oh, it doesn't matter what his name is. We went out a couple of times."

"Are you in love with him?" Ralph asked outright.

"Yes," Jill whispered slowly. It hurt to admit, and for a moment she dared not look at Ralph.

"It doesn't seem like a lot of time to be falling in love with a man. You were only gone a week."

Jill didn't tell him Jordan was in Hawaii only three days. Nor did she mention the two brief times she'd seen him since. There was no reason to analyze the relationship. It was over. She'd made certain of that when she told him she was marrying Ralph. She'd never hear from Jordan again.

"Love happens like that sometimes," was all she could say.

"If you're so in love with this other guy, then why did you agree to marry me?"

"Because I'm scared and, oh, Ralph, I'm sorry. I should never have involved you in this. You're a wonderful man and I care for you, I really do. You've been a good friend and I've enjoyed our times together, but I realized this morning that I can't marry you."

For a moment he said nothing, then he reached for her hand and held it gently between his own. "You don't need to feel so guilty about it."

"Yes, I do." She was practically drowning in guilt.

"Don't. It took me about two minutes to realize something was troubling you last night. You surprised me completely when you started talking about getting married."

"I surprised you?"

"To be honest, I assumed you were about to tell me you'd met someone else and wouldn't be seeing me anymore. I've known for a long time that you're not in love with me."

"But I believed that would've changed," Jill said almost desperately.

"That's what I figured, too."

"You're steady and dependable, and I need that in my life," she said, although the rationale sounded poor even to her own ears. True, if she married Ralph she wouldn't have the love match she'd always dreamed about, but she'd told herself that love was highly overrated. She'd decided she could live without love, live without passion—until Jordan showed up on her doorstep. And this morning, Shelly had told her what she already knew. She couldn't marry Ralph.

"You're here because you want to call off the engagement, aren't you?" Ralph asked.

Miserably, Jill nodded. "I didn't mean to hurt you. That's the last thing I want."

"You haven't," he said pragmatically. "I figured you'd call things off sooner or later."

"You did?"

He grinned sheepishly. "You going to marry this other man?"

Jill shrugged. "I don't know."

"If you do…"

"Yes?" Jill reluctantly raised her eyes to his.

"If you do, would you consider subletting your apartment to me? Your place is at least twice as big as mine, and your rent's lower."

Despite everything, Jill started to laugh. Leave it to Ralph, ever practical, ever sensible, to brush off a broken engagement and ask about subletting her apartment.

The week that followed was one of the worst of Jill's life. She awoke every morning feeling as though she hadn't slept. She was depressed and lonely. Several times she found herself close to tears for no apparent reason. She'd be reading a prescription and the words would blur and misery would grip her heart with such intensity she'd be forced to swallow a sob.

"Jill," her supervisor called early Friday afternoon, walking into the back room where she was taking her lunch break. "There's someone out front who wants to talk to you."

It was unusual for anyone to visit her at work. She immediately feared it was Jordan, but quickly dismissed that concern. She knew him too well. She was out of his life. The instant she'd told him she was engaged to Ralph, he'd cut her out, surgically removed all feeling for her. It was as if she no longer existed for him.

But as she'd been so often lately, Jill was wrong. Jordan stood there waiting for her. His gaze was as hard as flint. Something flickered briefly in the smoky-gray depths, but whatever emotion he felt at seeing her was too fleeting for Jill to identify.

She'd had far less practice at hiding her own feelings, and right now, they were wreaking havoc with her pulse. With great effort she managed to remain outwardly composed. "You wanted to speak to me?"

A nerve twitched in his jaw. "You might be more comfortable if we spoke elsewhere," he said stiffly.

Jill glanced at her watch. She had only fifteen minutes of her lunch break left. Time enough, she was sure, for whatever Jordan intended. "All right."

Wordlessly, he walked out of the drugstore, obviously expecting her to follow, which she did. He paused beside his car, then turned to face her. A cool, disinterested smile slanted his mouth.

"Yes?" she said after an awkward moment. She folded her arms defensively around her middle.

"I need you to explain something."

She nodded. "I'll try."

"Your friend Shelly Brady was in to see me this morning."

Jill groaned. She hadn't talked to Shelly since the morning she'd dropped off the wedding dress. Her friend had phoned several times and left messages, but Jill hadn't had either the energy or the patience to return the calls.

"How she managed to get past security and my two assistants is beyond me."

It was a nightmare come true. "What did she say?" As if Jill needed to know.

"She rambled on about how you were making the worst mistake of your life and how I'd be an even bigger fool if I let you. But, you know, if you prefer to marry Roger, then that's your prerogative."

"His name is Ralph," she corrected.

"It doesn't make any difference to me."

"I didn't think it would," she said, keeping her gaze lowered to the black asphalt of the parking lot.

"Then she started telling me this ridiculous story about a legend behind a certain wedding dress."

Jill's eyes closed in frustration. "It's a bunch of non-sense."

"It certainly didn't make too much sense, especially the part about the dress fitting her and her marrying Mark. But she insisted the dress also fits you."

"Don't take Shelly seriously. She seems to put a lot of credence in that dress. Personally, I think the whole thing's a fluke. You don't need to worry about it."

"*Then* she told me an equally ridiculous tale about a vision she had of you in Hawaii and how happy you looked. It didn't make any more sense than the rest."

"Don't worry," she said again. "Shelly means well, but she doesn't understand. The wedding dress is beautiful, but it isn't meant for me. The whole thing is ridiculous—you said so yourself, and I agree with you."

"That's what I thought—at first. A magic wedding

dress is about as believable as a talking rabbit. I don't have any interest in that kind of fantasy."

"Then why are you here?"

"Because I remembered something. You had a wedding dress with you in Hawaii. When I asked you about it, you said a friend had mailed it to you. Then, this morning, Shelly arrived and told me why she'd sent you the dress. She told me the story of her aunt Milly and how she'd met her husband. She also said Milly had mailed the dress to her and she'd fallen into Mark Brady's arms."

"Did she leave anything out?" Jill asked sarcastically.

He ignored her question. "In the end I phoned Mark and asked him about it. I don't know Brady well, but I assumed he'd be able to explain the situation a little more rationally."

"Shelly does tend to get a bit dramatic."

"That's putting it mildly."

"I just wish she hadn't said anything to you."

"I imagine you do," he remarked dryly.

"What did Mark say?"

"We talked for several minutes. By this time Shelly was weeping and nearly hysterical, convinced she was saving us both from a fate worse than death. Mark was kind enough to inject a bit of sanity into the discussion. What it boiled down to is this."

"What?" Jill wasn't purposely being obtuse.

"Me confronting you. I'm here to ask you about Aunt Milly's wedding dress."

He could ask her whatever he wanted, but she didn't have any answers.

"Jill?"

She heaved a sigh. "I returned the dress to Shelly."

"She explained that, too. Said you'd brought it back the morning after my visit."

"It wasn't meant for me."

"Not true, according to Shelly...and Mark." He remained standing where he was, unwilling to divulge his own feelings.

"So you're going to go ahead and marry Roger."

"Ralph."

"Whoever," Jordan snapped.

"No!" she shouted, furious with him, furious with Shelly and Mark, too.

A moment of shocked silence followed her announcement. Several feet separated Jill from Jordan, and although neither of them moved, they suddenly seemed much closer.

"I knew that," he said.

"How could you possibly know?" Jill hadn't told anyone yet. Not Shelly and certainly not Jordan.

"Because you're marrying me."

Eight

All of Jill's defenses came tumbling down. She'd known they would from the moment she'd walked out of the lunchroom and confronted him. Known in the very depths of her soul that he'd eventually have his way. She didn't have the strength to fight him anymore.

He must have sensed her acquiescence because he moved toward her, pausing just short of taking her in his arms. "You will marry me, won't you?" The words were gentle yet insistent, brooking no argument.

Jill nodded. "I don't want…don't *want* to love you."

"I know." He reached for her then, drawing her into his embrace as though he were comforting a child.

It should have eased her mind that settling into his arms felt more natural than anything she'd done in the past week. A feeling of welcome. A feeling of rightness. And yet there was fear.

"You're going to break my heart," she whispered.

"Not if I can help it."

"Why do you want to marry me?" The answer evaded her. A man like Jordan could have his pick of women. He had wealth and prestige and a dozen other attributes that attracted far more sophisticated and beautiful women than Jill.

The air between them seemed to pulse for a long moment before Jordan answered. "I've done some thinking about that myself. You're intelligent. Insightful. You feel things deeply and you're sensitive to the needs of others." He traced a finger along the line of her jaw, his touch light. "You're passionate about the people you love."

She should've been reassured that he seemed to know her so well after such a short acquaintance, but she wasn't. Because she knew that for a time she'd be a pleasant distraction. Their marriage would be like a toy to him. Then gradually, as the newness wore off, she'd be put on a shelf to look pretty and brought down when it suited his purposes. His life, his love, his personality, would be consumed by the drive to succeed, just the way her father's had been. Everything else would fade into the background, eventually to disappear. Love. Family. Commitment. Everything that was important to her would ultimately mean nothing to him.

"I want us to marry soon," Jordan whispered.

"I—I was hoping for a long engagement."

Jordan's eyes were adamant. "I've waited too long already."

Jill didn't understand what he meant, but she didn't

question him. She knew Jordan was an impatient man. When he wanted something, he went after it with relentless determination. Now he wanted *her*—and heaven help her, she wanted him.

"A bride should be happy," he said, tucking his hand under her chin and raising her face to his. "Why the tears?"

How could she possibly explain? She loved him, although she'd fought it with everything she had. She'd been willing, for a time, to consider marrying Ralph in her effort to drive Jordan from her life. Yet even then she'd known it was useless and of course so had Ralph. Nothing could save her. Her heart had been on a collision course with Jordan's from the moment she'd been assigned the seat next to his on the flight to Hawaii.

"I'll be happy," she murmured, silently adding *for a while.*

"So will I," Jordan said, his chest expanding with a breath and then a sigh that seemed to come all the way from his soul.

The small private wedding took place three weeks later in Hawaii at the home of Andrew Howard. Shelly was Jill's matron of honor and Mark stood up for Jordan. Elaine Morrison was there, too, weeping through the entire ceremony. But these weren't tears of joy. Her mother, like Jill, recognized Jordan's type and feared what it meant for her daughter's life, her happiness.

"Jill," Elaine had pleaded with her earlier that morning, before the wedding. "Are you sure this is what you want?"

Jill had nearly laughed aloud. With all her heart, with all her being, she longed to be Jordan's wife. And yet, if the opportunity had availed itself, she would've backed out of the marriage.

"He needs me." Repeatedly over the past few weeks, Jill had been reminded how much Jordan did need her. He didn't realize it himself, of course, not on a conscious level, but something deep inside him had acknowledged his need. And in her own way, Jill needed him.

Andrew Howard had seen that they belonged together. He'd been the first one to point it out to Jill. From the time Jordan was a child, his life had been devoid of love. As an adult he'd closed himself off from emotion; he'd refused to allow himself to become vulnerable. That he should experience something as powerful as love for her in so short a time was close to a miracle. But then, Jill was becoming accustomed to miracles.

"All I want is your happiness," her mother had gone on to say, her eyes, so like Jill's, blurred with tears. "You're my only child. I don't want you to make the same mistakes I did."

Could loving someone ever be a mistake? Jill wondered. Her mother had loved her father, sacrificed herself for him even though, as the years went on, he'd barely seemed to reciprocate her love. And when he died prematurely, without warning, she'd become lost and miserable.

Jill knew she loved Jordan enough to put aside her fears, to bind herself in a relationship that might ultimately cause her pain. But she vowed she wouldn't lose her own identity. She wouldn't, couldn't, let Jordan's personality swallow her own.

He hadn't understood that in the beginning, despite her attempts to explain it. To him, Jill's desire to continue working after their marriage seemed utterly foolish. For what purpose? he'd asked. She didn't need the income; he'd made certain of that, lavishing her with gifts and more money than she could possibly spend. Her insistence on continuing her job resulted in their first real argument. But in the end Jordan had reluctantly agreed.

Andrew Howard had gone to a great deal of trouble to arrange their wedding, warming Jill's heart with his generosity. She'd come to understand that the older man looked upon Jordan as the son he'd lost. He was more than a mentor, far more than a friend. He was the only real family Jordan had—until now.

Flowers filled every room of Andrew's oceanfront home, their fragrance sweet in the summer air. An archway of orange blossoms stood outside on the lush green lawn that overlooked the roaring ocean. A small reception and dinner were to follow. Tables laid with white linen tablecloths were placed around the patio.

The warm wind whispered over Jill as Andrew Howard came to escort her into the sunshine where Jordan was waiting. Andrew paused when he saw her, his eyes vivid with appreciation. "I've never had a daughter," he said softly, "but if I did, I'd want her to be just like you."

Tears of love and gratitude gathered in her eyes. Her mother, fussing about Jill, arranged the long, flowing train of the dress, then slowly straightened. "He's right," Elaine said, stepping back to examine Jill. "You've never looked more beautiful."

It was the dress, Jill thought. The dress and its magic. She ran her glove along the bodice with its Venetian lace and row upon row of delicate pearls. The high collar was adorned with pearls, too, each one sewn on by hand. The skirt flared from her waist, the hem accentuated with a flounce of lace and wide satin ribbons.

Andrew Howard stood beside her mother as the minister asked Jordan and Jill to repeat their vows. Jill's gaze met Jordan's as she made her promises. Her voice, although low, was steady and confident. Jordan's eyes held hers with a look of warmth, of tenderness.

A magic wedding dress? The scenario seemed implausible. Yet here they were, standing before God, their family and friends, declaring their love for each other.

"You look so beautiful," Shelly told Jill shortly after the ceremony. "Even more beautiful than the day you first tried on the dress."

"My hair wasn't done and I didn't have on much makeup and I—"

"No," Shelly interrupted, squeezing Jill's fingers, "it's more than that. You hadn't met Jordan yet. It's complete now."

"What is?"

"Everything," Shelly explained with characteristic

ambiguity. "Aunt Milly's wedding dress, you and Jordan. Oh, Jill," she whispered, her eyes brimming with tears, "you're going to be so happy."

Jill wanted to believe that—how she wanted to believe it!—but she was afraid. So afraid of what the future held for her and Jordan.

"I know what you're thinking," Shelly said, dabbing her eyes. "I loved Mark when I married him. I'd loved him for months, but deep down I wondered how long a marriage between us could last. We're totally different."

Jill smiled to herself. Shelly was right; she and Mark *were* different, but they were perfectly matched, balancing each other's strengths and weaknesses.

"I was sure my lack of domestic skills would drive Mark crazy, and at the same time I thought the way he organizes everything would kill our relationship. Did you know that man makes lists of lists? Even before I walked to the altar, I was worried this marriage was doomed."

"It's been all right, though, hasn't it?"

Shelly smiled. "It's been so easy—love does that, you know. Love takes something that's difficult and makes it feel so effortless. You'll understand what I mean in a few months."

Unfortunately Jill shared little of her friend's confidence. She was delighted that things had worked out between Shelly and Mark, but she didn't expect that kind of happiness for her and Jordan.

"When you think about it, it's not all that surprising,"

Shelly had gone on to say. "Take Aunt Milly and Uncle John for example. She's educated and idealistic, and John, bless his heart, was a realist and a mechanic with a grade-school education. Yet he was so proud of her. He loved her until the day he died."

"Mark will always love you, too," Jill said, smoothing the satin of the wedding dress.

"Jordan feels the same way about you."

Jill's heart stopped. It hit her then, for perhaps the first time—Jordan loved her. His love had guided Jill through her uncertainty. It had helped her understand what had led her to this point, helped her look past her mother's tears and her own doubts.

The small reception and dinner held immediately after the ceremony featured a light, elegant meal and a festive atmosphere. Jill met several of Jordan's business associates, who seemed both surprised and pleased for them. Even the Lundquists put in a jovial appearance, although Suzi was absent.

When it came time for them to leave, Jill kissed Andrew Howard's cheek and thanked him once more. "Everything's been wonderful."

"I lost my only son," he reminded her, his eyes momentarily aged and sad. "For years I've hungered for a family. After my wife died, and even before, I shut myself away, locked in my grief, and watched the world go on without me."

"You're being too hard on yourself," Jill told him. "Your work—"

"True enough," he said, cutting her off. "For a while I was able to bury myself in my company, but two years ago I realized I'd wasted too much of my life struggling with this grief. Soon afterward I decided to retire." His gaze wandered away from Jill and toward her mother, and he smiled. "I think the time might be right for me to make other changes, take the next step. What do you think, my dear?"

Jill smiled, too. Her mother needed someone like Andrew. Someone to teach her that love didn't always mean pain.

"I'd forgotten what it was like to be young," he said, now smiling easily. "I've known Jordan nearly all his life. I've watched him build a name for himself and admired his cunning. He's good, Jill. But he's a man without a family, and I suspect I see a lot of myself in him. The thought of him growing old and disillusioned with life troubled me. I want him to avoid the mistakes I made."

Funny how her mother had said basically the same thing to Jill a few hours earlier. "There are certain mistakes we each have to make," Jill returned softly. "It's the only way we seem to learn, painful as it is."

"How smart you are," Andrew said, chuckling. "Much too clever for your years."

"I love him." Somehow it was important Mr. Howard know that. "I have no idea whether my love will make a lot of difference, but…"

"Ah, that's where you're wrong. It will change him. Love does that, my dear, and he needs you so badly."

"How can you be sure I'll have any influence over Jordan's life? I'm marrying him because I love him, but I don't expect anything to change."

"It will. Just wait and see."

"How do you know that?"

His smile came slowly, transforming his face, brightening his eyes and relaxing his mouth. "Because," he said, clasping her hand in his own, "because it once changed my life, and I'm hopeful that it will again." He glanced at her mother as he spoke, and Jill leaned over to give him another quick kiss.

"Good luck," she whispered.

"Jill," Jordan called then, approaching her. "Are you ready?"

She looked at her husband of less than two hours and nodded. He was referring to their honeymoon trip, but she…she was thinking about their lives together.

"Hmm," Jill murmured as the first light of dawn crept into their hotel room. She yawned widely, covering her mouth with both hands.

"Good morning, wife," Jordan said, kissing her ear.

"Good morning, husband."

"Did you sleep well?"

Eyes closed, she nodded.

"Me, too."

"I was exhausted," Jill told him, smiling shyly.

"No wonder."

Although her eyes remained closed, Jill knew Jordan

was smiling. Her introduction to the physical aspect of their marriage had been incredible, wonderful. Jordan was a patient and gentle lover. Jill had felt understandably nervous, but he'd been tender and reassuring.

"I didn't know it could be so good," she said, snuggling in her husband's arms.

"I didn't, either," he surprised her by saying. His lips were in her hair, his hands exploring her skin. "It's enough to make a husband think about wasting the morning in bed."

"Wasting?" Jill teased, a smile lifting the corners of her mouth. "Surely I misunderstood you. The Jordan Wilcox I've met wouldn't know how to waste time."

"It all has to do with the musical rest," he said seductively. "The all-important caesura. Who would ever have guessed something so small could change a man's entire life?" He kissed her with a hunger that moved her, then made love to her with a need that humbled her.

It was noon before they left the hotel room and one o'clock when they returned.

"Jordan," Jill said, blushing when he reached for her, "it's the middle of the day."

"So?"

"So…it's indecent."

"Really?" But as he spoke, he was lowering his mouth to hers. The kiss was intoxicating, and any resistance Jill might have felt vanished like ice in the sun.

She rested her palms against his shoulders as he kissed her again and again.

Unable to stop herself, Jill moaned softly.

Dragging his mouth from hers, he trailed kisses down the side of her neck. "There's that sightseeing trip you wanted to take," he reminded her. "To see the pineapple and sugarcane fields."

"It's not important. We could see them another time," she said breathlessly.

"That's not what you claimed earlier."

"I was just thinking…" She didn't get the opportunity to finish. Jordan's kiss absorbed her words and scattered the thought.

"What did you think?"

"That married people should occasionally be willing to change their plans," she managed to say.

Jordan chuckled, and lifting her gently into his arms, carried her to the bed. "I'm beginning to think married life is going to agree with me." His mouth found hers and gentleness gave way to urgency.

Five days later, when Jordan and Jill returned to the mainland, their honeymoon over, Jill was so deeply in love with her husband she wondered why she'd ever hesitated, why she'd fought so hard against marrying him.

The first person she called when they arrived at the penthouse was Shelly. Jordan had arranged to have her things moved there while they were away. Ralph lived at her previous apartment now and was elated with the extra space.

"Have you got time to meet an old friend for lunch?" Jill asked without preamble.

"Jill!" Shelly cried. "When did you get back?"

"About an hour ago." Although he hadn't said as much, she knew Jordan was dying to get to his office. "I thought I'd steal away for a few minutes and meet you."

"I'd love to see you. Just name the time and place."

Jill did, then kissed Jordan on the cheek while he was talking to his assistant on the phone in his study. He broke away, covered the mouthpiece with his hand and gave her a surprised look. "Where are you headed?"

"Out for lunch. You don't mind, do you?"

"No." But he didn't sound all that sure.

"I thought you'd want to go to the office," she said.

"I do." He wrapped his arm around her waist, bringing her close to his side.

"I know, so I thought I'd meet Shelly."

He grinned, kissed her lightly and resumed his telephone conversation as though she'd already left. Jill lingered at the door, waiting for the elevator. Part of her longed to stay with him, to hold on to the happiness before it escaped, before it was dispersed by everyday tensions and demands.

"Well," Shelly said a half hour later as she slid into the restaurant booth across from Jill, "how are the newlyweds?"

"Wonderful."

"I thought you'd be more tanned."

Jill blushed; Shelly laughed and reached for her

napkin. "It was the same with Mark and me. I swear, we didn't leave that hotel room for three days."

"We made several short trips," Jill said, but she didn't elaborate on exactly how short their sightseeing ventures had been.

"Married life certainly seems to agree with you."

"It's only been a week," Jill reminded her friend. "That's hardly time enough to tell."

"I knew after the first week," Shelly said confidently, her face animated by a smile. "I figured if Mark and I survived the honeymoon, our marriage had a chance. Mark wanted to honeymoon at Niagara Falls, remember?"

"And you suggested a rafting trip through the Grand Canyon." Jill smiled at the memory. Mark preferred tradition, while Shelly craved adventure, but in the end, they'd learned what she and Jordan had already discovered. All that mattered was their marriage, their love for each other.

"We couldn't agree," Shelly continued. "I was seriously worried about it. If we were at odds over a honeymoon site, then what on earth would happen when it came to dealing with the really important issues?"

Jill understood what Shelly meant. She loved Jordan; of that there could be no doubt. Now she had to place her trust in their love, hope it was strong enough to withstand day-to-day reality. She was still fearful, but ready to fight for her marriage, to keep it safe.

Suddenly Shelly set aside the menu, pressed her hand against her stomach and slowly exhaled.

"Shell, what's wrong?"

Shelly briefly closed her eyes. "Nothing bad. I just can't stand to read about food."

"About food?" That made no sense to Jill.

"I'm two months pregnant."

"Shelly!" Jill was so excited she nearly toppled her water glass. "Why didn't you say something sooner? Good grief, I'm your best friend—I'd think you'd want me to know."

"I do, but I couldn't tell you until I knew for sure, could I?"

"You just found out?"

"Not exactly." Shelly reached for a small packet of soda crackers, tore away the cellophane wrapper and munched on one. "I found out before your wedding, but I didn't want to say anything then."

Jill appreciated Shelly's considerateness, her wish not to compete with Jill's important day.

"Actually, it was Mark who told me. Imagine a husband explaining the facts of life to his wife. I'm such a scatterbrain, I made a mistake. I miscalculated and didn't even know it."

As far as Jill was concerned, this baby certainly wasn't a mistake, and from Shelly's happy glow, her friend felt the same way.

"I was afraid Mark might be upset. Naturally we'd talked about starting a family, but neither of us planned to have it happen so soon."

"He wasn't upset, though, was he?" Jill would've been shocked if Mark had been anything but thrilled.

"Not in the least. When he first told me what he suspected, I just laughed." She shook her head in mock consternation. "You'd think I'd know better than to question a man who sleeps with his daily planner by his side!"

"I'm thrilled for you."

"Now that I've adjusted to it, I can't wait. I'm looking forward to decorating the nursery and wearing maternity clothes and *everything*."

After the waitress had taken their order, Jill leaned back against the banquette cushion. "It happened just like you said it would," she said.

"What did?"

"Loving Jordan." Jill felt a little shy talking so openly about something so intimate. Although she and Jordan were married and deeply in love with each other, they never spoke of their feelings. Jordan was still uncomfortable with expressing emotion. But he didn't need to tell Jill he loved her, not when he went about proving it every way he knew how. She'd never pressured him, never demanded the words.

"The day we were married you told me love makes the difficult things seem effortless. Remember?"

Ever confident, Shelly grinned. "You're going to be so happy..." She paused, swallowed and reached for her napkin, dabbing her eyes. "I get so emotional these days, I can't believe it. The other night I found myself crying at a stupid television commercial."

"You? Seattle's drama queen? Impossible," Jill teased.

Shelly shook her head ruefully. "Yes, me." She began to laugh, and Jill joined in.

Laughter came easily since her marriage; it was all the happiness in her heart brimming over, spilling out. She'd never felt so carefree or laughed at so many silly things before.

When Jill returned from lunch two hours later, Jordan was gone. Exhausted from the flight and the excitement of the past week, she crawled into bed and slept, not waking until it was dark.

Rolling onto her back, she stretched luxuriously under the weight of the blanket and smiled, musing how thoughtful it was of Jordan to let her sleep.

She kicked aside the blanket and searched blindly for her shoes. Yawning, she walked into the living room, surprised to find it dark.

"Jordan?" she called.

She was greeted by silence.

Turning on the lights, Jill was shocked to discover it was after nine. Jordan must still be at the office, she supposed, her stomach knotting. Could it be happening so soon? Could he have grown tired of her already?

No sooner had the thought formed than the elevator doors opened and Jordan appeared. She didn't fly into his arms, although that was her first instinct.

"Hello," she greeted him, a bit coolly.

He was loosening his tie. "What time is it?"

"Nine-fifteen. Are you hungry?"

He paused, as though he needed to think about it. "Yeah, I guess I am. Sorry I didn't call. I didn't have a clue it was this late."

"That's okay," she muttered, although it really wasn't.

He followed her into the kitchen and slid his arms around her waist while she investigated the contents of the refrigerator.

"It won't be like this every night," he said, his words sounding very much like a promise her father had once made to her mother.

"I know," Jill said, desperately hoping that was true.

She couldn't sleep that night. Perhaps it was the long nap she'd taken in the middle of the afternoon; at least that was what she tried to tell herself. More likely, though, it was the gnawing fear that Jordan's love for her was already faltering. She tried to push the doubts aside, tried to convince herself she was overreacting. He'd been away from his office for a week. There must have been all kinds of important issues that required his attention. Was she expecting too much?

In the morning, she promised herself, she'd talk to him about it. But when she awoke, Jordan had left for the office.

Frowning, she dressed and wandered into the kitchen for a cup of coffee.

"Morning." Jordan's cook, Mrs. Murphy, a middle-aged woman with lively blue eyes and a wide smile, greeted her. Jill smiled back, although her cheerfulness felt a little strained.

"Hello, Mrs. Murphy, it's nice to see you again," she said, helping herself to coffee. "Uh, what time did Jordan leave this morning?"

"Early," the cook said with a disappointed sigh. "I was thinking Mr. Wilcox would stop working so hard once he was married. He hasn't even been home from his honeymoon twenty-four hours and he's already at the office at the crack of dawn."

Jill hated to disillusion the woman, but this wasn't Jordan's first trip to the office. "I'll see what I can do about giving him some incentive to stay home," Jill said, savoring her coffee.

Mrs. Murphy chuckled. "I'm glad to hear it. That man works too many hours. I've been telling my George that Mr. Wilcox needs a wife to keep him home at night."

"I'll do my best," Jill said, but she had the distinct feeling her efforts would make little difference. Checking her watch, she quickly drank the rest of her coffee and hurried into the bedroom to shower.

Within half an hour she was dressed and ready for work.

"Mrs. Murphy," she told the cook, "I'll be at work— PayRite Pharmacy—if Jordan happens to call. Tell him I'll be home shortly after five." Jill wished she'd had the chance to talk to him herself; she knew he was going to be tied up in meetings and conference calls, so she was reluctant to interrupt. Still, she was more than a little distressed that within a week of their wedding she was communicating with her husband through a third party.

Despite everything, Jill enjoyed her day, which was busier than usual. The pharmacy staff took her out for a celebration lunch, and dozens of customers came by to wish her well. Many of the people whose prescriptions she filled regularly had become friends. In light of how her married life was working out, Jill was thankful she'd decided to keep her job.

By five she was eager to get home, eager to share her day with Jordan and hear about his. She was met by the aroma of cheese, tomato sauce and garlic, and followed it into the kitchen, where she found Mrs. Murphy untying her apron.

"Whatever you're cooking smells absolutely delicious."

"It's my lasagna. Mr. Wilcox's favorite."

Jill opened the oven door and peeked inside. She was famished. "Did Jordan phone?" she asked, her voice rising on a note of longing.

"About fifteen minutes ago. I told him you'd be home a bit after five."

No sooner were the words out than the phone rang. Jill saw Jordan's office number on call display and answered immediately.

"This is Brian Macauley, Mr. Wilcox's assistant," a crisp male voice informed her. "He's asked that I let you know he won't be home for dinner."

Nine

"Jill."

Her name seemed to come from a long way off. Someone was calling her, but she could barely hear.

"Sweetheart." The voice was louder now.

She snuggled into the warmth, ignoring the persistent sound. After hours and hours of forcing herself to stay awake, she'd finally given up and succumbed to the sweet seduction of sleep.

"Honey, if you don't wake up, you'll get a crick in your neck."

"Jordan?" Her eyes instantly flew open, and she saw her husband kneeling on the carpet beside her chair. She straightened, throwing her arms around his neck. "Oh, Jordan," she whispered, "I'm so glad you're home."

"With this kind of reception, I'll have to stay away more often."

Jill decided to ignore that comment. "What time is it?"

"Late" was all he said.

She kissed him, needing him, savoring the feel of his arms around her. He looked dreadful. He hadn't been home for dinner in well over a week and spent all hours of the day and night at his office.

Although she'd asked him several times, Jordan's only explanation was that a project he'd been working on had developed problems. *A project.* For this he was willing to send both their lives into tumult; for this he was willing to place their marriage at risk. The upheaval had all but ruined the memory of their brief idyllic honeymoon. They'd been back in Seattle for two weeks now, and Jill hadn't been allotted a single uninterrupted hour of Jordan's time.

"Are you hungry?" She doubted he'd eaten a decent meal in days.

He shook his head, then rubbed his face wearily. "I'm more tired than anything."

"How much longer is this going to continue?" she asked, keeping her voice as steady as she could. She'd gone into this marriage with her eyes wide open. From the moment she'd met Jordan, she'd known how stiff the competition would be, how demanding his way of life was. She'd always known it would be difficult to keep their marriage intact. But she'd figured their love would hold the edge for at least the first couple of years.

Unfortunately she'd figured wrong. If anything, she'd underestimated the strength of his obsession with business and success. Jordan loved her; he might rarely have told her that, but Jill didn't need the words. What she did need was some of his time, his attention.

"I've hardly seen you all week," she reminded him. "You're gone before I wake up in the mornings. Heaven only knows what time you get home at night."

"It won't be much longer," Jordan said stiffly, standing. "I promise."

"Would it be so terrible if this project folded?"

"Yes," he returned emphatically.

"One failure isn't the end of the world, you know."

Jordan smiled wryly, and his condescension angered her.

"It's true," she said. "Did I ever tell you about trying out for the lead in the high-school play during my senior year?"

Jordan frowned. "No, but is this another story like the one about your piano-playing?"

Jill tucked her legs under her and rested one elbow on the chair arm. "A little."

Jordan sank down on the leather sofa across from her, leaned his head back and closed his eyes. "In that case, why don't you move directly to the point and skip the story?"

He wasn't being rude, Jill told herself, only practical. He was exhausted and in desperate need of rest. He didn't have the energy to wade through her mournful tale in search of a moral.

"All right," she agreed amicably enough. "You've probably already guessed I didn't get the lead. But I'd been so sure I would. I'd played major roles in several plays. In fact, I'd gotten every part I'd ever tried out for.

Not only didn't I get this part, I wasn't even in the play, and darn it all, even now I think I would've done a good job of playing Helen Keller."

He grinned. "I'm sure you would have, too."

"What I learned from that experience was not to fear failure. I survived not playing Helen Keller, and later, in college, when I was awarded a wonderful role, it heightened my appreciation of that success." When Jordan didn't immediately respond, she added, "Do you understand what I'm saying or are you asleep?"

His eyes were still closed but his mouth lifted in a gentle smile. "I was just mulling over the sad history of your musical and acting careers."

Jill smiled, too. "I know it sounds ludicrous, but failure liberated me. My heart and soul went into my audition for that role, and when I lost, I felt I could never act again. It took me a long time to regain my confidence, to be willing to hazard another rejection, but eventually I was the stronger for it. When I decided to try out for a play in my freshman year of college, I felt as though I was somehow protected, because failure wasn't going to rock me the way it had earlier."

"So you wanted to be an actress?"

"No, I'm not much good at waiting tables."

Jordan didn't immediately catch her joke, but when he did, he laughed out loud.

"You know what they say about hindsight being twenty-twenty? In this case it's true. If failure hadn't taught me to appreciate success when I got it, I might have fallen into a nasty trap."

"What was that?"

"Thinking I deserved it, believing I was so talented, so gifted, so good that I'd never lose."

Jordan fell silent. Jill waited a moment, then said, "Mr. Howard told me something…about the shopping-mall project. I didn't say anything to you at the time because…well, because I wasn't sure he wanted me to."

She had Jordan's full attention now.

He straightened, his eyes searching hers. "What did he say?"

"He hasn't often gone in on construction projects with you, has he?"

"Only a handful of times."

"There's a reason for that."

"Oh?"

"You've never failed."

Jordan's head came up sharply. "I beg your pardon?"

Jill knew he found such thinking preposterous. If anything, his successes should have been an induce-ment to his financial supporters.

"Mr. Howard explained that he doesn't like to deal with a man until he's been devastated financially at least once."

"That makes no sense," Jordan returned irritably.

"Perhaps not. Since my experience in the financial world is limited to paying my bills, I wouldn't know," Jill admitted.

"Who's going to lend money to someone who's failed?"

"Apparently Andrew Howard," Jill said with a grin. "He told me the man who's lost everything is much more careful the next time around."

"I didn't realize you and Howard talked business."

"We didn't." She did her best to appear nonchalant. "Mostly we discussed you."

This didn't please Jordan, either. "I'd prefer to think I owe my success to hard work, determination and foresight. I certainly wouldn't have come as far as I have without them."

"True enough, but—"

"Is there always going to be a but?"

Jill tried to hold back a laugh. Actually she was enjoying this, while her tired husband was left to suffer the indignities of her insights.

"Well," he said shortly, "go on, knock down my argument."

"Oh, I agree your intelligence and dedication have played a large role in your success, but others have worked just as hard, been just as determined and shown just as much foresight—and lost everything."

Jordan scowled. "My, you're full of cheer, aren't you?"

"I don't want you to put so much store in this one project. If it falls apart, so what? You're beating yourself to death with this." She didn't mention what it was doing to their marriage.

He considered her words for a few seconds, then his

face tightened. "I won't lose. I absolutely, categorically, refuse not to succeed."

"How much longer?" Jill asked when she could disguise the defeat and frustration she was feeling.

He hesitated, then massaged the back of his neck as though to ease away a tiredness that stretched from the top of his head to the bottom of his feet. "A week. It shouldn't be much more than that."

A week. Seven days. She closed her eyes, because looking at him, seeing him this exhausted, this spent, was painful. He needed her support now, not her censure.

"All right," she murmured.

"I don't like this any better than you do." Jordan stood and held her securely in his embrace, burying his face in the curve of her neck. "I'm a newlywed, remember. There's no one I want to spend time with more than my wife."

Jill nodded, because it would have been impossible to speak.

"I wish you hadn't waited up for me," he said, lifting her into his arms and carrying her into their bedroom. Without turning on the light, he settled her on the bed and lay down beside her, placing his head on her chest. Jill's fingers idly stroked his hair.

Words burned in her throat, the need to unburden herself, but she dared not. Jordan was exhausted. This wasn't the right time.

Would it ever be the right time?

There'd been so many lonely evenings, so many

empty mornings. Every night Jill went to bed alone, and only when Jordan slipped in beside her did she feel alive. Only when they were together did she feel whole. So she waited night after night for a few precious minutes, knowing they were all he had to spare.

The even sound of Jordan's breathing told her he'd fallen asleep. The weight on her chest was growing uncomfortable, yet she continued to stroke his hair for several minutes, unwilling to disturb his rest.

She'd always known it would come to this; she just hadn't expected it to happen so soon.

A week. He'd promised her it would be over within a week.

And it would be—until the next time.

Jill awoke early the following morning, astonished to find Jordan asleep beside her. At some point during the night he'd rolled away from her and covered them both with a blanket. He hadn't bothered to undress.

Jill wriggled toward him and playfully kissed his ear. She knew she ought to let him sleep, but she also knew he'd be annoyed if he was late for the office.

Slowly he opened his eyes, looking surprised to see her there with him.

"Morning," she whispered, with a series of tiny, nibbling kisses.

"What time is it?" he asked.

"Almost eight." She looped her arms around his neck and smiled down at him.

"Hmm. An indecent hour."

"Very indecent."

"My favorite time of day." His fingers were busy unfastening the opening of her pajama top and his eyes blazed with unmistakable need.

"Jordan," she said breathlessly, "you'll be late for work."

"I fully intend to be," he said, directing her lips to his.

"It's happening already, isn't it?" Elaine Morrison said bluntly the next Saturday. She stood in Jill's living room, holding a china cup and saucer and staring out the window. The view of the Olympic Mountains was spectacular, the white peaks jutting against a backdrop of bright blue sky as fluffy clouds drifted past.

Jill knew precisely what her mother was saying. She responded the only way she could—truthfully. "Yes."

Elaine turned, her face pale, haunted with the pain of the past, the pain she saw reflected in her daughter's life. "I was afraid of this."

Until recently, Jill had found communicating with her mother difficult. After her husband's death, Elaine had withdrawn from life, hidden herself away in her grief and regrets. In many ways, Jill had lost her mother at the same time as she had her father.

"Mom, it's all right," Jill said in an attempt to reassure her. "It's only for the next little while. Once this project's under control everything will be different."

Jill knew better. She wasn't fooling herself, and she sincerely doubted she'd be able to fool her mother.

"I warned you," Elaine said, walking to the white leather sofa and sitting tensely on the edge. Setting the cup and saucer on a nearby table, she turned pleading eyes to Jill. "Didn't I tell you? The day of the wedding—"

"Yes, Mother, you warned me."

"Why didn't you listen?"

Jill exhaled slowly, praying for patience. "I'm in love with him, just like you loved Daddy."

It seemed unfair to drag her father into this, her much-grieved father, but it was the only way Jill could explain.

"What are you going to do about it?"

"Mother," Jill sighed. "It's not as though Jordan's having an affair."

"He might as well be," Elaine replied heatedly. "Here it is, Saturday afternoon and he's working. One look at him told me he had the same drive and ambition, the same need for power, as your father."

"Mother, please… It isn't like that with Jordan."

The older woman's eyes were infinitely sad as she gazed at her daughter. "Don't count on that, Jill. Just don't count on it."

Her mother's visit had unsettled Jill. Afterward, she tried to relax with a book, but couldn't concentrate. The phone rang at six, just as it had every night that week. One of Jordan's assistants had called to let her know he wouldn't be home for dinner.

One ring.

Walking over to the phone, Jill stood directly in front of it, but didn't pick up the receiver.

Two rings.

Drawing in a deep breath, she flexed her fingers. Twice in the past couple of weeks, Jordan had phoned himself. Maybe he'd be on the other end of the line, inviting her to join him for dinner. Maybe he was phoning to tell her he'd unscrambled the entire mess and he'd be home within the next half hour. Perhaps he was calling to suggest they take a few days off and vacation somewhere exotic, just the two of them.

Three rings.

Jill could feel her pulse throbbing at the base of her throat. But she didn't answer.

Four rings.

Five rings.

The phone went silent.

Her entire body was trembling when she turned away and walked into the bedroom. She sat on the bed and covered her face with both hands.

The phone began to ring again, the sound reverberating loudly through the apartment. Jill slapped her hands over her ears, unable to bear it. Each ring tormented her, pretending to offer hope when there was none. It wouldn't be Jordan, but his assistant, and his message would be the same one he'd relayed every night that week.

Making a rapid decision, Jill got her jacket and purse and hurried toward the penthouse elevator, purposely leaving her cell phone behind.

Not having any particular destination, she wandered downtown until she passed a movie theater and decided to go in. The movie wasn't one that really interested her, but she bought a ticket, anyway, willing to subject herself to a B-grade comedy if it meant she could escape for a couple of hours.

The movie actually turned out to be quite entertaining. The plot was ridiculous, but there were enough humorous moments to make her laugh. And if Jill had ever needed some comic relief, it was now.

On impulse she stopped at a deli and picked up a couple of sandwiches, then flagged down a taxi. Before she could change her mind, she gave the driver the address of Jordan's office building.

She had a bit of trouble convincing the security guard to admit her, but eventually, after the guard talked to Jordan, she was allowed inside.

"Jill," he snapped when she stepped off the elevator, "where have you been?"

"It's good to see you, too," she said, ignoring the ir- ritation in his voice. She kissed his cheek, then walked casually past him.

"Where were you?"

"I went out to a movie," she said, strolling into his office. His desk, a large mahogany one, was littered with folders and papers. She noted dryly that he was alone. Everyone else was gone, but he hadn't afforded himself the same luxury.

"You were at a movie?"

She didn't answer. "I thought you might be hungry," she said, neatly stacking a pile of folders in order to clear one small corner of his desk. "I went to Griffin's and bought us both something to eat."

"I ate earlier."

"Oh." So much for that brilliant idea. "Unfortunately, I didn't." She plopped herself down in the comfortable leather chair and pulled a turkey-on-rye from the sack, along with a cup of coffee, setting both on the space she'd cleared.

Jordan looked as though he wasn't sure what to do with her. He leaned over the desk and shoved several files to one side.

"I'm not interrupting anything, am I?"

"Of course not," he answered dryly. "I was staying late for the fun of it."

"There certainly isn't any reason to hurry home," she returned just as dryly.

Jordan rubbed his eyes, and his shoulders slumped. "I'm sorry, Jill. These past few weeks have been hard on you, haven't they?"

He moved behind her and grasped her shoulders. His touch had always had a calming effect on Jill, but she wanted to fight it, wanted to fight her weakness for him.

"Jill," Jordan whispered. "Let's go home." He bent down and kissed the side of her neck. A shiver raced through her body and Jill breathed deeply, placing her hands over his.

"Home," she repeated softly, as if it was the most beautiful word in the English language.

"Jill!" Shelly's eyes widened when she opened the front door one evening a few weeks later. "What's wrong?"

"Wrong," Jill repeated numbly.

"You look awful."

"How kind of you to point it out."

"I've got it!" Shelly said excitedly. "You're pregnant, too."

"Unfortunately, no," she said, passing Shelly and walking into the kitchen. She took a clean mug from the dishwasher and poured herself a cup of coffee. "How are you feeling, by the way?"

"Rotten," Shelly admitted, then added with a smile, "Wonderful."

Jill pulled out a kitchen chair and sat down. If she spent another evening alone, she was going to go crazy. She probably should have phoned Shelly first rather than dropping in unannounced, but driving over here had given her an excuse to leave the penthouse. This evening she badly needed an excuse. Anything to get away. Anything to escape the loneliness. Funny, she'd lived by herself for years, yet she'd never felt so empty, so alone, as she had in the past two months. Even the conversation with Andrew Howard earlier in the evening had only momentarily lifted her spirits.

"Where's Mark?"

Shelly grinned. "You won't believe it if I tell you."

"Tell me."

"He's taking a carpentry class."

"Carpentry? Mark?"

Shelly's grin broadened. "He wants to make a cradle for the baby. He's so sweet I can hardly stand it. You know Mark, he's absolutely useless when it comes to anything practical. Give him a few numbers and he's a whiz kid, but when he has to change a lightbulb, he needs an instruction manual. I love him dearly, but when he told me he was going to build a cradle for the baby, I couldn't help it, I laughed."

"Shelly!"

"I know. It was a rotten thing to do, so Mark's out there proving how wrong I am. This is his first night, and I just hope the instructor doesn't kick him out of the class."

Despite her unhappiness, Jill smiled. It felt good to be around Shelly, to laugh again, to have a reason to laugh.

"I haven't talked to you in ages," Shelly remarked. "But then I shouldn't expect to, should I? You and Jordan are still on your honeymoon, aren't you?"

Tears sprang instantly to Jill's eyes, blurring her vision. "Yes," she lied, looking away, praying that Shelly, who was so happy in her own marriage, wouldn't notice how miserable Jill was in hers.

"Oh, before I forget," Shelly said excitedly, "I heard from Aunt Milly."

"What did she have to say?"

"She asked me to thank you for your letter, telling her about meeting Jordan and everything. She loves a good romance. Then she said something odd."

"Oh?"

"She felt the dress was meant to be worn one more time."

"Again? By whom?"

Shelly leaned forward. "You and Jordan were too wrapped up in each other on your wedding day to notice, but your mother and Mr. Howard got along famously. Milly wouldn't have known that, of course, but…it's obviously meant to be."

"My mother." Now that she recalled her conversation with Andrew at the wedding, it made sense. In the weeks since their return from Hawaii, she'd forgotten about it. He'd phoned Jill twice, but he hadn't mentioned Elaine, nor had her mother mentioned him.

"What do you think?"

"My mother and Mr. Howard?" Jill experienced a feeling of rightness.

"Isn't that incredible?" Shelly positively beamed. Until recently—the arrival of the wedding dress, to be exact—Jill hadn't realized what a complete romantic her friend was.

"But Mom hasn't said a word."

"Did you expect her to?"

Jill shrugged. Shelly was right; Elaine would approach romance and remarriage with extreme caution.

"Wouldn't it be fabulous if your mother ended up wearing the dress?"

Jill nodded and, placing her fingertips to her temples, closed her eyes. "A vision's coming to me now…."

Shelly laughed.

"I think we should call my mom and tell her that we both had a clear vision of her standing in the dress next to a distinguished-looking older man."

Once again, Shelly giggled. "Oh, that's good. That's really good." She sighed contentedly. "The dress definitely belongs with your mother. We'll have to do something about that soon."

Jill pretended her tears were ones of mirth and dashed them away with the back of one hand.

But the amusement slowly faded from Shelly's eyes. "Are you going to tell me what's wrong, or are you going to make me force it out of you?"

"I— I'm fine."

"No, you're not. Don't forget I know you. You've been my best friend for years. You wouldn't be here if something wasn't wrong."

"It's that crazy wedding dress again," Jill confessed.

"The wedding dress?"

"I should never have worn it."

"Jill!" Shelly exclaimed, then frowned. "I don't understand what you're saying."

"It clouded my judgment. I was always the romantic one, remember? Always a sucker for a good love story. When Milly first mailed you the dress, I thought it was the neatest thing to happen since low-fat ice cream."

"Not true! Remember how you persuaded me—"

"I know what I said," Jill interrupted. "But deep down, I could hardly wait to see what happened. When you and Mark decided to marry, I was thrilled. Later, after I arrived in Hawaii and you had the dress delivered to me, I kind of allowed myself to play along with the fantasy. I've wanted to get married for a long time. I'd like to have children."

"Jill," Shelly said, looking puzzled, "I'm not sure I follow you."

"I think I might even have felt a little...jealous that you got married before I did. I was the one who wanted a husband, not you, and yet here you were, so much in love. Somehow it just didn't seem fair." The tears slipped down her cheeks and she absently brushed them away.

"But you're married now and Jordan's crazy about you."

"He was for about a week, but that's worn off."

"He loves you!"

"Yes, I suppose in his own way he does." Jill didn't have the strength to argue. "But not enough."

"Not enough?"

"It's too hard to explain," she said. "I came over to tell you I've made a decision." As hard as she tried, she couldn't keep herself from sobbing, "I've decided to leave Jordan."

Ten

Shelly's eyes narrowed with disbelief. "You can't possibly mean that!"

Leaving Jordan wasn't a decision Jill had made lightly. She'd agonized over it for days. Unable to answer her friend, she pushed back her hair with hands that wouldn't stop shaking. Her stomach was in knots. "It just isn't going to work. I need some time away from him to sort through my feelings. I don't *want* to leave, but I'm afraid I'll just fall apart if I stay."

Shelly had never been one to disguise her feelings. Anger flashed from her eyes. "You haven't given the marriage a decent chance. It hasn't even been two months."

"I know everything I need to know. Jordan isn't married to me, he's married to his company. Shelly, you're my best friend—but there are things you don't know, things I can't explain about what's happening between me and Jordan. Things that go back to my childhood and being raised the way I was."

"You love him."

Jill closed her eyes and nodded. She did love Jordan, so much her heart was breaking, so much she didn't know if she'd survive leaving him, so much she doubted she'd ever love this deeply again.

"I don't expect you to understand," Jill continued, choking over the words. "I wanted you to know... because I'm going to be living with my mother for a while. Just until I can sort through my feelings and figure out what I'm going to do."

"Have you told him yet?" Shelly's voice sounded less sharp.

"No." Jill had delayed that as long as possible, not knowing what to say or how to say it. This wasn't a game, or an attempt to manipulate Jordan into devoting more time to her and their marriage. She refused to fall into that trap. If she was going to make the break, she wanted it to be clean. Decisive. Not cluttered with threats.

"You *do* plan to tell him?"

"Of course." She could never be so cowardly as to move out while Jordan was at the office. Besides, the sorry truth was that she might be gone for days before he noticed.

Confronting him wasn't a task she relished. She could predict his reaction—he'd be furious with her, more furious than she'd ever seen him. Jill was prepared for that. But in the end he would let her go as if she meant nothing to him. His pride would demand that.

"When do you plan to tell him?" Shelly asked softly,

seeming to understand for the first time Jill's torment. A true sign of their friendship was that Shelly didn't ply her with questions, but accepted Jill's less-than-satisfactory explanation.

"Tonight." She hadn't packed yet, but she intended to do that when she got home.

Home.

The word echoed in her mind. Although the penthouse was so distinctly marked with Jordan's personality, it did feel like home. She'd only lived there a short while, but in the lonely weeks following her honeymoon with Jordan, she'd become intimately acquainted with every room. She was going to miss the solace she gained from looking out over Puget Sound and the jagged peaks of the Olympics. And Mrs. Murphy had become a special friend, almost like a second mother, who fretted over her and worried about the long hours Jordan worked. Jill would miss her, too. Although Jill hadn't mentioned it to the cook, she guessed that Mrs. Murphy wouldn't be surprised.

"You're sure this is what you want?" Shelly asked regretfully.

Leaving Jordan was the last thing Jill wanted. Yet it had to be done—and soon, before it was too late, before she found it impossible to go.

"Don't answer that," Shelly whispered. "The pain in your eyes says everything I need to know."

Jill stood and searched in her purse for a tissue. The tears were rolling freely down her cheeks now. She had to compose herself before she encountered Jordan. Had to draw on every bit of inner strength she possessed.

Shelly hugged her, and once again Jill was grateful for their friendship. They were as close as sisters, and Jill had never needed family more than she did right then.

The penthouse echoed with emptiness when she arrived home. Jill stood in the middle of the living room, then slowly moved around, skimming her hand over each piece of furniture. Her gaze gravitated toward the view, and she walked over to the window, staring into the night. Far below, lights flashed and glowed, but she was far removed from the brilliance. Far removed from the light…

Finally she entered the bedroom she shared with Jordan. Her breath came in shallow, painful gasps as she dragged out her suitcases and set them on the bed. Carefully, she folded her clothes and deposited them inside.

Several times she had to stop, clutching an article of clothing, crushing the fabric, until she composed herself enough to continue. Tears stung her eyes, but she refused to succumb to them.

"Jill?"

She froze. She hadn't expected Jordan to come home for several hours yet. They'd barely seen one another all week.

"Where are you going?" he asked.

Pulling herself together, Jill turned to face him. Jordan stood on the other side of the room, his expression confused.

"My mother's," she eventually said.

"Is she ill?"

"No…" Drawing a deep breath, hoping it would calm her frantic heart, she forged ahead. "I'm leaving for a while. I—I need to sort out my feelings…make some important decisions."

The fire that leapt into his eyes was filled with anger. "You plan to divorce me?" he demanded incredulously.

"No. For now, I'm just moving in with my mother."

"Why?"

Jill could feel her own anger mounting. "That you even have to ask should be answer enough! Can't you see what's happening? Don't you care? At this rate our marriage isn't going to last another month." She paused to gulp in a much-needed breath. "My instincts told me this would happen, but I was so much in love with you that I chose to ignore what was obvious from the first. You don't need a wife. You never have. I don't understand why you wanted to marry me because—"

"When did all this come on?"

"It's been coming on, as you say, from the minute we got home from our honeymoon. Our marriage has to be one of the shortest on record. One week. That's all the time you allotted to it. I need more than five minutes at the end of the day when you're so exhausted you can hardly speak. I wish I was stronger, but I'm not. I need more from you than you can give me."

"You might have said something to me earlier."

"I did. A hundred times."

"When?" he barked.

"I'm not going to get involved in a shouting match with you, Jordan. I won't sit by and watch you work yourself to death over some stupid project. You'd said ages ago that it'd be finished in a week. I was foolish enough to believe you. If this project is so important to you that you're willing to risk everything to keep it from folding, then fine, it's all yours."

"When did you tell me?" he asked a second time.

"Do you remember our conversation last night?" she asked starkly.

Jordan frowned, then shook his head.

"I didn't think you had."

The previous afternoon, Jill had been so lonely that she'd reached for the phone, planning to call Ralph to invite him to a movie. She'd nearly dialed his number before she remembered she was married. The incident had had a profound effect on her. She didn't *feel* married. She felt abandoned. Forgotten. Unimportant. If she was going to live her life alone, she could accept that. But she wasn't interested in a one-sided marriage.

This time apart would help her gain perspective, show her what she needed to do. Explaining it to Jordan was impossible. But in time, a week perhaps, she might be able to tell him all that was in her heart.

"What was it you said last night?" Jordan wanted to know, clearly confused.

Jill neatly folded a silk blouse and put it in the suitcase. "I told you how I almost called Ralph to ask him if he wanted to see a movie…and you laughed. Remember? You found it humorous that your wife had forgotten she was a married woman. You didn't bother to understand what had led me to the point of wanting to call an old boyfriend."

"You're not making any sense."

"No, I suppose not. I'm sorry, Jordan. I wish I could explain it better. But as I already told you, I need more from our relationship than you can give me…"

"I've said this project would be settled soon. I'll grant you it's taking longer than I thought, but if you'd just be patient for a little while… Is that so much to ask? You'd think…" He hesitated, then jammed his hands in his pockets and marched across the room. "These past few weeks haven't been a picnic for me, either. You'd think a wife would be willing to lend her husband some support, instead of using threats to bully him into doing what *she* wants."

It didn't surprise Jill that Jordan assumed her leaving was merely a ploy. He didn't realize how serious she was.

"I can't live like this. I just can't!" she cried. "Not now, not ever. I want my children to know their father! My own was a shadow who passed through my life, and I couldn't bear my children to suffer what I did."

"This is a fine time for you to figure it all out," Jordan growled, his hold on his frustration and anger obviously precarious.

"If I could go back and change everything, I would… I would." Hurrying now, she closed her suitcases.

"Are you pregnant?" The question came at her like a bolt of lightning.

"No."

"You're sure?"

"Of course."

A moment of silence followed as she collected her purse and a sweater.

"Nothing I can say is going to change your mind, is it?"

"No." She took the handles of the two suitcases and pulled them off the bed. "If…if there's any reason you need to get hold of me, I'll be at my mother's."

Jordan stood there unmoving, his back toward her. "If you're so set on leaving," he said, "then just go."

"Jill, sweetheart." Her mother knocked lightly, then walked into the darkening bedroom. Jill sat on the padded window seat, her knees tucked under her chin, staring out the bay window to the oak-lined street below. Often as a child she'd sat there and reflected on her problems. But now her problems couldn't be worked out by staring out her bedroom window or by pounding on a piano for an hour or two.

"How are you feeling?"

"Fine." She wasn't ready to talk yet.

"I've made dinner," Elaine said, her voice sympathetic. There was a radiance about her these days. Andrew Howard had called almost daily since Jill had been living with her mother, although he didn't know about her separation from Jordan. Jill had sworn her mother to secrecy. The last Jill had heard, Andrew planned to fly to the mainland early the next month so he and Elaine could spend some time together. Jill was delighted for her mother and for Andrew. Her own situation, though, was bleak.

"Thanks, Mom, but I'm not hungry."

Her mother didn't argue, but sat on the edge of the cushion and leaned forward to hug Jill. The unexpected display of affection moved Jill to tears.

"You haven't eaten anything to speak of all week."

"I'm fine, Mom." Jill didn't want her mother fussing over her just now, and she was grateful when Elaine seemed to realize it. Elaine lovingly stroked Jill's hair, then got to her feet.

"If you need me…"

"I'm fine, Mom."

Her mother hesitated. "Are you going back to him, Jill?"

Jill didn't answer. Not because she didn't want to, but because she didn't know. She hadn't heard from Jordan even once in the week she'd been gone. A concerned Shelly had dropped by twice, unobtrusively leaving the wedding dress, in its original mailing box, on Jill's window seat. Even Ralph had called. But she hadn't heard from Jordan.

She shouldn't miss him this much. Shouldn't feel so empty without him, so lost. Jill had hoped their time apart would clear her thoughts. It hadn't. If anything, they were more confused than ever. Her musings were like snagged fishing lines, impossible to untangle.

She hadn't really expected him to get in touch with her, but she'd hoped. Foolishly hoped. Although if he had, Jill didn't know how she would've reacted.

The doorbell chimed in the distance. A minute later Jill heard her mother talking with another woman. The voice wasn't familiar and Jill pressed her forehead to her knees, suddenly weary. Part of her had wanted the visitor to be Jordan. Fool that she was, Jill prayed that he'd be willing to put aside his pride enough to come after her, to convince her they could make their marriage work. She ached for the sight of him. Obviously, though, any move would have to come from her. But Jill wasn't ready. Not when her heart was in such turmoil.

"Jill?" Her mother knocked at her bedroom door again and opened it a crack. "There's someone here to see you. A Suzi Lundquist. She says it's important."

"Suzi Lundquist?" Jill repeated incredulously.

"She's waiting for you in the living room," her mother said.

Jill hadn't the slightest idea why Suzi would want to see her. Jordan had used her to ward off the younger woman's affections. Perhaps Suzi still loved Jordan and intended to rekindle the fire. But in that case, she wasn't likely to announce her plans to Jill.

After quickly changing her clothes, Jill went downstairs. Suzi was pacing the living room, her movements tense and agitated, when Jill appeared.

"I hope you're happy."

Jill blinked. "I beg your pardon?"

"He's done it, you know, and it's all because of you."

"Done what?"

"Given up the fight." Suzi was staring at her as though Jill was completely dense.

"I hate to seem ignorant, but I honestly don't know what you're talking about."

"You're married to Jordan, aren't you?"

"Yes." They stood several feet apart from each other, like duelists preparing to choose their weapons.

"Jordan's handed control of the firm to my father and brother," Suzi said impatiently.

"Isn't this rather sudden? When did all this happen?" Surely if Jordan was in a proxy fight, he would've said something to her. Surely he would have let her know. She'd only been away for a week. Nothing could have threatened his hold on the company in that short a time, could it?

"This proxy battle's been going on for months," Suzi snapped. "It all started while you and Jordan were on your honeymoon. He couldn't have chosen a worse time to leave. He knew it, too—that's what was so confusing. When he returned from Hawaii, he had a full-fledged revolt on his hands. Dad used that time against Jordan, buying shares until he controlled as large a percentage of the company as Jordan did. He wanted Jordan out as CEO and my brother in."

"What happened?"

"After months of gathering supporters, of buying and selling stock, of doing whatever he could to avoid a proxy fight," Suzi continued, "Jordan handed the whole thing over to my father, who'll hand it all to my brother on a silver platter. You met Dean, and we both know he doesn't have the leadership or the maturity to be a CEO. Within five years, he'll wipe out everything Jordan's spent his life building."

Jill didn't know what to say. Her immediate reaction was to argue with Suzi. Jordan would never willingly surrender control of his company. She didn't need the younger woman to tell her that Jordan had worked his entire adult life to build the company; he'd invested everything in it—everything.

Although it seemed a long time ago, she remembered that he'd told her about buying the controlling shares. He'd also said he'd soon be forced to battle to remain in power. Jill remembered what she'd said to him. She'd told him she couldn't imagine him losing.

"Jordan's resigned?" she repeated, breathless with disbelief.

"This morning, effective immediately."

"But why?"

"You should know," Suzi said harshly. "Because he's in love with you."

"What has that got to do with anything?"

"Apparently he felt it was either you or the company. He chose you."

"He sent you here to tell me?" That didn't sound like

something Jordan would do. He preferred to do his own talking.

Suzi gave a short, humorless laugh. "You've got to be joking. He'd have my hide if he knew I was within a mile of you."

"Then why are you here?"

"Because I fancied myself in love with him not long ago. He was pretty decent about it. He could have used me to his own advantage if he'd wanted, but he didn't. Beneath that surly exterior is a real heart. You know it, too, otherwise you'd never have married him."

"Yes…" Jill agreed softly.

"He needs you. I don't know why you left him, but I figure that's between you and Jordan. He's not the kind of man who'd be unfaithful, so I doubt there's another woman involved. If anything, he's too honorable. If you don't realize what you've got, you're a fool."

Jill's emotions were playing havoc with her. Jordan had resigned! It was too much to take in.

"Are you going to him?" Suzi demanded.

Jill hesitated. "I, uh…"

Suzi shook her head. "If it's pride that's stopping you, I don't think you have anything to worry about. Eventually Jordan will come to you. It may take a while, though, if you're determined to wait him out."

"I'm going to him." Recovering somewhat, Jill looked at Suzi, struggling to speak. "I can't thank you enough for coming. I owe you so much."

"Don't thank me. I just hope you appreciate what

he's done," Suzi muttered as she picked up her purse, tucking it under her arm.

"I do," Jill assured her, leading the way to the front door. No sooner had Suzi left than Jill went looking for her mother.

She found her in the kitchen. "I heard," Elaine said before Jill could explain the purpose of the other woman's visit. "It might not last, you know."

"I'm going to him."

Her mother's eyes searched Jill's face before she nodded. "I knew that, too."

As they embraced briefly, Jill whispered, "There's a box in my room, Mom. Shelly brought it over for you— and for Andrew Howard."

The drive into downtown Seattle seemed to take forever. It was rush hour and the only parking space she could find was in a loading zone. Without a qualm, she took it, then hurried toward Jordan's office. Luck was with her because the building hadn't been locked yet, but she was waylaid by a security guard. Fortunately, he was the same man she'd met earlier, and he let her stay.

"Has Mr. Wilcox left yet?" she asked.

"Not yet."

"Thank you," she said, sighing with relief.

She hurried to the elevator. Jordan's office was on the top floor. When the elevator doors opened, she ran down the wide corridor to the outer office where his assistants worked. No one was there, but the double doors leading into Jordan's massive office were open. He was packing the things from his desk into a cardboard box.

Jill stared at Jordan, unable to move or speak. He looked haggard, as though he hadn't slept at all during the week she'd been gone. Dark stubble shadowed his face, and his hair, ordinarily neat and trim, was rumpled.

He must have sensed her presence because he paused in his task, his eyes slowly meeting hers. His hands went still. The whole world seemed to come to a sudden halt. In that unguarded moment she read his pain and it became hers.

"You can't do it!" she cried, choking on a sob. "You just can't."

Jordan's face hardened and he seemed to clamp down on his emotions. He ignored her and continued packing up the objects from his desk. A smile, one that spoke more of sadness than joy, came into his eyes. "Your husband is unemployed as of five o'clock this afternoon."

"Oh, Jordan, why would you do such a thing? For me? Because I left you? But you never told me… Not once did you explain, even when I pleaded with you. Didn't you trust me enough to tell me what was happening?" That was what hurt most of all, that Jordan had kept everything to himself. Not sharing his burden, carrying it alone.

"It was a mistake not to tell you," he admitted, the regret written clearly across his face. "I realized that the night you left. By nature, I tend to keep my troubles to myself."

"But I'm your *wife*."

He grinned at that, but again his smile was marked with sadness. "I'm new to this marriage business. Obviously I'm not much good at it. The one thing I was hoping to do was keep my business life separate from my personal life. I didn't want to bring my company problems home to you."

"But, Jordan, if I'd known, if you'd explained, I might have been able to help."

"You did, in more ways than you know."

Tears blurred Jill's eyes. She would have given everything she owned for Jordan to take her in his arms, but he stood so far away, so alone.

Jordan picked up a small photograph, one of their wedding day. He stared at it for a moment, then tucked it into the box. "I loved you almost from the day we met. Don't ask me to explain it, because I can't. After that first night, when we kissed on the beach, I knew my life would never be the same."

"Oh, Jordan."

"Being with you was like standing in the sun. I never knew how lonely I was, how my heart ached for love, how much I longed to share my life with someone...."

Tears ran unashamedly down Jill's face.

"The day we were married," he went on, "I swear I've never seen a more beautiful bride. I couldn't believe you'd actually agreed to be my wife. I vowed then and there that I'd never do anything to risk what I'd found."

"But to resign..." Trembling a little, nervous and

unsure, Jill moved across the room to Jordan's side. He tensed at her approach, his expression a blend of undisguised longing and hope.

"I can't lose you," he said.

"But to walk away from your life's work?" What he'd done remained incomprehensible to Jill.

"I have a new life," he said, gently pulling her into his arms. He buried his face in her hair and inhaled deeply. "None of this means anything without you. Not anymore."

"But what are you going to do?"

"I thought we'd take a year off and travel. Would you like that?"

Jill nodded through her tears.

"And after that, I'd like to start our family."

Once again Jill nodded, her heart pounding with love and excitement.

"Then, when the time's right, I'll find something that interests me and start over, but I'll never allow work to control my life again. I can't," he said quietly. "You're my life now."

"You're sure this is what you want?" He'd given up so much.

She felt him smile against her hair. "Without a doubt. I don't need a business to fill up the emptiness in my life. Not when I have you."

"Oh, Jordan," she whispered, her throat tight. "I love you so much." She squeezed her eyes shut and murmured a prayer of thanksgiving for the wonderful man she'd married.

"Shall we go home, my love?" he asked her.

Jill nodded and slipped her hand into his. "Home," she repeated. With her husband. The man she loved. The man she'd married.

REQUEST YOUR
FREE BOOKS!

2 FREE NOVELS
FROM THE ROMANCE COLLECTION
PLUS 2 FREE GIFTS!

YES! Please send me 2 FREE novels from the Romance Collection and my 2 FREE gifts (gifts are worth about $10). After receiving them, if I don't wish to receive any more books, I can return the shipping statement marked "cancel." If I don't cancel, I will receive 4 brand-new novels every month and be billed just $5.74 per book in the U.S. or $6.24 per book in Canada. That's a saving of at least 28% off the cover price. It's quite a bargain! Shipping and handling is just 50¢ per book in the U.S. and 75¢ per book in Canada.* I understand that accepting the 2 free books and gifts places me under no obligation to buy anything. I can always return a shipment and cancel at any time. Even if I never buy another book, the two free books and gifts are mine to keep forever.

194 MDN E4LY   394 MDN E4MC

Name	(PLEASE PRINT)
Address	Apt. #
City	State/Prov. Zip/Postal Code

Signature (if under 18, a parent or guardian must sign)

Mail to **The Reader Service:**
IN U.S.A.: P.O. Box 1867, Buffalo, NY 14240-1867
IN CANADA: P.O. Box 609, Fort Erie, Ontario L2A 5X3

Not valid for current subscribers to the Romance Collection
or the Romance/Suspense Collection.

Want to try two free books from another line?
Call 1-800-873-8635 or visit www.morefreebooks.com.

* Terms and prices subject to change without notice. Prices do not include applicable taxes. N.Y. residents add applicable sales tax. Canadian residents will be charged applicable provincial taxes and GST. Offer not valid in Quebec. This offer is limited to one order per household. All orders subject to approval. Credit or debit balances in a customer's account(s) may be offset by any other outstanding balance owed by or to the customer. Please allow 4 to 6 weeks for delivery. Offer available while quantities last.

Your Privacy: Harlequin Books is committed to protecting your privacy. Our Privacy Policy is available online at www.eHarlequin.com or upon request from the Reader Service. From time to time we make our lists of customers available to reputable third parties who have a product or service of interest to you. If you would prefer we not share your name and address, please check here. ☐

Help us get it right—We strive for accurate, respectful and relevant communications. To clarify or modify your communication preferences, visit us at www.ReaderService.com/consumerschoice.

DEBBIE MACOMBER

(limited quantities available)

TOTAL AMOUNT	$ _____
POSTAGE & HANDLING	$ _____
($1.00 for 1 book, 50¢ for each additional)	
APPLICABLE TAXES*	$ _____
TOTAL PAYABLE	$ _____

(check or money order—please do not send cash)

To order, complete this form and send it, along with a check or money order for the total above, payable to MIRA Books, to: **In the U.S.:** 3010 Walden Avenue, P.O. Box 9077, Buffalo, NY 14269-9077; **In Canada:** P.O. Box 636, Fort Erie, Ontario, L2A 5X3.

Name: _____

Address: _____ City: _____

State/Prov.: _____ Zip/Postal Code: _____

Account Number (if applicable): _____

075 CSAS

*New York residents remit applicable sales taxes.
*Canadian residents remit applicable GST and provincial taxes.

MIRA®

www.MIRABooks.com

MDM0909BL